PRAISE FOR

THE
CHRONICLES OF NEVER
AFTER SERIES

"Satisf[ies] the fractured fairy tale itch."

—*School Library Journal*

"Fans of fantasy and fairy tales of all kinds will delight in catching all the references to classics."

—*Booklist*

"A fast-paced fantasy that Land of Stories fans will enjoy."

—*Publishers Weekly*

"Equal parts whimsical and adventure-packed, Filomena's journey will entrance readers and have them rooting for the young, witty heroine . . . A refreshing twist on well-known fairy tales."

—*Kirkus Reviews*

ALSO BY MELISSA DE LA CRUZ

THE CHRONICLES OF NEVER AFTER

The Thirteenth Fairy

The Stolen Slippers

The Broken Mirror

THE DESCENDANTS SERIES

The Isle of the Lost

Return to the Isle of the Lost

Rise of the Isle of the Lost

Escape from the Isle of the Lost

Because I Was a Girl: True Stories for Girls of All Ages
(Edited by Melissa de la Cruz)

THE
MISSING
SWORD

MELISSA DE LA CRUZ

ROARING BROOK PRESS
New York

Published by Roaring Brook Press
Roaring Brook Press is a division of Holtzbrinck Publishing Holdings Limited Partnership
120 Broadway, New York, NY 10271 • mackids.com

Our books may be purchased in bulk for promotional, educational, or business use.
Please contact your local bookseller or the Macmillan Corporate and Premium
Sales Department at (800) 221-7945 ext. 5442 or by email at
MacmillanSpecialMarkets@macmillan.com.

Library of Congress Cataloging-in-Publication Data is available.

First edition, 2023
Series design by Aurora Parlagreco
Printed in the United States of America by Lakeside Book Company,
Harrisonburg, Virginia

ISBN 978-1-250-86629-5 (hardcover)
1 3 5 7 9 10 8 6 4 2

For my heroes,
Mike and Mattie, always

CONTENTS

Prologue: Of Avalon, Curses & Queens 1

Part One 3

Chapter One: Filomena, Toto, and
Ira, Oh My! 5

Chapter Two: Brocéliande Forest. 14

Chapter Three: A Grand Reunion 25

Chapter Four: Lance and Gwen 34

Chapter Five: Sparkflies and Sparks Fly . . . 44

Chapter Six: Putting the Breakfast in
Bed-and-Breakfast for Questing Heroes 52

Chapter Seven: The Water's Warm. 62

Chapter Eight: The Pools of Camelot 69

Chapter Nine: Cavern of Crystals 78

Chapter Ten: Gita the Good Witch? 88

Chapter Eleven: The Literal Yellow
Brick Road. 97

Chapter Twelve: Only the Best at
Exit West! 107

Prologue: The Sacred Island 121

Part Two 123

Chapter Thirteen: The Emerald City. 125

Chapter Fourteen: There's No Place like
Home, but Where's Home? 136

Chapter Fifteen: Meeting in the
Town Square 144
Chapter Sixteen: Gita's Lair 150
Chapter Seventeen: How to Melt a Witch . . . 154
Chapter Eighteen: Landed or Stranded? 165
Chapter Nineteen: From Wonderland's
Ocean to Avalon's Shore 174
Chapter Twenty: The Keeper of the Gate . . . 183
Chapter Twenty-One: Talking Mirror,
Meet Talking Owl 189
Chapter Twenty-Two: A Bunch of Roots . . . 198
Chapter Twenty-Three: Underground
Invasion 204
Chapter Twenty-Four: Filomena and the
Ogre Queen 212
Chapter Twenty-Five: The Teenage King . . . 220
Chapter Twenty-Six: The King's Summer
Castle 231
Chapter Twenty-Seven: Marlon's Cauldron . . 237
Chapter Twenty-Eight: A Dragon-Sized
Favor 245
Chapter Twenty-Nine: Home: There's No
Place like It 254

Prologue: Two Worlds 261
PART THREE 263
Chapter Thirty: Westphalia or West
Hollywood? 265
Chapter Thirty-One: The Opal Blade 272

Chapter Thirty-Two: The End of the
    Quest 280
Chapter Thirty-Three: One Last Twist. 285
Chapter Thirty-Four: Under the
    Jacaranda Tree 292
Chapter Thirty-Five: The Last Goodbye 302

Prologue: Of Choices and Consequences . . . 307
PART FOUR 309
Chapter Thirty-Six: Back to the Future. 311
Chapter Thirty-Seven: From Paris with
    Love 320
Chapter Thirty-Eight: Pastries and Portals. . . 327
Chapter Thirty-Nine: Alistair Discovers
    Televisions. 335
Chapter Forty: Back to the Waters of
    Avalon 340
Chapter Forty-One: The Decision,
    Reprised 346
Chapter Forty-Two: Filomena's Choice 352
Epilogue 355

ACKNOWLEDGMENTS 357

OF AVALON, CURSES & QUEENS

From the broken mirror
the prophecy came.
A mother's cursed illness,
A crying shame!
The ogre queen cast it,
And there's only one cure:
To find the sacred sword
Excalibur!

But the sword is hidden
deep in Camelot,
And this Never After kingdom
is not like the rest,
Each pathway a challenge;
Each encounter a test.
Filomena Jefferson-Cho
has newly taken her throne,
But in order to save her mother,
She must travel alone.
Things in Camelot
are not as they seem.
Is what you see real?
Or simply a dream?

PART ONE

Wherein . . .

Filomena travels through fields
and forests, only to meet some
familiar faces.

A pit stop brings miscommunication,
dating advice, and an exit stage left.

Everyone learns that even tests,
witches, and plot twists are more
complicated in Camelot.

CHAPTER ONE

FILOMENA, TOTO, AND IRA, OH MY!

Filomena Jefferson-Cho of North Pasadena, known to some as Eliana, daughter of the fairy Rosanna, and now also known as the rightful queen of Westphalia (Filo can still hardly believe that part) is riding a horse down a long, empty, winding path. For the first time since landing in Never After several months, many adventures, and three books ago, Filomena is alone. Though she's fought ogres as often as a normal twelve-year-old has sleepovers, and though she's rescued kingdoms, outwitted thieves, reversed enchantments, and escaped evil queens—this might be the strangest thing she's faced in all of Never After.

Because she's alone. Well, not completely alone, she supposes. She does, after all, have her newly created built-in mentor, guide, and friend, the formerly broken but now repaired magic talking mirror, Ira Glassman. Right now Ira's napping, hanging from a strap at Filomena's hip, because hey, talking mirrors need rest, too. It's quite a lot of work, possessing mirror world knowledge. Plus, telling the truth can be tiring! So Ira's fast asleep while Filomena rides her new steed, Toto. Ira named Toto only a few hours ago, when they set off from Northphalia. Filomena agreed with him that the name seemed to fit. Like Dorothy's little dog, Toto has a lot of personality.

Has it been only a few hours? It's hard to tell since the landscape has remained the same for most of the journey. The endless rolling green hills in every direction, punctuated now and then only by a smattering of trees. Sometimes Filomena catches a glimpse of a village in the distance. This journey has felt eternal! For Filomena, being without friends always makes time move more slowly. Oh, how she wishes they were here! Alistair would be keeping Filomena company with his jokes; Gretel would be bantering with Filomena. And Jack, well . . . whenever Filo thinks of him, she gets a roller-coaster feeling in her stomach. Or maybe that's just the feeling of Toto taking a particularly big step on the rocky path. Filomena is not used to riding a horse, after all.

Princess Jeanne swore it would be easy.

They'd all been standing in Princess Jeanne's stables at the Northphalian castle before Filomena left. "It's just like riding a bike!" Gretel had piped up.

"I think that expression means that once you've learned it, you never forget it," Filomena replied, glancing worriedly at the large white-and-brown-spotted horse whose neck Princess Jeanne was patting. "Learning to ride a bike for the first time is not that easy."

But what choice did she have? Filomena had just found out that her mother's illness was caused by cursed beauty products sold to Bettina by evil Queen Olga.

"Now that's taking being a beauty influencer to a very dark place," Gretel had whispered to Alistair, though Alistair had no idea what she was talking about. Sometimes Gretel and Filomena still forgot how little Jack and Alistair knew about the mortal world.

And of course there's the fact that Ira told Filomena that a cure was to be found in Excalibur. Yet another story Filomena knows from the mortal world that she now has to carry out herself. But that wasn't even the worst of it; Ira also told Filomena that she had to go on this quest alone. Ira is a magic mirror, so Filomena was taking this prophecy seriously. But why in all of Never After did she have to go alone? She still couldn't understand it. The only thing that made being in another world bearable while her mom was sick was having friends with her.

So she took Princess Jeanne up on her kind offer of a noble horse, who had whinnied at Filomena in a rather charming manner upon meeting. After a hasty riding lesson, Filo set off on her next adventure. All on her own.

Filomena hears a yawn come from her hip.

"All right, all right, I'm awake," Ira Glassman says. "What did I miss? Can you flip me around so I can see everything? Oh, we're still traveling? So I missed nothing?"

Filomena laughs. "Not too much, Ira. So far, it's been acres of green pasture as far as the eye can see. We've just been traveling the path you told me to follow."

Ira seems to nod, if it's possible for a talking mirror to nod, and looks out onto the landscape ahead. Verdant grasses sway in the breeze. The fields are empty in every direction. Toto continues clopping forward, and the rhythm of his movement is relaxing despite the anxiety Filomena feels.

"Can you tell me a bit more about where we're going? I'd like to be a little more prepared and maybe not completely reliant on a horse I just met to lead me to the cure for my terminally ill mother."

Toto gives a disgruntled sniff in response, not pleased with having his directional skills questioned.

"Filomena, how many times do we have to go over this?"

Ira sighs. "You know I would love to dish everything I know. I love to gossip; I love to chat. You know this. I know this. But I'm as bound to the rules the fairies created as any other talking mirror. I can reveal things only at the right time, the time they're meant to be revealed."

They've had this sort of conversation a few times already in the hours they've been traveling, and each time, Filomena still doesn't quite get it. Does Ira know all? When she and Jack discussed talking mirrors in Snow Country, Jack kept mentioning mirror world knowledge, but what did that actually mean? Filomena understands there are only thirteen talking mirrors in all of Never After—each animated by a fairy—plus Ira the handheld talking mirror Filomena animated thanks to the fairy mark on her forehead. She keeps picturing Ira on the other side of the mirror, sitting in a chair in an empty room, gazing at everything on Filomena's side, with every piece of knowledge about her world swirling around him.

She has learned, however, that Ira can heal and regenerate just like a person. Though Robin Hood smashed him to pieces a few days ago, Ira had already started to recover. Ira thinks that soon he'll be able to show images in his mirror face again, as he was made to do.

"Let me put it this way," he says. "It's not just that I'm prevented from telling you things I know. It's that there are many things I don't know until the moment they are to be shared with you. Does that make sense? I didn't know about the Excalibur thing before I said it. I'm like an oracle; it just comes to me. I'm a mere vessel. Get it?"

"I think so. It's starting to make a bit more sense. There's nothing like this in the mortal world, like, at all, so I'm playing catch-up. I'm not like Jack. He's understood the dynamics of the mirror world since he was born!"

"Ah yes, Jack the Giant Stalker. I've been meaning to ask you about him. How did you two meet, after all?"

Filomena blushes slightly. She leans forward, laying her head along Toto's soft neck and wrapping her arms around him. "Isn't that something your mirror world knowledge would cover?"

"Perhaps, but I like to hear things right from the source." He winks.

Filomena gives in. She doesn't have to be prompted too hard to talk about her favorite people in all the worlds. She tells Ira about their first meeting: running into Jack and Alistair in the mortal world. How they brought her to Never After, how Gretel joined them, how she and Gretel are both biportal, how they've been battling the evil ogre queen Olga ever since Filomena arrived in Never After, with little victories here and there but always a larger battle to be won. She tells Ira about meeting Hori and Bea; Cinderella's ball; being captured by the Beast, Byron; then breaking his curse. How the fairy Zera asked for their help, but then they got sidetracked helping Princess Jeanne rescue her kingdom from evil King Richard and his army.

She talks about how Robin Hood is Princess Jeanne's childhood friend and how he was in love with Jeanne, wanted to run away with her and leave the kingdoms behind, but she refused because she was committed to finding her crown and ruling Northphalia. Not to mention Jeanne is quite keen on Lord Sharif of Nottingham. So Robin Hood became a thief working with evil Queen Olga, though they have no idea where either Robin or Olga are now. Filomena also tells Ira about Rosie and meeting her and the dwarves in Snow Country, and Colette the fairy, aka Rosie's mom, also known as Snow White, who died at the hand of evil Queen Christina. And then of course, it was with the help of Rosie that Filomena was able to create Ira in the first place.

It's only after she says all this that she realizes Ira isn't listening. "You're not even paying attention. I just told you the whole story, and you were totally zoned out, weren't you?"

"It's just . . . I know about all that. And I know you, Princess Jeanne, Hori, and Prince Charlie were all recently crowned kings and queens of your kingdoms. That's not what I'm asking, dear. I know the plot. I want to know about *you*. And about Jack," Ira teases.

About her? About Jack? Filomena's been so focused on the action over the past few months that it's only in rare moments when she really reflects on herself. On what's going on inside her, in her heart, and in her mind.

"Well, what do you want to know?"

"Is this Jack kid good enough for you? He's handsome, I'll give you that, but that's not everything."

Filomena laughs. Jack's pretty much the best person she can think of. He's kind and brave, and it's true that he's very handsome, but more importantly, he's so fun to be around. Well, except for that time in Snow Country when he was being Jack the Giant Jerk, but to be fair he had just found out that Zera was captured, so Filo can't really blame him too harshly. Zera was basically a mother to Jack, a mentor and a role model and a protector. Zera was captured and drained of her life by none other than Olga. And Jack had since apologized, of course.

"Yes, yes, I can confidently say he is a good guy, Ira. More than good enough."

"So, what happens with you two now? You've smooched a few times . . . now what?"

Her cheeks flush red in the way they do when anyone asks about her and Jack. She's still getting used to the fact that they're . . . well, what are they? They definitely like each other. But they didn't smooch; they kissed briefly. That was all.

"I have no idea. Absolutely no idea."

Ira chuckles. "I'd say we have a long road ahead on which to figure it out, but it in fact appears as though we may be reaching the next leg of our journey."

Filomena was so wrapped up in their conversation that

she didn't see what was coming into view. All along the horizon, as far as the eye can see, stretches a forest like a border protecting one side of Never After from the other. It's apparent that, whatever this is, there's no choice but to go through it.

CHAPTER TWO

BROCÉLIANDE FOREST

As they get closer to the forest, Toto begins whinnying loudly. If Filomena were traveling without Toto, she wouldn't be concerned upon coming to the forest. It looks nothing like the grim darkness of the enchanted Sherwood Forest. Instead, it's leafy and bright, with trees as tall as mortal world skyscrapers. It stretches as far as she can see to either side, into a horizon of green grasses. A forest without end. How had she not seen this before? It's as if it just appeared while she was talking to Ira. And it's quiet, too. Everything feels still, except for a cold breeze rushing through the branches. But Toto whinnies again as they step up to the edge of the forest. Filomena knows from living with her beloved Pomeranian puppy, Adelina Jefferson-Cho, that animals have great instincts. Adelina always gets flustered about two minutes before someone knocks on the door, as if she can sense a potential intruder or a dangerous presence.

"What is this place, Ira?" Filomena whispers. She's not sure why she's whispering, but it's so quiet, she feels compelled.

"I believe this is the border between the parts of Never After that you know and, well, where we're trying to go," Ira says solemnly.

"Okay, great!" Filomena says in what she hopes is a bright, casual manner. "So we'll just ride on through the forest and see what's on the other side."

She tries to speak with confidence, but her heart is pounding. Doing this alone feels so completely different from when she was with the League of Seven. Having Jack, Alistair, Gretel, Rosie, Byron, and Beatrice by her side had made her feel capable, protected. Six people had had her back whatever the situation. Now it's just her. Ira may be smart, but he can't exactly swing a sword or block an attack. And Toto, Filomena can already tell, is much more *flight* than *fight*.

Filomena gently gives Toto a tap with the stirrups, indicating she's ready to move forward, just like Princess Jeanne showed her. Whatever lies ahead there's no choice now. She has to get through it. It's not like they can go around the forest. And what's the problem, really? It's just a nice-looking forest. She's been in plenty of forests before.

As Toto steps forward, into the forest, the trees appear to shift just slightly. He walks on the soft brown earth of the forest floor, the tall ancient trunks standing around them feeling as if they're leaning closer. The sun is softly dappling through the treetop canopy twenty, thirty, forty feet overhead. The more steps Toto takes, the more the trees' bark and leaves begin to shift, to be shrouded in slight mist. The mist seems to rise from the forest floor itself, and the trunks start shimmering. Soon Filomena, Ira, and Toto appear to be surrounded by trunks that reflect like mirrors, obscured by a soft haze.

"What is this place?" she whispers again to Ira, hoping for a more specific answer.

Ira doesn't respond. She looks into the antique handheld mirror that Rosie gave her to animate, Ira's home, and all she sees is her own reflection. It's just a regular mirror. A chill runs up her spine. Where did Ira go?

Even Toto is silent, pacing in a slow rhythm forward, forward.

"Okay, time to test my galloping skills," Filomena whispers to herself. The faster she gets through this, the better. If they just charge through to the other side . . .

But Toto won't gallop. They'd practiced this many times at the Northphalian castle when Princess Jeanne and Beatrice had taught Filomena how to ride. But now Toto isn't responding to the signal. He's just slowly taking steps, one after another. Something is off.

Filomena looks around, scanning the trees for danger. She sees nothing. But even if she did, what would she do about it? She's no real fighter. How would she know if she can hold her own in a fight? The whole time she's been in Never After, Jack has protected her. She's no talent; she's no hero. She just stumbled across the League of Seven. She's just along for the ride, so to speak. Her friends are the real heroes. She's just a girl who read a book series. Just that she was born a princess doesn't mean anything. She didn't earn it.

A deep gloom covers Filomena's chest. It's like molasses has stuck itself around her heart. An overwhelming sense of despair coats her. Who is she kidding? She's not fit to run a kingdom. How is she going to do this quest alone? She's going to fail everyone, especially her mom.

"Filomena!"

A voice echoes from what seems like miles away, but it's loud.

"Filomena! I need you!"

Through the trees the voice calls. It's familiar . . . It's her mother's!

"Filomena, come home! I need you!"

Suddenly, on a mirrored tree trunk to her left, a misty vision appears. It's Filomena's mother, Bettina, lying in bed in their house in North Pasadena. She looks so weak, and she's crying an endless stream of tears.

"I need my daughter. I need my Filomena. Why won't she come home? Why does she insist on staying in Never After? Why doesn't she care about me?"

Filomena is struck with fear. What are these trees? Are they portals? Are they talking mirrors? Her mother is calling out for her, and she's not there. She's a horrible daughter!

Another tree trunk, to her right this time, presents an image. It's of her friends, the League of Seven, at Northphalia Castle. They're sitting around a dining table, having a feast.

"I'm so relieved she's finally gone," Gretel says. "She can be so annoying. It's *exhausting* to pretend we like her."

"Tell me about it!" Rosie chimes in. "Those trolls from her school had it right: Filomena is such a loser. I mean, what kind of name even is *Filomena*?"

"If only she weren't a gift from the fairies, then we wouldn't have to pretend we like her!" Alistair says. "It's too bad we need her for our missions."

"You think you have it bad?" Jack says. "I have to pretend I have feelings for her!"

They all laugh and laugh and laugh.

"At least once we're done saving Never After, we'll never have to talk to her again!" Gretel says with a big smile on her face.

"Yes, the sooner Filomena finishes her quest, the sooner we'll be rid of her!" Jack says. "She can stay in Westphalia, all alone."

Filomena sees them all cheer in the mirrored tree trunk.

Filomena can feel hot tears running down her cheeks. Are her friends talking about her right now at the castle? They're only pretending to like her because they need her to save Never After? All the loneliness she felt from being bullied by the trolls in middle school comes rushing to her. But this is way worse. She thought these people were her best friends in the worlds, that they would love and protect her no matter what. A wave of betrayal washes over her, sharp, like being stabbed by a thousand little knives. She feels like she could fall through to the center of the Earth. If she doesn't have these friends, then what is she doing here? What is she trying to save? If they don't care about her, what's the point?

She feels the urge to turn around. To abandon this whole quest. What's the point? She can't do this alone! But apparently she can't do this with friends, either. Because they aren't really her friends. Everything she thinks she knows is wrong. She's not a hero, she's not special, she doesn't know anything. She's just a silly loser girl who's been tricked.

Filomena cries, sobs heaving up from her chest. All she wants to do is crawl into bed with her mom and watch a movie. She wants to cuddle Adelina and read about Never After, not live it!

Toto, meanwhile, has been silently, slowly trudging along. They now come to another trunk, this one with a vision of Scheherazade, or Zera, the fairy. Filomena wants to look away, afraid of what she'll learn, but she finds that she can't.

In the vision, Zera and Jack are speaking. Zera is shaking her head pitifully. "Why did you choose this Filomena girl, Jack?"

"Zera, you know I'll do whatever it takes to save Never After. Even if it means pretending to have feelings for someone as bland and boring as Filomena."

Zera nods sadly. "You are brave to take this on, Jack. Filomena has no real talent or courage, but it's true that we need to use her as a tool in order to save Never After."

"I'll do whatever I can to help, Zera. Including something as horrible as this. I even kissed her, so hopefully she'll really believe I like her."

Another jolt of pain stabs Filomena in the heart. Jack is just using her? Because she's the queen of Westphalia? He's using her as a political tool? How can that be? That's so cruel!

This is too much. Tears stream down Filomena's face. All she wants to do is sit on the couch between her parents, eat takeout, and watch a silly TV show. She wants to never leave the house again, let them keep her locked up and away from this horrible place. The idea is so comforting that she begins to turn Toto around. *That's it; I'm out of here.* She's going back to where she belongs, to the mortal world with her parents. Her mom is sick! Her mom needs her!

As Filomena turns Toto around, a glittering path lays itself out on the forest floor, leading her back the way she came. She leads Toto to take a few steps down the path—until dread drops into the pit of her stomach.

Suddenly Filomena remembers why she's here in the first place. Because things aren't normal at home. She can't just sit on the couch between her parents, because her mother is bedridden. She can't dance around the kitchen with them, because Bettina, her mom, can hardly move. That's why she's on this mission alone—to save her mom.

She stops Toto.

The urgency she feels now for her mission clears her mind for just a moment, and that moment of clarity is enough to realize that some of the things that were said in those tree visions were off.

Jack telling Zera that he and Filomena had kissed—that couldn't be right. Their first kiss happened after Zera died, right before Filomena and Jack battled ogres and Filomena was crowned queen. So there's no way that vision could be real. It never could have happened, because there was never a time in which Jack could have told Zera about their kiss.

Filomena feels a jolt, a sparkle of recognition that lights up in the back of her mind. She never told Rosie about the middle school trolls, either. So why would she say those things? And come to think of it, in the vision of Filomena's mother, the bedroom window didn't have the right view. Usually it looks out on a big lemon tree. But the vision's tree had oranges.

Wiping the tears from her cheeks, Filomena sits up straight. Something is definitely off here. These visions . . . they aren't what they seem.

If she can just get to the other side of the forest, things will make sense. She doesn't know why, but this feels true, essential.

"We're turning around, Toto! We're almost there! We're close," she says.

As she forces herself to turn Toto around again, away from the glittering path and back into the mists, a weight covers her, one so heavy it feels like a hundred of her mom's weighted blankets are resting on her shoulders. In the center of her chest, all her doubts about herself are flourishing. But deeper still, inside herself, Filomena can feel her intuition telling her that something is wrong. These visions, this feeling . . . something is not right.

Toto's pace is getting slower and slower. This won't do. Filomena hoists her leg over the saddle and hops to the ground to walk beside Toto. She looks into Toto's face. His neck is drooped, and his eyes are blurry with eyelids half closed. Can a horse look tragic? Like it just had its heart broken? Because that's what Toto looks like right now, Filomena thinks. As if all joy has been sucked from his body.

Filomena pats Toto's neck and pulls his reins to pick up the pace. They're almost at the forest edge.

A whisper like a thousand buzzing bees sweeps through the forest.

"You can't have it all, Filomena. You want to live in both worlds, but you can't have it all. One day, you will have to choose."

With one last push of strength, Filomena forces herself

to step away from the lulling voice. Finally, Filomena and Toto step over the border of the forest and into the bright hot sun of a meadowed clearing. Filomena collapses to the ground. It feels as though all weight has been lifted from her. She begins to laugh and sob, every emotion coursing through her body at once. The grass is soft, and she touches her forehead to the ground as she lets it all out, both the laughter and the tears.

Most of all, she feels a deep sense of relief. It's so obvious, so apparent to her now. Those were just visions! All that doubt she felt about herself—none of it was real! Right?

Behind her, Toto whinnies and shakes his head, as if clearing out cobwebs.

From her hip, Ira perks up. "What's going on? Where are we?"

Still sitting on the grass, she lifts Ira up to her face.

"Thank goodness you're back, Ira! Where did you go?"

"I just sort of turned off, I think. I'm not sure how exactly. Oh, you have been crying, young lady! Thank goodness you aren't wearing mascara. Is everything okay?"

Filomena laughs, then sighs, shakes her head. She feels like she's just run an emotional marathon. "I'm not really sure what happened back there. At first, I felt so much doubt in myself. Like I'll never be able to make this work, like I'm worthless without Jack, Alistair, and Gretel. Then, in the trees, I saw all these visions of my friends saying horrible things about me, of my mom calling out for me—it was awful, Ira! It made me question everything I'm doing and everything that's happened since I came to Never After."

Ira nods solemnly, considering this.

"Were those visions real? Did my friends really say that about me? It can't be, right? But what other explanation is there?"

"Can you turn me around, to face the forest?" Ira asks.

She does as he requests, standing up, next to Toto. She sees Ira nod.

"Brocéliande Forest," he says.

"What's that?"

Ira answers. "Welcome to Camelot."

CHAPTER THREE

A GRAND REUNION

Camelot. Filomena takes a breath and nods. Camelot never appeared in the Never After books she's read, but she's familiar with it from mythology in the mortal world. A lot of stories take place in the mythical kingdom of Camelot, but Filomena's not exactly sure which of them translate to the fairy world. As Filomena has learned the hard way, the fairy-tale stories the ogres fed the mortal world rarely line up with the stories' real versions in Never After.

"Great, so if we're in Camelot, we must be close to King Arthur's sword Excalibur, right?" Filomena asks.

She still isn't sure how a sword is going to heal her mom, but Ira said the sword is key, and Filomena trusts Ira's wisdom completely.

"I'm not so sure about that. There's a lot for you to learn about Camelot, my dear."

While they talk, Filomena mounts Toto again. She figures they may as well start heading to wherever they're going. Ira points them west, and they walk along the forest border.

"You called this Brocéliande Forest," she says as Toto trots along. "What is that?"

"It's the only forest in Camelot," Ira starts.

"The only forest? In the whole kingdom? How can there be only one?"

"Camelot isn't like the rest of Never After, Filomena. If you think things are strange there, well, Camelot is a whole other level of strange. Brocéliande Forest is a mystic forest. It's not enchanted the way that some are in Never After. An enchantment can be broken. If something is mystic, then the magic of it is embedded in the very thing itself."

This is a lot for Filomena to wrap her head around, but she thinks she can keep up. There are so many rules in Never After. The elemental rules of magic almost feel like science class sometimes.

"The Brocéliande is the only forest in this kingdom because it moves around Camelot as needed. It appears and disappears at will. The other thing you should know is that

Camelot is not an easy place to be. I think your experience entering it taught you that."

As they walk west along the Brocéliande, Filomena peeks into the forest to her left. To her right is the wide expanse of Camelot, with rolling hills, deep valleys, and clumps of trees here and there for as far as the eye can see. But no other forests, Ira is right. She supposes she sees no other forests because the Brocéliande is still right there, on her left. However, it now looks a lot less mystic than it did a few minutes ago. No mirrors, no mist. Just your average forest, albeit with forty-foot trees.

"What was all that in there, Ira?"

"That was a test, I believe. In order to prove that you deserve to enter Camelot, you had to pass the test. You had to prove that you can come here alone. Camelot is not for the faint of heart, Filomena. Actually, there's a lot I should tell you about Camelot before we get too deep in—"

But just as Ira is about to reveal more, Filomena tenses up, and Ira falls quiet. There's a group of people emerging from the forest up ahead. They appear to be falling all over themselves and onto the ground. Filomena places a hand on her Dragon's Tooth sword hanging from her hip, and readies herself for a fight. She takes a deep breath. She can do this. If they're unfriendly travelers, she can fight. They're so far in the distance, it's hard to tell exactly how many people there are, but she thinks she counts one, two, three, four, five, six . . . No. It can't be.

She gives Toto a tap and suddenly he's galloping—it looks like he remembers the signal after all. As she gets closer, Filomena's heart leaps. There's a girl in an elaborate chain mail jumpsuit with her hands on her knees. There's a sweet young boy dry heaving by a tree. There's a guy with huge muscles who's delicately patting his forehead with a kerchief. There's a redhead chugging liquid out of a thermos that changes color. There's an elegant girl doing deep-breathing exercises. And most important, there's a dashing young man who's looking around urgently. His eyes land right on the galloping horse, and when he sees Filomena, his face breaks into so much relief that her heart soars.

It's him! It's them! Filomena can't believe it. She's so thrilled that, in a fit of joy and disbelief, she accidentally loses her balance and tumbles off Toto just as he reaches the group—

"Hey! I missed you, too, but don't hurt yourself before we even get started!"

Here he is. She tripped and landed right in the strong arms of the one and only Jack the Giant Stalker.

Once again Filomena feels she could laugh and cry at the same time. Instead, she yells. "YOU'RE HERE!"

"Yowza, easy on the ears, Fil! I'm still a little dizzy!" Alistair says. He's now lying flat on his back and covering his ears.

Filomena doesn't care. She's too happy. "It's you," she breathes.

"It's me," Jack agrees. He's holding her so tightly, she can feel his heart pounding, and when they break apart reluctantly, she wishes she hadn't let him go. But she goes to hug Gretel after jumping over Alistair on the ground.

Gretel laughs, patting Filomena's back. "You're crying!"

"I'm so confused! You're all here? How are you here?" Filomena asks.

"That's a great question," a very woozy-looking Byron says. He's standing with his back against a tree trunk. Filomena runs and hugs Beatrice, Rosie, and Byron, too.

Rosie gasps as Filomena bear-hugs her. "I-I can't—breathe."

"We knew you had to get into Camelot alone," Jack starts.

Filomena leans down to hug Alistair, who's still looking green. "There's a lot about Camelot we don't know," Alistair says, "But if Ira said you have to go alone, we knew it meant there was a test you had to confront in order for us all to gain entry into the kingdom."

"You knew the whole time that you were going to meet me here?" Filomena says, shocked, shoving Jack's shoulder. Jack blushes again, which makes Filomena do the same. He runs his hand through his hair nervously. No one else seems to notice the awkward, fizzy, strange, electric energy between her and Jack, thank goodness.

"We couldn't tell you," Gretel says with a shrug. "It's just the rules. But gosh, I almost flubbed up a few times!"

Rosie laughs, turning to Gretel. "Remember when you said, 'See you soon,' to Toto when they left?"

Gretel raises her hands innocently. "What can I say? We bonded!"

Rosie laughs and passes around her thermos.

"Helloooo," Ira says from Filomena's hip.

"Oh right, sorry, Ira," Filomena says, unhooking the talking mirror and attaching him to Toto's saddle so Ira can be at eye level with everyone.

"Did you know about this, Ira?" she asks.

"If I could shrug, I would. Look, I told you there are certain things I just can't tell you until the time is right. This is one of them! But now the gang's back together. Although you're all looking a bit rough, I have to say."

Surveying the scene, it's true. Everyone looks like they just drank far too much peony punch, or got punched in the stomach, or both.

Gretel melts to sit on the ground and tips her head back, downing water from Rosie's color-changing thermos. They all look exhausted.

"Imagine the worst jet lag you've ever had in your life. And you definitely didn't fly first class. You flew on a tiny little plane with a ton of turbulence. Now multiply that by a thousand. Literally a thousand. I'm not exaggerating. That's how I feel right now," Gretel says.

"How did you all get here?" Filomena asks.

"Swoop hole," Jack says, "but getting to Camelot isn't like going between swoop holes in the rest of Never After."

"There's a far thicker barrier between Camelot and the rest of Never After," Ira explains. "It's much more difficult to get into Camelot via swoop hole. And the only reason this lot was even allowed to is because you passed the test and you're all on the same quest."

"All right, everyone, I know we're feeling rough, but we have to get moving," Jack says, hoisting a reluctant Alistair to his feet. "We need somewhere to recover from that journey, and if I know Camelot, we do not want to be outside when it gets dark."

The group begrudgingly stands up and starts walking.

"We can all take turns riding Toto," Filomena offers.

Toto sniffs at her with disdain in response, rolling his eyes, but he concedes. Gretel calls dibs on the first ride.

The rest of them drag themselves away from Brocéliande Forest and down the first of many rolling hills, toward the idea of shelter.

Toto, Ira, and Gretel lead the way with Byron, who's carrying Bea in a piggyback, behind them. Rosie and Alistair are trying to hold each other up as they walk at the rear.

Filomena can hear Alistair ask, "Rosie, what is this?" as he takes a sip from her thermos.

"A new invention for traveling," she says. "The ever-replenishing water source. So you'll never run out!"

Alistair considers this. "Do you think we could fill it with cream soda?"

Jack and Filomena laugh, falling behind the group by a few paces. They're both quiet for a moment, unsure what to say, especially after their affectionate reunion.

"Are you okay?" Jack whispers. "I was worried about you."

"I didn't know how long it would be until I got to see you again. I'm so glad you're here. Uh, that you're *all* here."

Jack smiles, looking at the ground, and Filomena sees slight dimples form in his cheeks.

Taking a breath, Jack surveys the evening spreading out in front of them. A single star flickers in the distant light blue sky. In front of them are verdant rolling hills and golden valleys, and they can see far into the horizon. It's beautiful. There's a certain clarity here, a purity to the air. Everything looks crisp, clear, and slightly melancholy in the setting sun.

"It's been a long time since I've been here," he says.

"You've been to Camelot?"

"Only once, a long time ago. And not for very long. It was when we were gearing up for the Last Battle."

Filomena wants to hear more, but it seems like Jack doesn't want to say anything else. The Last Battle is always a touchy subject for him. They walk in silence for a moment. The path they're on is atop a hill now, and Filomena looks down at the valley below.

She almost wants to tell Jack about the test just so he can reassure her that none of the visions were true. But would that counter the point of the test itself? Maybe she's not sup-posed to rely on reassurance from others. Maybe she just has to trust herself—and trust them. She banishes the questions from her mind. Like Ira said, it was just a test, and she passed.

But still something nags at her. Even more than the horrible things everyone said, which she realizes were just make-believe mirages, depictions of her worst fears to be overcome. That's not what lingers with her now. It's what that voice said, the buzzing-bees voice. About her eventually having to choose between her two lives, between Never After and the mortal world. Because as much as she can dismiss the rest as mere mirages, something within is giving her the sense that the voice might have been telling the truth. Will she have to choose one day? And if that day comes, what will she choose?

CHAPTER FOUR

LANCE AND GWEN

"Bed-and-breakfast! Bed-and-breakfast!" Alistair screams, pointing to a large stone house tucked up on a hill and set a few yards back from the path. A wooden sign with gold lettering swings on hinges. It reads BED-AND-BREAKFAST FOR QUESTING HEROES.

It sounds almost too good to be true, but instinctually everyone turns to the left and starts toward it. Right now they don't have a lot of energy for distinguishing a benevolent bed-and-breakfast from an evil or tricky one, so Filomena just prays that Alistair's B and B instincts are up to snuff.

Invigorated by a potential rest stop, Alistair gathers his energy and bounds up the stone steps first, then uses the wooden door's large brass handle to knock. Behind him, the group holds their breath. The door opens. A beautiful woman answers it. She's dressed in a light green empire-waist dress. Dark brown curls frame her face, and she smiles, tilting her head sympathetically.

"¡Hola! You look like a weary bunch of travelers!" she says brightly, laughing at the bedraggled bunch. Filomena turns around to see Rosie falling asleep on Beatrice's shoulder. Beatrice nudges Rosie awake, and Rosie's eyes dart open in surprise. Filomena stifles a laugh.

"Buenos días, my fair maiden," Alistair says, bowing. He always gets overly formal when comfort is at stake. "My name is Alistair Bartholomew Barnaby, and these are my companions. I'm not sure if word of the League of Seven, the group of prophesied heroes, has reached this side of Brocéliande Forest?"

Alistair motions to the group behind him with great importance. Unfortunately, at that moment Byron lets out a loud yawn and Rosie gives herself a slap to stay awake.

"It's been a long day," Alistair says, turning back around to the woman.

The woman nods.

"We are, as you can probably tell, in desperate need of rest."

The woman smiles serenely. Filomena wonders, *Can we trust this stranger?*

As if reading her mind, Jack speaks: "May I inquire as to whose residence we've stumbled upon?" he says.

"*¡Por supuesto!* I'm Lady Guinevere Sánchez, and I run this bed-and-breakfast with my partner, the knight Lancelot de León."

This seems to put Jack and Alistair at ease a bit. They must have heard of these people. Guinevere and Lancelot . . . Why do those names ring a bell for Filomena?

Of course! They're one of the most famous love stories in all of the mortal world!

Guinevere laughs at Filomena's shocked face. "You have heard of us?" she asks.

"I have, my lady," Filomena says, bowing. "My name is Filomena, or you can call me Eliana."

"Eliana. *¿Eres la reina de Westphalia?*"

Filomena bows again, blushing. It still feels unbelievable that the title belongs to her.

"And you are seeking a place to rest?" Guinevere asks.

The group nods ferociously, even Toto.

"*Por favor, pasa.*" Guinevere smiles. "I would be honored to have you as my guests tonight. A group of knights just left this morning, so the whole manor is empty. We have a stable for your horse as well!"

Toto huffs, unhappy to be separated from the group, but horses can't lodge inside, not even in Never After. Guinevere rings a bell, and a stable boy comes to collect Toto. The rest of the group is led by Guinevere to the main room of the manor, where a fire is roaring in a stone hearth. Large windows flank the fireplace, overlooking a vista of hills. The seven weary travelers and one weary talking mirror rest on the sheepskins and leather chairs around the fire. Guinevere sits with them.

"So tell me," she begins, "*¿por qué estás en Camelot?* You have a quest to complete, I presume?"

Filomena is suddenly gripped with a slight panic. She should have had Ira brief her before they entered. How much should she say? How do they know who to trust, to whom they should reveal themselves? What if Guinevere is on the side of Queen Olga?

Thankfully, Ira, who's set upright in Filomena's lap, pipes in. "Yes, my lady, we do. But before we get into that, might we get more acquainted first?"

Guinevere gasps. "¡Ay! Is that a talking mirror?"

"Rosie, here, and Filomena animated him!" Beatrice says proudly. She looks over to Rosie, whose head has fallen back against the leather couch. Her eyes are fluttering shut. Bea pinches Rosie's ankle from her place on the rug.

Rosie yelps. "What? Inventions! Yes! We did!"

"That is *muy* impressive indeed." Guinevere nods. "I've never heard of such a thing."

"We're all quite proud," Ira says. "But back to making your acquaintance?"

"Oh, of course!" Guinevere says, and nods again. "I understand these are strange times. It feels difficult to trust anyone. Perhaps I should tell you my history, so you can know whose home you are staying in."

The group nods, enraptured by Guinevere's beauty and grace. Even Rosie is awake now.

"I have lived in Camelot *toda mi vida*. King Arturo has always been *un querido amigo*. As you perhaps have heard, I met Lancelot long ago, and we fell very much in love. After Lancelot decided to retire from life as a knight, having completed more quests than any other hero in Camelot, Arturo gifted us this manor to thank us. It's been our duty ever since to house heroes at the beginning of their quests in Camelot and help send them on their way."

Just as she finishes speaking, the group hears the front door to the manor swing open.

"¡Hola, Guinevere!" a melodic voice echoes.

Guinevere smiles to the seven. "That's Lancelot now." "Lance, ¡aquí!" she calls over her shoulder. "With some guests!"

A tall, lean woman with short cropped hair and a silver choker necklace appears in the doorway to the sitting room. In her brown muscled arms are a bushel of ripe red tomatoes, a bunch of rosemary, and bright yellow potatoes.

"I'm just back from the market." Her smile is charming. "Look at this bounty!"

The seven all nod approvingly, their stomachs starting to growl at the sight of food.

"I'm Lancelot." The woman grins. "But you can call me Lance. And who are you all?" she says, putting down the vegetables and sitting on the arm of Guinevere's chair.

"I was just about to find out, *mi amor*," Guinevere says, "but this is Queen Filomena of Westphalia, that much I know."

Guinevere points to Filomena, and Lancelot bows her head slightly in respect. "Quite young for a queen," she says. "You must be exceptionally gifted."

Filomena shrugs. "That or we're in a sort of a crisis," Filomena laughs, but then the laugh tapers off when she realizes how true it is. "You know what's going on all over Never After."

"Ah, yes," Lancelot says, suddenly grown solemn.

Filomena meant it as a joke, but it doesn't seem to have landed. Too real. They're suddenly aware of an elephant in the room. An elephant . . . or an ogre.

"Guinevere was just telling us about how you completed the most quests of any hero in Camelot," Jack says, seemingly in an effort to change the tone. "I'm Jack the Giant Stalker, by the way."

Filomena can see that Lancelot recognizes the name by the way her eyebrows shoot up in surprise. She nods. "Gwen loves to brag about me," Lance says, nudging Guinevere's shoulder playfully. "It's true. It was my honor to protect Avalon for a long time. But for every knight comes the time to step back and let new heroes take over."

Filomena is enraptured and confused. She shuffles forward from her place on a rug, toward Lance. "So it's true that there are other heroes in Never After?"

"You mean besides the League of Seven?" Lance smiles.

The group members look at one another in surprise.

"Yes, I've heard of you." Lance chuckles. "I like to keep tabs on what's happening in the rest of Never After. I must congratulate you on your many successes so far."

The group stutters and stammers, overwhelmed by the praise. Even Byron waves off the compliment with his meaty hand.

"But yes, Filomena, there are other heroes in Never After. Though almost all of them are here, in Camelot," Lance goes on. "Before we get too far with the chatting, though, let's put you all to work. *Vamos a la cocina.* Let's get started on dinner. I'm assuming you're hungry?"

"YES!" Alistair, Gretel, and Rosie answer at once.

The League of Seven plus Gwen follow Lance down the hall and into an enormous kitchen with windows overlooking more of Camelot.

"*¿Quien sabe cocinar?*" Lance asks.

Everyone points to Alistair.

"*Perfecto*. Alistair, is it? You'll be my sous-chef. The rest of you, get chopping."

Lance passes cutting boards and knives across a large wooden island, and soon enough everyone is chopping herbs and vegetables and mixing vinaigrettes. Gwen kneads a loaf of sourdough. Lance starts to pace and toss a tomato in the air. Filomena is amazed by Lancelot's combination of coordination and grace—the tomato remains unbruised as Lance tosses it. She places it in front of Filomena to slice.

"You should know that something has changed in Camelot as of late."

Filomena tries to focus on slicing the juicy red tomatoes on her cutting board, but it's hard to concentrate.

"As I'm sure you know," Lance goes on, "Camelot guards the sacred island of Avalon. I'm not sure what your quest is, and it's not my place to ask, but I'm guessing that finding Avalon has something to do with it."

"You're right, Lance," Jack says, eavesdropping from where he's chopping basil. "We do seek Avalon. We're looking for Excalibur."

Lance holds up a hand. "*¡No me digan más!* The fewer people who know the nature of your quest, the better. But you should know, in that case, that something has changed recently. Avalon has once again become shrouded in the Mists of Myth. This happens extremely rarely and only a few times in all of Camelot's history, when Avalon sought to protect itself from the outside world even more than usual."

Filomena looks to her friends to see if this phrase—Mists of Myth—registers with any of them. But all have furrowed brows; they're concentrating on their tasks at hand.

"Things have felt off in Camelot for a while," Gwen says, her rolling pin sliding over floured dough. "It used to be a place where pure bravery or honor could get a hero through a test. It's not so anymore. The tests of Camelot have become more obscure, complicated. There's a darker element to them. In order to pass them . . . well, the typical means aren't the only way anymore."

"And," Lance says, hopping up to sit on a countertop, "there's another thing. Arturo has been missing for several fortnights. We assume he has taken permanent shelter on Avalon, but we can't be sure. Perhaps . . ." Lance trails off. She looks out a window. It seems she can't bring herself to finish the sentence.

Gwen looks at her and sighs. "We've been asking any heroes who pass through to keep an eye out for dear Arturo. But so far, none have gone to Avalon. You're the only ones heading that way. Perhaps while you're there, you might keep an eye out for him and bring us word or news? If you can."

Filomena gets a sinking feeling at this. Avalon and Camelot having changed, King Arthur missing . . . Something about this all feels sickeningly familiar.

"Of course, Guinevere. It would be our honor," Jack says.

Lance snaps out of her daze and hops down from the counter, then claps her hands. "All right, heroes, let's get this feast started. You look like you need all the energy you can get."

CHAPTER FIVE

SPARKFLIES AND SPARKS FLY

After dinner, Lance and Gwen show everyone to their rooms. Gretel, Rosie, and Filomena bunk together, Beatrice and Byron next door, and Alistair and Jack down the hall. Despite the beautiful forest-to-table, market-fresh dinner, everyone is still completely wiped from the day's swoop hole and forest travel, so they all go to bed. But Filomena can't fall asleep. She lies awake between a snoring Gretel and a drooling Rosie and decides she needs some fresh air. This past day has been a whirlwind. She needs a moment to clear her head.

Filomena pads quietly down the staircase and sneaks out the back door of the kitchen to a small garden and a courtyard that overlook the hills. She sits down on a bench, takes a deep breath of crisp night air, and tries to calm her mind.

But then she notices a shadowy figure in the garden. Her heart jumps into her throat, and she instinctively touches her hip for her Dragon's Tooth sword. Lily Licks—she left it in the bedroom!

The figure steps closer, and a face emerges from the darkness, lit by the kitchen's light. It's Jack. Now Filomena's heart jumps in her throat for a different reason. He smiles, flustered.

"You're lucky I don't have my Dragon's Tooth sword on me!" Filomena whisper-yells. "I would've totally sliced you out of instinct!"

"I have to remember not to surprise you when you're armed." He laughs. "Can I sit?"

She shifts over on the bench to make room for him.

He points. "Look, sparkflies."

In the flower garden before them are little floating globes of light. Occasionally one bumps into a flower and a spark, like a minuscule firework, fills the air.

"I've never seen anything like that! They're so beautiful."

"Native to Camelot, I think," Jack says. "They spark when they touch something to protect themselves. It doesn't hurt too badly, though. It's just a little pinch. I've heard that some-times heroes in Camelot use them to stay awake at night when they're on a quest."

They laugh, then are quiet for a moment. Moments like this with Jack are always confusing. Filomena's never sure: Are they going to talk about what's going on between them, about their feelings, or about their mission? Sitting in this garden, on this bench, with him now makes her think of the moment they shared in Snow Country, outside the giants' cottage. They held hands that time. It was one of the first moments when she'd felt like Jack might have feelings for her. And since then, so much has happened between them, and so little at the same time. They've kissed—twice. But what does that mean?

Filomena wants to ask Jack about their relationship. Are they dating? Are they a couple? How do couples work in Never After? Well, Gwen and Lance seem very in love; how do they do it? Did Lance ask Gwen to be her girlfriend? Or did Gwen ask Lance? Or was it more subtle, natural? How in the worlds does all this work? And what if you have to com-plete a life-endangering quest with your partner? Are you still supposed to go on dates while you do it?

"So—" Filomena starts, just as Jack says, "I wanted—"

They laugh, both flustered.

"You go," Jack says.

"Oh, I was just going to say, uh . . ." Filomena didn't really know what she was going to say. She was just hoping that as soon as she started talking, the right words would come out. "I was going to ask you to tell me what you know about Camelot."

Silently she curses herself. Going for the safe option . . . again.

A look of surprise and disappointment flickers on Jack's face for a moment, but he quickly composes himself. "Right. You're coming to all this cold, I suppose."

"Just when I think I know everything about Never After . . . ," she says, trailing off.

"So you know now that Camelot is the border between Avalon and the rest of Never After," he starts.

"No one's really explained exactly why Avalon is so special, though. I mean, I know Excalibur is there . . ."

A look of sadness sweeps across Jack's face. "Avalon is where the fairies come from," he says. "It's the source of their magic, their home. That's why it's so sacred. That's why all of Camelot is so dangerous—to protect the fairies and the magic that lies there. The fairies are able to pass through Camelot easily, but everyone else has to pass each test that appears. If you pass the tests, it assures your purity of heart, which deems you worthy of being welcomed to Avalon."

"So Camelot is like a safeguard for the fairies," Filomena says, nodding.

"Exactly."

They both fall silent, thinking of Zera, Colette, and all the other fairies who don't need safeguarding anymore.

"It worries me, what Gwen and Lance said. About the tests being different now. Something is afoot here. I haven't been in Camelot for ages. Since the war between the fairies and the ogres, Camelot has been sort of sealed off from the rest of Never After," Jack says. His brows furrow as he looks at the dark horizon.

"Is that why you're out here?" Filomena asks, her heart pounding. "To think about all this?"

Jack turns to look at her. He nods. "That and . . . other things."

There's a moment of silence between them. They look ahead, at the sparkflies making sparking noises in the gardens and electrocuting petals left and right.

Jack turns to her. "How are you doing, Fil? With your mom, with everything?"

Filomena takes a deep breath. "I've been trying not to think too much about her, to be honest. Knowing that her health, her life, all depends on me . . ."

"On *us*," Jack says. He puts an arm around her shoulders. She feels nervous at his touch but then relaxes into it. His arm is warm, and he smells like a campfire.

Filomena tries to draw courage to broach the relationship subject. If she can ride through Brocéliande Forest, she can do this. She can talk to a boy about her feelings. Right? Right?!

"Jack, I've been wondering something," she starts.

"I think I know what you're going to say," he says, pulling away his arm and facing her. She misses his arm instantly.

"Well, that's a surprise, because even I don't know what I'm going to say," she says, and then laughs.

"Sorry, go ahead," he says. "I didn't mean to interrupt."

The energy between them has turned frigid somehow. Filomena doesn't know why. They usually have such a sparking dynamic, teasing, laughing, natural. What happened to it? What's this awkwardness she feels? Is this what happens when friendship turns to romance? Do things always get weird?

"I was just wondering, uh, what's going on with us?" she finally says.

"Oh, right," Jack replies, suddenly seeming nervous.

If he just asks me to be his girlfriend, Filomena thinks, *then all this will make sense. That's what's supposed to happen, right?*

Jack quickly stands up and starts pacing around. "I think you're really great, Filomena, and, uh, I think you're awesome and cool, and uh, and I think . . ."

Here it comes! Her hands start to clam up. A thumping starts in her chest. Are they about to officially become boyfriend and girlfriend?

"I think you're a great friend . . ."

Her heart sinks. Friend? In a split second, she feels so silly. It was a mistake. He thinks it was a mistake. The kiss, the feelings. He thinks it'll just get in their way.

"Right, friend," she says.

"Well, yeah, and also—"

But she can't let him go on anymore. She doesn't want him to go on about how they're just *friends*.

"You don't need to explain, Jack," she says coldly.

"Explain what?"

"Like you said, we're friends. We're friends on a quest, and that's it. Anything else would be too complicated, right?"

There are sparkflies in her stomach now. Why is she saying this? She doesn't even believe it! Does she?

"Oh, well, is that what you think?" Jack asks, frowning.

"It doesn't matter what I think. It is what it is." Filomena shrugs, though inside she feels the opposite of casual. "I think we should probably get some sleep. It's getting late, and we have a big day tomorrow. You know, with the quest and all," she continues.

"Oh, all right," he says brusquely. "I guess we should get some sleep."

They both stand, hovering there in the cold night air. What just happened? Filomena can't even remember what she just said, what he said. Who said what first. And they landed on just being friends? How did that happen? How can he pretend there's nothing between them? That it's not at least worth trying to see where it goes? It all happened so fast.

Filomena feels hurt in a way she doesn't recognize. She feels cold toward Jack, like she wants to make him feel a little hurt, too. Jack goes in for a tentative hug. She walks away, through the kitchen door, leaving Jack in the garden with his arms hanging wide in the air.

When she reaches her room, she feels sick with regret. Why did she leave Jack standing like that? Why didn't she hug him? What was he going to say before she interrupted him? No—that part she knows: He was just going to say that he wants to stay friends and be nothing more. So she had to take the reins before he could reject her. She also feels a gross sense of satisfaction, that he made her feel bad, and maybe she made him feel bad, too, for offering a hug that went unreciprocated. But that satisfaction fades quickly. The whole thing resulted in two people who feel weird now.

Filomena lies back down between Gretel and Rosie, who are each still snoring and drooling, respectively. She wants to wake them up, tell them about what just happened, and try to parse out what it means. None of it makes sense! But no, she can't do that to them. They were so tired. It can wait until morning, until tomorrow. For now, she closes her eyes and tries to fall asleep.

CHAPTER SIX

PUTTING THE BREAKFAST IN *BED-AND-BREAKFAST* FOR *QUESTING HEROES*

The next morning, Filomena wakes up alone. She sits up quickly, in a panic. A dream jolted her awake. She was dreaming of standing on a tiny island that was only the size of a bed. She knew, somehow, that the bed was Avalon. Around her, swimming in water that shifted colors like

Rosie's glasses and thermos, were the League of Seven. Farther out in the water, her mom was drowning, calling for help, but Filomena couldn't get to her, and none of Filo's friends would listen when she told them to go rescue her mom. Filomena was all alone on the bed island. She couldn't get into the water, and she couldn't bring anyone onto the island. She felt so, so alone.

Where is she? She looks out a window to her left. She's high up in green hills. It's so bright outside; there's blindingly bright sunlight on the endless green. She sees a tall woman picking a bunch of flowers, which look slightly fried, from a garden. Who is that person? A silver choker glints on her neck. Something clicks: Filomena's in Camelot, staying with Gwen and Lance. But her friends—where are her friends? That wasn't all a dream, was it?

She rushes down the stairs and breathes an audible sigh of relief as Rosie, Gretel, Byron, and Beatrice come into view. They're sitting around the large stone table, passing plates of food. Filomena runs over to sit beside Gretel and gives her a huge hug.

"There you are, sleepyhead!" Gretel says, ruffling Filomena's hair.

"I had the worst dream! I thought you all were gone and I was in Camelot alone again!" she says, her head on Gretel's shoulder.

"Oh, silly! We just wanted to let you sleep a little longer.

You seemed like you were having a hard night. You were tossing and turning a lot," Rosie says, pouring syrup on a stack of waffles.

Filomena notices Jack and Alistair aren't sitting at the table. "Where are Jack and Alistair?"

"Alistair's been making breakfast," Rosie says, nodding her head toward the kitchen.

"So you see," she hears Alistair saying, "if you press the flowers, you can actually infuse them *into* the syrup!"

"He's giving them bed-and-breakfast tips," Gretel says, rolling her eyes affectionately.

Filomena takes a lemon scone and starts buttering it. She takes a big bite. Having nightmares makes one ravenous, it turns out. "And Jack?" she says, her mouth stuffed full with scone.

"Here," a voice says from behind her. Jack walks down the stairs and sits at the table. "Just a *friend* reporting for duty."

The last part was said under his breath, but everyone still caught it. The members of the table look at one another, immediately sensing the tension. Before any of them can say anything, Gwen comes in from the kitchen.

"*¿Alguien necesita algo?* Coffee? Tea? *¿Tocino?*" she asks.

Everyone shakes their head no. The spread that's laid out on the table is more than adequate.

"*Está bien*, let me know if you do. You're going to need your strength to make it through Oz."

Filomena's head snaps up from buttering her scone.

"Gwen! *¡Vuelve aquí!*" Lance shouts from the kitchen. "Alistair's showing me how to infuse maple syrup into bacon! And also how to infuse bacon into maple syrup!"

"Oh, excuse me!" Gwen says to the group. "Can't miss that!"

"Wait, did you just say 'Oz'?" Filomena calls after Gwen, but Gwen is already in the kitchen and doesn't hear. Filomena turns to the table. "Did you guys hear that?"

They all shrug.

"What's Oz?" Rosie asks.

"I'm not sure exactly what it means here, but in the mortal world it's another famous story. Kind of like a fairy tale," Filomena responds.

"I think we should wrap up here," Jack cuts in. "Let's go pack our stuff. We should get going."

Jack leaves the table and calls to Alistair in the kitchen.

"Do we have to go?" Alistair whines. "I'm having so much fun!"

While everyone else goes to grab their stuff, Filomena walks into the kitchen to find Lance and Guinevere cleaning up.

"Hi, can I talk to you two for a minute?"

"*¡Sí!*" Lance says. She's drying breakfast plates.

"I was just wondering, Gwen, before, when you said we'll need strength to make it through . . . Oz. Not Camelot, but Oz."

"Oh," she says, "*sí*. Camelot, Oz, you know, different names for the same place."

"Wait, what?" Filomena asks. Camelot and Oz belong in two completely different stories in the mortal world . . . How can they be the same place here?

Lance doesn't seem to notice Filomena's agitation. "Listen, dear, I wanted to give you some advice before you all head out. Make sure, when you're moving through your quest, not to take anything at face value. These days, things are not what they seem in Camelot. That's always been true, but now it's more true than ever. Pay attention, be careful, and don't trust things right off the bat. Keep your wits about you."

Filomena nods, trying to understand what exactly this cryptic message means. She hears the others upstairs, gathering their things, getting ready to go. She doesn't have much time.

"I have one last question," she says. "It's sort of, uh, unrelated to questing. But I feel like you two are good people to ask, anyway."

Sparkflies prick the inside of her stomach now. Lance and Gwen nod encouragingly at her. As she was falling asleep last night, she swore she'd ask them.

"How would you . . . ? Uh, how would I . . . ? How would you recommend, with feelings, and someone who's your friend . . . ? What's the best way to—"

"You have a crush on someone?" Gwen cuts in.

Filomena's relieved that Gwen picked up on it. She doesn't quite know how to phrase what she's asking. Like, *What do I do?* is basically what she wants to know.

"Yes, a big one," Filomena admits.

Lance and Gwen smile at each other.

"*Tan linda*," Lance says.

"You're wondering what to do about it?" Gwen asks.

"Yeah, pretty much."

"Does this person know that you have a crush on them?" Lance asks.

"I think so. We've kissed . . . twice. But recently we had this conversation where things got all confusing, and I thought he wanted to just be friends, but now I'm not sure that's what he meant, and now *he* thinks I want to be just friends . . ."

Lance and Gwen nod.

"It sounds like this person likes you back. So I think you can just let things unfold naturally! You don't have to label anything," Lance says. "*Eres joven*. Just see what happens."

"*Sí*, but also make sure to communicate what it is that you want. Be straightforward, and let them know how you feel," Gwen suggests.

"But what if I don't know what I want?" Filomena asks.

"Then maybe use this time to think about it and figure it out!" Gwen says. She walks over to Lance and puts her arm around the woman's shoulders. "There's no rush, remember that. In quests, yes. *En amor*, no."

This is not exactly the advice Filomena was hoping for— she was hoping for more of a step-by-step guide with very detailed instructions, including phrases to use and moves to make. But nothing is ever that easy, she's learning.

"Thank you, both of you. I really hope that we get to see each other again. I really liked spending time with you."

Lance puts her head on Gwen's shoulder, and they both smile at Filomena.

"It was a pleasure spending time with you, Queen Eliana," Lance says.

Filomena turns away and starts walking out the kitchen door to go grab her bag.

"Oh, and Filomena, that reminds me: There's one last thing we should tell you," Lance says. "In Camelot, you can't go backward, only forward. So just remember, whenever you leave somewhere, you won't be able to return until your quest is complete."

Filomena heads to her room to pack her things. Surprisingly, her thoughts are no longer occupied by only Jack. Now she's thinking about what Lance said as she fills her backpack. *You can't go backward, only forward.* What does that mean, exactly? It sounds like a rule for a story, a fairy tale. What does it mean for their quest?

The League of Seven is all packed up, ready, and waiting outside the front door. A stable boy brings Toto to them. Filomena has Ira on one hip and her Dragon's Tooth sword on the other. But just as they're leaving, walking down the porch's stone steps, Gwen comes running out.

"League of Seven," she yells, "I just received a message!"

The stable boy had retrieved a letter from town that morning. Word had been sent to Camelot regarding the whereabouts of King Byron and Queen Beatrice of Wonderland. Apparently Robin Hood had decided to take advantage of both Never After's current calm and the king and queen's time away—and partake in some petty theft. This had led to something more intense: Citizens of Wonderland were starting to rally . . . around him in the absence of their king and queen.

After reading the missive, Byron and Beatrice turn to each other.

"We can't let this get out of hand," Bea says. "The longer we're gone, the longer we leave this, the worse it could get. If Robin Hood starts to get people on his side, it could be really bad news for us in the long term."

Everyone is quiet, considering this for a second. It's true that Robin Hood is working with Olga, and while he could be doing it for money, it could be out of spite too, after Princess Jeanne's rejection. Could he be spreading her lies around Wonderland?

"What are you thinking? Should we leave?" Byron asks his wife.

"I think we must. We need to show our faces and try to figure out a way to get people back on our side."

"You're leaving?" Gretel says, her eyes tearing up.

"We don't have a choice," Beatrice says stoically but sadly. "I'm so sorry, Filomena. I really wanted to help you on this quest for your mother."

"I understand, Bea," Filomena says. And she does. Completely.

"I want to come with you, Bea," Rosie says. "Maybe I can use my inventions . . . ? I'm not sure. But I can help. Would that be okay, Fil?"

Rosie looks at Beatrice sweetly. Filomena realizes that Rosie bonded intensely with Beatrice and Byron when the group last split up for their quests. Rosie must find it hard to be apart from them now. Just like how Filomena feels about Jack, Alistair, and Gretel.

"Of course, Rosie. You'll be a huge help to Wonderland," Filomena says, giving Rosie a hug.

"But maybe it's better this way." Beatrice shrugs sadly. "It will be easier for you to travel around as a foursome."

"The League of Seven's breaking up?!" Alistair cries, throwing his arms around Rosie. "Nooooo!"

"Alistair, come on now," Jack says, patting him on the back. "We're not breaking up! Byron and Beatrice have to take care of their kingdom. It's just one quest."

Alistair wipes a tear from his eye. "Oh. Right. I'm not crying, I'm totally not crying."

Filomena feels a mixture of emotions. On one hand, she's sad to be losing three of the League of Seven. On the other hand, she wishes they would stay—now she has even less of a buffer between her and Jack! Okay, so it's not so much a mixture of emotions as a mixture of *bad* emotions.

"Please be safe, you three," Gretel says, hugging Beatrice tightly. "Come back to us in one piece."

"Same goes for you!" Beatrice says.

The two groups all exchange hugs, then stand back and look at one another sadly for a moment.

"I think this calls for a group hug," Filomena says.

"Thank goodness you said that! I need one!" Alistair says. His face is already in Byron's chest.

And with that, the League of Seven splits in two: one half to Never After's other kingdoms, the other half deeper into Camelot. Or is it Oz? Filomena has a feeling there's still a lot to find out.

CHAPTER SEVEN

THE WATER'S WARM

"All right. Dish."

Gretel raises her eyebrows for emphasis. Gretel and Filomena are riding Toto sidesaddle. Filomena is in front with her legs on Toto's right, and Gretel's behind with her legs on Toto's left. This way, they can talk face-to-face. Several yards ahead, Jack and Alistair walk with Ira, arguing with him about which way leads to Avalon. Filomena and Gretel figure they'll let Jack and Ira argue in peace. The two seem to have slightly different ideas on which path to take.

All around them, sloping hills and valleys rise and fall. Is

Camelot just one hill and valley after another? Where are the buildings? Where are the villages? Filomena wants to ask Jack, but he's been avoiding her. Or at least, that's what it seems like. He's not ignoring her, exactly, but he seems to get really involved in doing other things anytime she comes near.

"Dish what?" Filomena replies.

"Come on, don't hide from me. You and Jack are obviously having a weird thing," she says.

"I wanted to talk to you about it last night, but you were dead asleep."

"Something happened last night?"

Filomena relays the events in the garden to Gretel. How he wants to be just friends and how she agreed preemptively so that he couldn't fully reject her.

"But you didn't hear what he had to say! It sounds like he was just saying that you're a great friend *and* that you'd be great at something else . . . like being his girlfriend," Gretel says.

"Do you really think so?" Filomena says quietly. She starts reassessing everything.

"Jack is obviously wild about you. You need to give him a peace offering. Smooth things over so you can get back on track to your *cruuuuuush*," Gretel teases, tickling Filomena's stomach.

"Careful!" Filomena giggles. "If I laugh too hard, I'm going to fall off Toto!"

Filomena wants to ask Gretel for ideas of peace offerings,

but before she can, Jack calls to them: "We found something up here!"

Jack and Alistair wait until Toto catches up to where they are at the base of yet another hill. Jack points to a speck on the horizon.

"I don't see anything," Gretel says.

"It's . . ." Jack squints. "I'm almost sure that's Avalon."

"What, that smudge in the distance?" Filomena says. She didn't mean to sound harsh.

"Isn't Avalon an island?" Gretel says.

"Yes, but maybe we just can't see the water? Anyway, let's walk in that direction," Jack says.

"Giant Stalker, I'm telling you, you can't just *walk toward Avalon*. It's not one place; it's a journey," Ira says from Jack's hand.

"Does Avalon move?" Filomena asks. "Like the forest?"

"Not exactly, darling," Ira answers, "but you can't see Avalon until you've completed the necessary tests."

"So that's not Avalon?" Alistair asks.

"Who knows? We need to pick a direction, so let's just go, all right?!" Jack snaps.

Alistair widens his eyes, mouthing *Yikes* to Gretel, who stifles a laugh. But Filomena isn't laughing. Is this what happens when feelings get involved with questing? You end up with snappy friends?

They walk in silence for a while, with Gretel and Filomena still riding Toto a few paces behind Jack and Alistair.

"I had some fabulous ideas for new designs while we were at Gwen and Lance's," Gretel says. "Jack, if we can get to a village post office so I can mail them to Lillet, that would be great. Do you think we can find one?"

Jack looks over his shoulder at Gretel while keeping pace. "We're on a quest and you're thinking about dresses and outfits?"

Gretel's mouth opens wordlessly in hurt surprise.

"Jack, that's not very nice," Alistair says. "Gretel's dresses and outfits are incredible."

Jack shakes his head, as if trying to rid himself of something. "You're right, you're right. I'm sorry, Gretel. I didn't mean that. I'm just feeling worked up. We'll try to find somewhere so you can send your designs."

Jack says this without looking back at Gretel, then speeds up his pace to get away from the group. He walks alone, ahead of them.

"Don't listen to him, Gretel," Filomena says.

Gretel's silent for a moment. "Do you think he's right? Is it silly of me to be focusing on these things?" she asks, wringing her hands.

"Hey," Filomena says as she puts her hand on Gretel's shoulder, "tell me about Lillet! You've been designing clothes for her?"

Gretel wipes her eyes and smiles through her tears. Filomena remembers when Gretel first told her about the carriage ride from Snow Country to Eastphalia, when Gretel and Alistair decided to hitchhike to get to Prince Charlie and Princess Hortense. They'd lucked out by catching a ride with none other than Lillet, the most famous opera singer in all of Never After. She travels around the kingdoms, performing for royal courts, and she had let them ride with her because Gretel promised to make her a beautiful outfit. It turns out that Lillet loves Gretel's designs and now wants to exclusively wear Gretel's creations for her performances.

"We've been sending parcels with sketches and notes back and forth from wherever I am ever since I designed that first gown. I'm designing a collection for her next opera kingdom tour." Gretel smiles modestly.

"See? That's incredible, Gretel!"

Filomena is genuinely impressed and bursting with pride. This whole time, when they've been on quests, Gretel's also been growing her business. It's amazing that she has the capacity to work toward her passion, even amid all the chaos.

Toto stops walking, and the girls look up from their conversation. They've come to a semicircle of trees. Jack and Alistair are leaned over, looking at something on the ground.

"Guys, come over here," Jack says.

They dismount Toto and walk over to the boys. The four plus Toto stand in the middle of the tree semicircle.

Before them are four small circular pools of water, each about the size of one Alistair, lengthwise. The water is crystal clear. Filomena leans over to peer into one pool and see how deep it goes. As she does, the pool turns an opaque shimmering silver that shows her reflection. Around the top edge of the pool bloom little pink flowers in quick succession. Their buds spell out *Filomena*.

Filomena jumps a little and gasps. She looks to her friends. "What is this?" she asks.

She sees that the other pools have done the same—turned from clear water to silvery liquid that shimmers with their reflections. Above each pool is a name spelled out in flowers. Another sentence spelled out with flowers appears underneath each pool:

Jump in, the water's warm.

The four adventurers glance at one another, confused.

"What is this?" Alistair asks.

"I think this might be our first test," Jack answers.

"Speak for yourself; I already went through a harrowing test to get here," Filomena adds.

"That's right, and you never told us what the test was like! Maybe you can tell us quickly now, and that can help us pass this one," Gretel says.

"Kids, I don't think there's time," Ira says from Jack's hand.

Unsure what he means, Filomena glances back at her pool. A beam of light flashes the number ten on the surface of the water. Then it changes to a nine, an eight . . .

"It's a countdown! We have to get in!" Filomena yelps.

Jack quickly ties Ira to Toto.

"Good luck, everyone," Jack says. "We can do this."

He jumps.

"See you on the other side," Alistair says, trying to smile, and dives in headfirst.

Gretel blows Filomena kisses, then hops feetfirst into the pool.

Filomena takes a breath.

Three . . . two . . .

She jumps.

CHAPTER EIGHT

THE POOLS OF CAMELOT

Filomena imagines this is what walking the bottom of a lake is like. It's hard to move, slow to walk. But it must not be water, because she can breathe. Ten feet or so above her, where the sky should be, is a ceiling of some kind with a skylight. The skylight must be the opening of the pool that she jumped through.

Right away, Filomena tries to keep her wits about her, like Lance advised. In Brocéliande Forest, she totally lost herself and became instantly doubtful of her capabilities, and she almost failed the test that way. There must be something in these obstacles that tricks your mind into doubt. She reminds herself now that she is in a test, that this isn't real. But for some reason that thought is hard to hold on to. It keeps slipping away.

She tells herself to keep walking. That seems like the only thing there is to do. Keep walking slowly through this thick substance. It's hard to see clearly; everything is slightly blurry. Around her sway large clumps of seaweed, flowing up from the ground like small trees and she has to swat her way through them.

Then, in front of her, a wooden sign emerges from the sandy ground. Writing is carved into it.

You have to choose, Filomena.

Choose what? She takes a few more blurry steps through the seaweed until a clearing appears. There is a blank wooden sign, and on either side of the sign float two bodies. One of the bodies is Filomena's mother, Bettina. The other is Jack. Their eyes are open, but they have no expressions on their faces. A jolt of panic rushes through Filomena's body. Are they dead? But no, their chests are moving; they're both breathing.

On the sign, a phrase carves itself with an invisible hand: Choose one.

Choose one?! How can she choose one? If she chooses one, what will happen to the other? Will the other die? She can't choose one. There must be a loophole.

She slowly walks closer to these two people, these people she loves so much. What will happen if and when she chooses? Where will they be taken? Where will *she* be taken? Nothing about this makes sense, but she feels an urgency so intense that she tries to grab both their hands and swim through the gooey thick substance with them in tow. But as soon as she grabs their hands, the skin on each turns burning hot. She recoils.

The sign has carved new words now.

You must play by the rules, Filomena.

Choose one. If Filomena has to choose, who should it be? Her mother or Jack? It should be her mother, of course. Right? But the thought of leaving Jack here, floating silently, makes her feel nauseous. An itch forms at the back of her brain. This feels too real. But no, wait—what was it she was trying to remind herself of coming into this? How did she get here again? She looks up. She sees the skylight. Of course! This isn't real! This is a test!

Relief floods her chest. She doesn't have to choose because this isn't real.

Victoriously Filomena jumps and swims up toward the

skylight. She's cracked it; all she has to do is remember that she is in a test, and then she doesn't have to choose. Like in the forest, when she just had to keep walking. She reaches up through the skylight and finds the edge of the ground. She pulls herself up, out of the pool, and back into the normal, thin, non-gooey air of Camelot.

She coughs and heaves for fresh air on the side of the pool, relief coursing through her. Did the others figure this out?

When she looks up, she sees a figure in the trees. Not Jack, nor Gretel, nor Alistair, but someone she's never seen before.

"You really think it will be that simple, Filomena?"

She didn't notice it before, but there's a little house in the semicircle of trees around the pools. A treehouse, actually. It's up in the treetops overlooking the water. And now a woman is floating down from the treehouse, down toward where Filomena is coughing for normal air. The woman seems to be sitting on something.

The woman *tsks* at her, shaking her head with disapproval. Thick red hair trails all the way down her back, covering a red velvet robe. Filomena—rubbing her eyes from the confusion of the test, still sitting on the ground by the edge of the pool—fully takes in the woman for the first time.

"What kind of hero would you be if you just ran away from all the tough decisions you had to make?" the woman says with faux sympathy, bending down to pat Filomena on the head. "We can't have our heroes making those kinds of choices, can we?"

The woman begins to pace around the clearing. She's using a broomstick as a cane. *That's what she was floating down on: a broomstick,* Filomena realizes. The woman stops and puts her chin on the end of the broomstick. Her heels sink into the forest floor. Filomena notices a glimpse of sparkling red peeking out from beneath the hem of the red robe.

"Unfortunately it doesn't seem like your friends fared much better," the woman says, motioning to the rest of the pools.

One by one, Gretel, Jack, and Alistair hoist themselves over the edges of their respective pools, gasping for air. They all shake their heads and look around, reacquainting themselves with their surroundings.

"What's happening?" Jack says, immediately on alert.

The woman in red pouts, her chin still on the broom handle.

"What's happening, cutie, is that you all failed the test miserably. I mean, Jack, my boy, I know that was pretty traumatizing, what we put you through. But come on, you're still not over it? That happened years ago! You have to learn to love, baby, and to not be afraid! Did you like that little twist we added? That was my idea." She looks at them with a mocking sympathy. "It's too bad. I was rooting for you. Really! I was! But it seems like none of you even knows yourself at all!"

The woman in red begins to pace around them. "I mean, Gretel, come on, was that really too hard for your sweet little noggin? Tsk tsk. I guess it's true what they say about blonds and brains. Better to stick to playing dress-up, dear."

She walks over to Gretel and pats her on the head. Gretel pulls her head away instinctively and scowls at the woman with an expression of pure hatred that Filomena has never seen her make.

"And, Alistair! It figures that you're too scared to go into battle on your own, without your protector by your side."

Alistair looks at his hands ashamedly.

The woman in red smiles, then turns to Filomena.

"And of course, Filomena. You can't have it both ways forever, girl. That's a little greedy, don't you think?"

Filomena looks at her three companions like, *What in the worlds just happened?* She's gathering that the others ran away from whatever their challenges were, too.

"But we passed, right?" Filomena says. "We realized this was a test, and we escaped. So we passed?"

"Oh!" The woman in red cackles. She screeches with laughter so hard that she actually bends over, her hands on her knees. Then, abruptly, she stops, clears her throat. She turns her broom horizontal, where it floats in midair, and takes a seat on it. The broom lifts her up in the air, a few feet above where the adventurers sit.

"No, Filomena, no. That's not how these tests work. You

completely missed the point of the test, dearies. None of you went through with your test; you all ran away. So none of you passes."

Filomena looks at Jack in a panic. No one ever told her what happens if they don't pass a test. Do they get booted from Camelot?

"Unfortunately, that means I'm going to have to kill you." The woman in red shrugs. A jolt runs through Filomena as she reaches for her Dragon's Tooth sword. She can see Jack, Alistair, and Gretel stiffen as well. But none of them dare move just yet.

"It's a shame, really. I was looking forward to watching you fumble a bit more on the way to your eventual deaths. You four had a particularly interesting course ahead of you in Camelot. It would've been so fun to watch. But alas, I don't always get to choose! And we can't dillydally too long—another round of heroes will be here soon. Oh, don't worry, they're not on the same quest as you or anything. Not that it would matter now."

The woman in red points a long finger, and out from it jets a fiery strike. Alistair jumps up and away quickly; the fireball lands exactly where he was sitting and burns a black hole into the earth.

"Good reflexes, Alistair!" The woman sitting on the broomstick chuckles. She glides back and forth in the air above them.

Filomena panics. They can't escape her, can't run away; she'll just follow them on her magic broomstick. There's no way they can outrun her. They're going to have to battle her. But how can they battle her with Dragon's Tooth swords if she'll just float away from them at every turn?

Suddenly Filomena has an idea. It strikes her like a blast of fire.

She runs up to the treehouse where the woman first appeared.

"What are you doing? Don't touch my things!" the woman screeches.

She aims a spray of fire at Filomena, who dodges it. It lands beneath the treehouse, on some branches that support the structure. Filomena starts to climb the tree trunks, dodging the fire. The fire continues to strike the tree holding up the house.

Filomena hopes she can keep this up. Do the others understand what she's trying to do here? She hopes so.

"What's your game here, girlie?" the woman in red says.

The woman is so focused on Filomena that she doesn't notice Alistair sneak up behind her. When the treehouse is starting to teeter on singed branches, Alistair pushes the woman in red on her broom toward the house. The broom glides quickly and seamlessly underneath it. Filomena jumps out of the way, and at the last moment, when she's away from the house, Jack lets his vines loose. They wrap around the treehouse and yank, pulling the remaining branches apart. The house falls, quickly, suddenly, thuddingly, onto the woman in red. Her broom flies out from under her, and she shrieks a horrible, painful shriek.

Once the dust clears, all that's left are her feet sticking out from under the house. On them are a pair of ruby-red slippers.

CHAPTER NINE

CAVERN OF CRYSTALS

In the aftermath, they're all frozen. Filomena stands mere feet from the collapsed house, staring at the feet and the ruby slippers in horror. Jack stands with his vines slowly retracting. Alistair stares from where he pushed the woman. And Gretel, a mere bystander in all this, stands near the pools. Toto and Ira are behind a tree, where they've been hiding ever since the four jumped into the pools.

"What the . . . ," Alistair starts.

"Did we just . . . kill her?" Filomena says.

It feels different from when they killed ogres. The ogres

were evil hulking masses of pure destruction. But killing this strange, cackling woman . . . it doesn't feel good. It feels quite horrible, actually.

"We had to, didn't we?" Alistair says. "She was going to kill us!"

"We need to get out of here, now," Jack says, his voice like concrete. "I have a bad feeling about this."

Filomena whistles, and Toto comes trotting over to her. She hops on his back, ready to make a run for it.

"Wait a second," Gretel says. "What about this?"

She motions to the magic broomstick, which is hovering in the air. It isn't alive per se, but it also doesn't seem *not* alive. It somehow seems to bow to them. Is the broomstick switching allegiances?

"I think we should take it. That way you and Jack can ride Toto, and Alistair and I can ride the broomstick. It'll make our trip faster."

"Great thinking, Gretel. That's smart," Jack says, as Filomena hoists him up to sit behind her on Toto.

Gretel smiles, pleased with herself. Then she looks at the ruby slippers.

"Okay, don't laugh at me, guys, but it would be a crime against fashion to leave these slippers here. They're so gorgeous!"

The four of them look at the feet and the slippers. They are stunning otherworldly shoes. The heels are sleek, and a similar shape to that of Cinderella's glass slippers, but these are a deep, infinite red, with sparkles like a thousand stars. It's impossible to see what material they're made from; they're too beautiful to look at too closely.

"We don't have any room in our packs, Gretel," Jack says.

"Well, I can't wear them. I promised myself I would stop wearing heels on our adventures. Plus, I made myself these combat boots," Gretel says, holding up a foot to admire the custom-made soft brown leather boots with thick pink rubber treads.

"Filomena, would you mind wearing them? At least just while you're riding? I'll repack my bag and make room for them the next time we get to a rest stop. I might want to model a collection inspired by them!"

Filomena looks at her own worn-out purple combat boots. They're ratty, with the soles almost falling apart. She looks at the beautiful slippers and Gretel's beautiful pleading face.

"How can I resist those puppy-dog eyes? Sure, sure, I'll wear them."

So Gretel swaps the ruby slippers from the woman in red's feet with Filomena's combat boots.

"It feels wrong, leaving her shoeless," Gretel says.

Then Gretel hops onto the broom, nodding for Alistair to sit behind her. The broom dips slightly from Alistair's weight.

Alistair laughs. "Oh come on, you can handle both of us, can't you? That woman was, like, twice our height!"

The broom seems to concede and rises.

Filomena gazes at Ira. "What was all that, Ira?" she asks. "Let's walk and talk, kid."

Eventually, after much bickering around directions, Ira and Jack settle on a path. It seems to Filomena that neither really knows which way he's going, but Ira seems to have figured out the general direction they have to head in. So what if they didn't pass the test? They made it *beyond* the test, and that has to count for something. Right? She passes Ira to Gretel.

Finally Jack comes up with an idea—to go through a cave system, where they may find a bit of time and a safe spot in which to catch their breath—and Ira concedes.

As they prepare to ride, Jack puts his arms around Filomena's waist. Filomena knows this is just for safety, but she gets a bubbling sensation of excitement in her stomach nonetheless. And then she feels dread and regret when she thinks of their conversation. Of how she said they should just be friends. Jack tightens his grip around her, and Toto starts to walk.

They come to a cave opening soon after leaving the clearing: a tunnel on the side of a hill. It's pitch-black inside, and Toto stops moving as soon as they enter.

"Filomena," Ira says from Gretel's hand, "why don't you light this up for us?"

At first, Filomena doesn't know what he means. But of course, of course! Filomena lights her mark of the thirteenth fairy to illuminate their path. The sides of the tunnel aren't the damp earth or rock that she was expecting but rather a spectacular white marble. Everywhere, coming up from the ground and down from the ceiling, are stalagmites and stalactites, but they appear to be made from solid crystals. Rose quartz, amethyst—all the sorts of crystals Filomena's mom scoffed at when they'd go to the market in North Pasadena. Bettina's erudite British sensibilities found these sorts of crystals, with their New Agey powers, to be laughable. But then again, whoever thought her mom would be cursed by an ogre, or that a magic sword would be the only way to save her? Filomena tries to push these thoughts from her mind. Thinking of her mom is too painful. Filomena has to focus on saving her.

"Wow, what is this place?" Alistair marvels. "These crystals look like candy . . . I wonder if I can just give them a little lick . . ."

Gretel laughs and pulls Alistair back onto the broom but keeps them from teetering over.

"It's very beautiful, isn't it?" Jack says. His voice quiet, just behind Filomena's ears.

Because they're riding a horse, she can't look at Jack directly, and somehow this makes talking to him easier.

"It is. How do you know about this place?" she asks.

"Zera brought me here when we were gathering people for the Last Battle. It's a cave system created by the fairies."

"That explains why it's so wonderful," Filomena says. She

pauses, unsure if she should say what she's thinking. But she decides, here and now, that from now on, she wants to say to Jack what she's thinking without worrying about his reaction. Otherwise what's the point of this friendship or whatever it is? She can't always treat Jack like he's some damaged hero with a broken heart.

"It must bring back a lot of memories, being here," she says after a few beats.

"It does," he says, his breath soft in her ear. "But I'm glad to be making new memories now."

A jolt in her stomach. The good kind. Are they back on? Are things going back to normal now?

Toto walks and the broom flies in silence for a few moments as everyone takes in the beauty of the cavern and decompresses from the scene they just left behind. As they ride, Filomena lets another thing she's been pushing out of her mind finally wash over her. When the house landed on the woman in red, Filomena felt like she was having déjà vu. It's a feeling she's had several times since coming to Never After. The feeling that she is living something vaguely familiar, something that echoes in a secret part of her mind. Usually this happens when she realizes she's living a familiar story. When she saw the woman in red's feet sticking out from under the house, she knew. She finally knew what was happening. Now she has to tell her friends what she knows.

"Gretel," she says to her left, where Gretel and Alistair are hovering. "Do you know the mortal world story called *The Wizard of Oz*?"

"Of course! It's one of my dad's favorite movies. I've watched it a million times." Gretel smiles.

"What is it?" Alistair asks. "I've never heard of it."

"Have you, Jack?" Filomena asks, turning her head slightly to see him from over her shoulder.

He shakes his head.

Looks like there's another story to add to the thirteenth book. Gretel and Filomena quickly explain the plot to the boys.

"What are you thinking?" Gretel asks Filomena when they're finished.

"I think we should maybe share what our experiences in the pools were," Filomena says.

She's met with silence. Alistair looks at his feet, Gretel looks away, and Jack is quiet behind her.

"I know, I know," Filomena goes on, "they're probably really personal. Maybe even embarrassing. But if we can't share that stuff with one another, who can we share it with?"

Again, silence.

"Plus, I think we might *need* to share, in order to know what we're dealing with on this quest."

"What about your test in Brocéliande Forest?" Alistair asks. "What happened there?"

Filomena isn't sure if he's just using this as a distraction technique or what, but either way, she figures she should tell them.

She tells them everything. Well, almost everything. She

leaves out the parts about Jack. Those are suddenly getting too real.

They take it all in, but they are all too embarrassed to share what happened in the pools. Filomena gets an idea.

"What if I turn my light off while we're talking? So it seems less embarrassing? And I'll go first, okay?"

"Sure, fine, whatever," the others mutter. She turns the light off. It's pitch-black in the tunnel now. They stop to chat.

"Okay." Filomena takes a breath. This is a big reveal, massive. She left Jack out of her explanation of the first test, but she can't exactly exclude him from this one, too. But whatever. Their lives are at stake, right? And didn't she *just* promise herself that she'd be more straightforward?

"So when I dove into the pool, I came to a wooden sign that said, *You have to choose, Filomena.* And beside the sign were my two choices: two people sort of floating in the water. One was my mom. And one was . . ."

Is she really going to do this? Is she going to reveal what feels like such an intense secret? Yes. She has to. *Be brave, Filomena,* she tells herself. *Be brave.*

"One was Jack."

She feels Jack tense up behind her. Good sign? Bad sign? Is he embarrassed for her? That he's important enough to her that she had to choose between him and her own mother?

There's total silence. Then she feels his arms tighten around her waist and give her a squeeze, like a hug. Her skin feels like it's on fire. Thankfully Gretel chimes in.

"In mine," Gretel starts, "I had to complete this really complicated puzzle. It was like a logic puzzle: putting together this coded language with blocks to try to unlock an answer that would free all of you. But I couldn't do it. I tried, but I just couldn't. I think I got close, but these voices kept whispering to me, saying I am so stupid, that I have no brains, that I'd never be able to do it. So I just gave up."

They're quiet again. Then Alistair's voice comes through the darkness.

"In mine, I had to face off against the ogres without Jack. I was all alone, and I felt like I couldn't fight on my own, like any ounce of bravery I have only comes from being sidekick to someone with real bravery and following his lead."

Jack sighs heavily from behind Filomena. "When I went down, I saw my village burning all over again. My family was trapped, and there was nothing I could do to save them. And I thought, *Okay, this has already happened, this has already happened.* But then there was someone else in my family's house who was burning, too. It was Filomena. And I thought, *No, I can't watch this.* And I left."

They wait in silence for a few more moments.

"Is it okay if I turn the light on?" Filomena asks.

"Yeah, sure," the others say.

The tunnel lights up with her mark again.

"I think I know what's happening, guys," Filomena says. "I'm Dorothy. Gretel, you're the scarecrow. Alistair, you're the lion. Jack, you're the tin man. And we're in Oz."

The realization washes over her friends.

"Does that mean . . . ?" Gretel starts. "Does that mean we just killed the Wicked Witch of the East?"

"Fallen house? Ruby slippers? I'm pretty sure we did," Filomena says, "and if that's the case, you know what that means . . . The Wicked Witch of the West is still out there."

CHAPTER TEN

GITA THE GOOD WITCH?

After Filomena's declaration about Oz, Gretel and Alistair decide they need to test just how fast their new magic broom can go in case they need a quick getaway from a certain witch who might be after them. They say they want to try flying up ahead and that they'll be back shortly, so as they zoom through the cavern system, Toto clops on, steady as always.

But that leaves Filomena alone with Jack for the first time since the previous night in the garden. She's sure he's thinking about what they've just revealed to each other. He was in her vision in the pool, and she was in his. What does it all mean?

"Sort of weird that we can't face each other, huh?" she says.

He laughs. "Yeah, it is a bit odd, talking to the back of your head."

"Hey, I have an idea. Back up a bit."

Jack slides backward on Toto's long back, sitting more toward Toto's rear. Filomena shifts herself around to sit side-saddle, so they're now facing each other.

"Toto, is this okay?" she asks, patting the horse's neck.

He whinnies contentedly in response—the horse version of "Go ahead."

Now here they are, face-to-face, on the back of a horse.

"So about the other night . . . ," Filomena begins.

"I'm sorry," Jack says right away.

This surprises her; she wasn't expecting an apology. She was more so expecting to *give* an apology.

Jack goes on: "I'm sorry I was so abrupt when you asked me what's going on with us. The truth is . . ."

Filomena holds her breath.

"The truth is, it's just hard to know with everything going on . . ."

Dread drops into her stomach. Is he taking back the kisses? Is he taking back liking her? Is he taking it all back? Again?

"It's just hard to know what to do, you know?" he finishes.

That's it? That's all he has to say to her?

"Uh, sure, yeah," she says.

Her head is swimming again. Are they always going to speak in these vague generalities? Does anything they say even *mean* anything?

"So we're on the same page?" he says.

Filomena has no idea what page they're on. She wants to just ask, *What's going on?! Do you like me? Do you* love *me? Do you want to be with me? Was our conversation in the garden for real, are we really just friends?* But what if they're on different pages? She's always been on the same page as Jack, ever since they met and became best friends. She loves the feeling of being the one who understands him like no one else does, the one who knows what move he's going to make before he even makes it. Why do *feelings* have to change that? What if she admits her feelings and they're *not* on the same page? Plus, there's still so much to do on their quest. She can't risk being fully heartbroken *and* trying to save her mom. If he doesn't like her anymore, maybe it's just easier to not know.

"Yeah," she says. "Yeah, we're totally on the same page. Sure."

He leans in, but before she realizes what he's doing, she pats him on the shoulder. He leans back and chuckles dismissively, nervously.

Wait, did he just try to kiss her? Did she just pat him on the shoulder? Why did she do that? She laughs lightly, to match his tone. Now they're both just giggling nervously at each other. *Uh, what just happened?*

The confusion doesn't break when they emerge from the tunnel and into sunlight. They've come to an exit from the cavern system.

The sunlight is bright, almost blinding, after the soft marble glow of the caves. A few seconds after they emerge, still on Toto's back, their friends on the broomstick come shooting out of the cave mouth after them.

"Woooooo-hoo!" Alistair pumps his fist. "We lapped you guys twice! This thing is *fast!*"

"I think I feel sick," Gretel says, holding her stomach. "But that was totally awesome." She and Alistair high-five.

At least someone had fun in the caves, Filomena thinks. She turns on Toto, so she's not facing Jack anymore, and looks around. They've come to another hill.

"So where to now, kids?" Ira says from Gretel's hand.

No one seems sure of the next move. There looks to be no clear path to Avalon. Filomena supposes that this is yet another protection method. But in that case, how does one get to Avalon if one is pure of heart and holds good intentions? If only there were a clear-cut path or a road . . .

Oh! A flash of recognition pops in her head.

"The yellow brick road!" she cries out.

Jack and Alistair exchange confused glances, but Gretel smacks her forehead. "Of course!" she says.

"*Follow the yellow brick road . . . Follow the yellow brick road . . . ,*" the girls sing.

"Okay, is this, like, another cheeseburger-FaceTime-mortal-world thing we don't know about?" Alistair says.

"Sort of." Filomena laughs. "In *The Wizard of Oz*, Dorothy and her companions have to follow the yellow brick road to get to the Emerald City, where the Wizard of Oz is. I'm betting that if, like Gwen said, Camelot is Oz, then Avalon must be the Emerald City."

A wave of excitement washes over the group as they're renewed with energy.

"But wait, Filomena," Gretel says, tamping down the excitement for a second. "If that's true, then why are they from different stories in the mortal world?"

Filomena considers this. Every other time she's discovered a character or a story from the mortal world in Never After, the Never After version—the *real* version—has been totally different. But why are these two separate stories combined? "I'm not sure, Gretel. I think we'll have to keep an eye out for more about that."

"And, more importantly, how do we get to the yellow brick road?" Alistair asks.

A good question. Filomena's pretty sure that in the *Wizard of Oz* movie, the yellow brick road just appeared. It appeared when . . .

"So you finally figured it out!"

The four jump. The voice comes from above. Filomena

looks up and sees a pink puffy skirt floating down from the sky. That can't be too threatening, can it?

"Ugh, why does it always take forever to float down?" the voice mutters. "This really lessens my dramatic impact."

The four wait as the figure continues to float. Finally she stops in front of them, a few feet above the ground: a tiny woman in a pink puffy dress that's covered in silver stars and has giant puffed sleeves. A pink headscarf covers her hair and neck. The woman pats down her dress, trying to make it less puffy, and checks to make sure her hijab is not crooked. It seems like her gown is trying to swallow her whole.

"I love her look," Gretel whispers to Alistair.

Still hovering, the woman plants a long, twinkling silver staff into the ground and crosses her arms. "Well, well, well. If it isn't four of the notorious League of Seven in my neck of the woods!"

Filomena is racking her brain for clues. Pink dress, silver stars, floating . . . Can this be Glinda the Good Witch? Of course, in the mortal world, Glinda is often depicted as golden haired. But Filomena has come to understand that the mortal world's versions of stories are not quite true.

"Hello! I'm Filomena, it's a pleasure to m—"

The woman holds up a hand, signaling Filomena to stop. "Did I not just call you the League of Seven? I know who you are, let's not waste time. And what about me? Do you know who I am?"

The four are silent for a moment.

"Glinda the Good Witch?" Filomena ventures.

The woman in pink cackles, tossing her head back. "Oh, is that what they call me in the mortal world? The good witch? That's rich. Oh that is rich!" She stamps her staff while laughing. "But it's not Glinda, it's Gita. *Gita* the Good Witch. Also known as Morgan le Fay." Gita points to Filomena. "You get it. You have two names, right? Filomena, or should I say, *Eliana?*"

Jack dismounts Toto and takes a knee before Gita, bowing. "Morgan le Fay, Gita, it's a pleasure to make your—"

"Stop this, stop this!" Gita waves her hands in front of Jack's face, motioning for him to get up. "What is it with heroes these days? So formal! Loosen up, why don't you? *'It's a pleasure to make your acquaintance,'*" she mocks. "What are you going to do next, try to kiss my hand?"

Filomena and Gretel look at each other nervously. It's hard to get a clear read on Gita. Is she going to help them? Hurt them? Dismiss them altogether? And wait, isn't Morgan le Fay evil in the Camelot stories? Isn't she intent on trapping Merlin and killing Arthur? Then how can Morgan le Fay be Gita the Good Witch?

But there's no chance to ask since Gita seems intent on moving them along.

"So this is the time in your quest when you're looking for the yellow brick road," Gita says quickly, looking bored. "You seek it, I show you, yada yada, blah blah blah."

"Uh, y-yes, ma'am—er, or t-totally, dude, or . . . ," Alistair stutters, trying to gauge the right thing to call her.

"Just call me Gita," Gita says. "It's easier than Morgan le Fay. And we don't have all day here."

Filomena relaxes a bit. Gita seems more bored with her job as the yellow brick road's gatekeeper than malicious.

"So here's the deal," Gita says. "To get to the Emerald City, you have to follow the yellow brick road, and the yellow brick road is thataway." She points with her staff to a path down the side of the hill. "Follow that path until you see a big boulder, and when you see the boulder, turn left through a patch of trees. Once you emerge from the patch of trees, voilà, yellow brick road. It's a brick road that's yellow. You really can't miss it."

"Thank you so much, Gita!" Gretel says. She and Alistair are still hovering on the broom.

"Hmm," Gita murmurs, scowling in Gretel's direction. "Nice broom you have there."

The four look at one another, freaked for a moment, but Gita gets back to business quickly. "The one thing you need to know is that partway down the road, you're going to come to a fork. Make sure you take the left path. I repeat: Make sure you take the left path!"

The four nod.

"Say it back to me now, so I know you got it."

"Make sure you take the left path," say the four plus Ira, and Toto whinnies in time.

"I'm sorry," Gita says, "where did that other voice just come from? Your hand? A mirror? You know what, don't tell me, I don't want to know. I sense a long story behind that one, and I don't want to hear it."

The four gaze at her, blinking.

"Well, what are you staring at me for? Don't you have a quest to go on? Get moving! Quick, quick!" she says.

Then, before they can ask a question or thank her or anything, Gita—Morgan le Fay, whoever she is—floats up into the air like a pink puffy balloon.

"See ya later!" they hear as she drifts away, into the sky.

CHAPTER ELEVEN

THE LITERAL YELLOW BRICK ROAD

F   *ollow the yellow brick road . . . Follow the yellow brick
        road . . .* Seems simple enough, right?

"Hey, guys," Filomena says as they stand in the clearing after Gita's takeoff, "I'm getting a bit sore from Toto's saddle. Do you think we can do a transportation swap?"

"I'll switch with you," Alistair says. "I haven't gotten to bond with Toto yet."

Filomena dismounts Toto and makes her way over to

Gretel and the magic broomstick. To be honest, Filomena's more in the mood for Gretel's company over Jack's than she is sore.

She takes a moment to get settled on the magic broomstick before they head down the path Gita pointed out.

"Whoa, this thing feels wild!" Filomena says. "I love it!"

The magic broomstick rises and dips slightly under their weight. It's as close to flying as she's ever felt.

"No offense, Toto. I still love riding with you, too," she says.

"Hey, I just remembered," Gretel says, "Toto is the name of Dorothy's dog in *The Wizard of Oz*!"

Filomena can't believe she didn't connect that sooner.

"Wait a second." She lifts Ira in front of her face. "You named Toto. Did you know Camelot is another name for Oz and that I'm Dorothy?"

"I thought it would be funny!" Ira shrugs as only a talking mirror can.

"You were really playing the long game with that joke." Gretel laughs.

Four heroes, one horse, one talking mirror, and one magic broomstick head in the direction Gita pointed. First in line are Toto, Jack, and Alistair, with Gretel, Fil, and Ira floating right behind. But as they keep pace, Filomena can't help but have doubts.

"Do you all think it's wise of us to just follow Gita's instructions, no questions?" she asks the others.

"It does put us in a tricky position," Gretel says. "If the Never After versions of things are always different from the mortal world versions, then doesn't that make Gita the Good Witch a bad witch?"

"And Morgan le Fay is pretty evil in Camelot as I remember from those stories," Filomena adds.

They think on this.

"What do you guys know about witches?" Filomena asks Alistair and Jack.

"*Witch* is just another word for an older woman who makes healing potions," says Jack. "But as I understand, they get a bad rap in the mortal world."

"That's true," says Filomena. She's always feared witches because of this. She thinks back to the Winter Witch in Snow Country, the one who gave Rosie the truth serum when Rosie was trying to rescue her brothers from Queen Christina's curse. Everyone was really taken aback when Rosie told them she went to go see the Winter Witch. Many say the Winter Witch rarely lets people out of her cave alive, but Rosie was fine.

"In the war between the ogres and the fairies, many witches took the ogres' side," Alistair agrees. "But some didn't. Some remained neutral."

"But that other witch, the Wicked Witch of the East?" Gretel says. "She was definitely bad, right? I mean, she was trying to kill us!"

Something Lance said is looping in Filomena's mind:

Things are not what they seem in Camelot. Before, Filomena would have said that such advice could apply to anything in Never After. It could be the fairy world's slogan. But Lance was right; something does seem different about Camelot. In the other kingdoms of Never After, things are almost the exact opposite of the fairy tales Filomena grew up with in the mortal world. If a character is bad in the mortal world's version of a fairy tale, then in Never After, that same character is misunderstood and has a good heart. If they are a hero in the mortal world's version of a fairy tale, they are a villain in Never After. But in Camelot . . . all bets seemed to be off. It wasn't as clear-cut. So what do they do now?

"I think we should follow Gita's instructions but proceed with caution," Jack says.

Filomena wants to disagree with him just on principle, just because she's annoyed and confused and weirded out by their whole dynamic. But she realizes that would be letting her feelings get in the way of their quest. And she won't let that happen.

So Filomena, Jack, Gretel, and Alistair follow Gita's instructions. On broom and steed, they head down the path, past the boulder, and through the patch of trees. On the other side, just like Gita said, they arrive at a yellow brick road.

"So it literally is a yellow brick road, huh?" Alistair says.

Gretel laughs. "What did you expect?"

"I thought maybe that was just an expression, you know,

like 'Follow the yellow brick road' is a metaphor for something."

Filomena laughs. "For once it looks like Never After is being straightforward!"

"Let's not jinx it," Jack says ominously.

Filomena ignores him, and they start their journey along the most famous brick road she knows.

She once again gets the strange feeling she's become accustomed to—the feeling that she's living out a fairy tale. Here she is: Dorothy! Only Filomena's traveling crew is a little different from the crew in the story she's heard. Mostly she's glad that the real Toto doesn't fit into a basket. That could make traveling a lot more difficult.

After a few rounds of I Spy in which all they are able to spy are grass, trees, yellow bricks, and the occasional sparkfly, the group arrives at that fork in the road.

"So we go left?" Jack asks.

"That is what Gita told us," Alistair replies.

"And we trust her, right?" Gretel asks.

"*Trust* might be a strong word for it," Jack ventures.

"I mean, she did appear out of nowhere at the exact time we needed her, which is a bit strange, but that's how it happens in the story. So I guess that makes sense . . . ," Filomena muses.

"But if we take the right path instead, what if something really bad awaits us there? What if Gita's warning is true?" Gretel says.

They all look at one another, puzzled. Do they trust Gita or not?

"Ira, what do you think?" Filomena asks the mirror.

"I'm not at liberty to say," Ira replies.

"What in the worlds does that mean?" Alistair says.

"There are just certain things I can't help with," Ira responds. "To be honest, I don't know what the right choice is here."

"What good is a talking mirror if he can't even tell us what road to take!" Alistair cries, leaning his head on Jack's back.

"What are you thinking?" Filomena asks Jack. Despite the weird feelings between them, the confusion and the almost kiss or not-kiss, the sort of apology or not-apology, she still turns to Jack when making decisions. Turns out that she still trusts him above all.

"I think we follow what Gita said. I don't know what other choice we have."

They all shrug. Left it is.

The yellow brick road is a lot longer than Filomena expected. After what feels like hours, they're still trekking the path. She supposes the *Wizard of Oz* movie never specified, exactly, the length of the road.

Still, everyone's been in good spirits. Gretel's sketching in her notebook—new ideas for a collection—while the magic broomstick carries them. Jack and Alistair are playing their favorite game of inventing things for Rosie to create. So far they've come up with a bacon-flavor infuser inspired by their time at the Bed-and-Breakfast for Questing Heroes; a horse couch ("Like a couch you can sit on while riding a horse!" Alistair said, his butt getting progressively more numb from the endless horse ride); and a kaleidoscope that, when you look through it, tells you whether someone is trying to trick you or be honest with you.

After they run out of ideas, the group is quiet for a while. They're starting to tire. As Gretel sketches the ruby-red slippers Filomena is wearing into her notebook for future reference, she sighs deeply.

"I feel guilty about what happened with the Wicked Witch of the East back by the pools. In a different way from when we've fought ogres. Jack, Alistair, you guys have more experience with this kind of thing," she calls to them. "Have you ever felt remorseful after a battle?"

They're both quiet for a moment, considering.

"Absolutely," Jack says softly.

"I guess that's the weird thing about all these quests," Alistair says. "Sometimes you hurt people, or worse."

"I guess it's something we'll all have to learn to bear together," Gretel says.

The four nod.

"Can I just say"—Filomena laughs—"how intensely thankful I am that I don't actually have to do this quest alone? Can you believe I really thought I was going to do that?!"

The other three laugh as well, eager for some levity.

"I never want us to be apart," Alistair says, hugging Jack from behind on Toto.

"Same!" Gretel yells.

Filomena hugs Gretel, but a little pinprick of dread forms in her stomach. She wants them to be together forever, too, but still there's that dread.

"Not to play into my trope too much," Alistair says, "but are you guys not, like, soooo hungry?"

As Alistair says this, a billboard appears on the side of the yellow brick road. Has that been there this whole time? Did they just not notice it? It's a huge billboard advertising a cheeseburger and fries. Underneath the photo, in cursive writing, the billboard says: Fuel up for your adventure at Exit West.

"Huh, did you guys notice that billboard before?" Filomena says as they pass it.

"No, but that looks *amaaaaazing*." Alistair drools. "I thought cheeseburgers were only a mortal world thing!"

"I wonder what's at Exit West," Gretel says. "A restaurant? On the side of the yellow brick road? That's strange."

"Maybe it's a roadhouse restaurant," Filomena says, remembering restaurants she'd been to with her parents on their road trip to Big Sur in California. She immediately shuts down the thought. It's impossible for Filomena to stay present and focus on the tasks at hand if she thinks too hard about her mom. And how much she misses her. And how scared she is for her. At least there's the fact that time moves very differently in Never After than in the mortal world. She's not sure of the exact ratio, but time passes much, much slower in the mortal world than it does here. When Filomena gets back, hopefully it will be like only a day or two has gone by for her parents. This is the one thing she can cling to.

"How long have we been riding?" Gretel whines. "Not to be a princess, but I'm getting *sooooo* tired."

As soon as Gretel says this, another billboard appears.

"Okay, that's just weird," Filomena says. "Are you guys finding this weird at all?"

But they're more focused on what this billboard says. On this one, there's a huge king-sized bed covered with soft-looking pillows and blankets. REST UP FOR THE ROAD AHEAD AT EXIT WEST, it reads in the same cursive.

"Do you think we should try this place?" Jack asks. "It is starting to get late. And we don't want to be out after dark. I could definitely use a cheeseburger and a bed. And to be honest, the pictures look like exactly what I'm craving."

"I guess it is getting late," Filomena says, looking at the sun, which is beginning to set over the horizon. "I wonder where the exit is?"

Suddenly, a signpost appears. EXIT: WEST, it reads.

"I'm not so sure about this, guys," she says. *Something about the whole thing feels fishy. It's too convenient.*

"Come on, Fil, we need to eat, don't we? We can't survive off Gwen and Lance's breakfast forever!" Alistair pleads.

He has a point. Filomena's stomach is growling wildly. But what Gwen and Lance told her echoes over and over in her head. *Things are not what they seem in Camelot.* Well, maybe it's not so serious in this case. Maybe what that means, in this case, is that they'll get hamburgers instead of cheeseburgers and queen-sized beds instead of king-sized beds. And that's the kind of switch that Filomena can live with.

Chapter Twelve

Only the Best at Exit West!

A large hotel—Exit West—appears before them immediately after they decide to go there. They're all too delirious from hunger and fatigue to really think anything of this, but in the back of Filomena's mind, it unsettles her.

"Looks like there's even a stable for Toto!" Alistair says as they walk up. "How much more perfect could this place get?"

"Hey, guys, I'm in need of a rest, too," Ira says. "Can you send me to the stables with Toto?"

The words are barely out of his mouth when a stable boy comes up to the group.

"May I take your steed for you?" he says. "And we can take the broom as well."

"Why, sure!" Jack says, dismounting Toto and tying Ira to his saddle. "Please take good care of them."

"Only the best here at Exit West!" the stable boy says.

"You can say that again," Alistair says. He's licking his lips as he watches a waiter with a big platter of food walk out the front door of the hotel and to a couple sitting on the front patio. "Let's go inside!"

After waving goodbye to Toto and Ira, the four make their way inside the hotel to get rooms for the night. Luckily Princess Jeanne sent them with a bit of money for their journey. Filomena just hopes the currency is accepted in Camelot.

The inside of the hotel is not what Filomena envisioned when she pictured them resting for the night. It's fancier than anywhere she's ever stayed before. It resembles photos she's seen of Las Vegas casinos. The floor is marble, a checkerboard pattern of greens. The ceilings are palatially high. There are palm trees and ferns everywhere, and, beyond the front desk, French doors lead to a dining room, and past that, gaming tables full of rowdy patrons.

"What is this place?" she says.

A woman pops up from behind the front desk. "Glad you asked," she says. "Welcome to Exit West, my emporium for weary travelers who need a rest!" The woman is dressed in a green sari that matches the palm leaves and the marble tiles. There's a bindi dot on her forehead. "What can I do for you weary travelers this evening?" she asks.

"We'd like to get two rooms for the night," Jack says.

"Perfect," the woman says, typing into a sleek silver computer. Her many stacked gold bracelets on either arm jangle. "I'll arrange that right away."

Jack pulls out some of the money Princess Jeanne gave them.

"No need to pay up front! Anything you get you can just put on your tab." The woman smiles. "Before you tuck in for the night," she goes on, "may I recommend dinner at our very own five-sparkfly restaurant?"

Gretel frowns. "'Five-sparkfly'?"

"Yes, dear, it's the highest rating Camelot restaurants have to offer!" The woman motions behind herself, to the dining room with white tablecloths and candles on each table.

"Looks fancy," Gretel says quietly. "Do we have enough money for this?"

"Oh, don't worry!" the woman says. "It's much more affordable than it looks."

Seated at a table at the restaurant, Filomena can't help but feel out of place. Dining at this luxurious hotel feels wrong when she's on a mission to save her mother. Oh, but the menu does look so good . . .

The snacks menu is particularly interesting. *A snack to improve your intelligence*, one item's description reads. *A snack to bolster your bravery. A snack to open your heart. A snack to take you home.* Oddly creative marketing, Filomena thinks, but before she realizes what she's doing, she's pointing silently to *A snack to take you home.* Then a waiter comes by.

Each adventurer orders one snack, and the foods come quickly on a silver platter.

"Now this is the life!" Alistair says. "I'll have to add this place to my list of favorite eateries in Never After. I've been keeping track."

Even Jack seems to have loosened up after eating. Filomena wonders what the description of his snack is.

"This food is great," Jack says, pinching the puff of his stuffed *bao*. He calls to a waiter. "Can I have another? On my tab!"

"It's so nice to just *relaaaax* together!" Gretel says, throwing her arm around Filomena. Filomena notices Gretel's plate is empty as well. "When do we ever just get to *chill*, you know? It's always *quest this, quest that*."

"I don't think the waiter heard me," Jack says, distracted. "We need another round of snacks, please!"

After taking a bite of her second pierogi, Filomena has to agree with Gretel. They're just kids, after all! They should be allowed to have some fun, hang out, and chat without all this life-endangering quest stuff happening. Right?

When Filomena blinks, she realizes there are ten plates

on their table, each covered in crumbs. How many snacks have they had?

"Yummm!" Gretel says after dragging a french fry through spicy mayo and chomping on it. "Ooh, there's a pinball machine. Let's go play!"

"I'm going to check out this place. Something doesn't feel right," Jack tells them, pushing away from the table.

Filomena and Alistair are left at the table. Alistair orders another round of snacks. There's a new server now. How long have they been here? Somehow Filomena is still hungry.

"All in all, this is pretty cool, huh?" Alistair says, leaning back in his chair. "Never a dull moment in Never After. Always a new place to visit, another place to discover."

Filomena nods slowly, taking in her surroundings. There's a tableful of teenagers in velvet robes sharing a platter of fondue. There's a group of twentysomethings in shiny silver armor snacking on a sashimi platter. Who are these people? Are these the heroes that Lance and Gwen talked about? The other heroes?

"I wonder how many different kinds of snacks there are," Alistair muses.

Filomena laughs nervously. She looks around and can't see where Jack has gone, which makes her nervous. She picks up one of Gretel's french fries and eats it to calm her nerves. It's stone-cold. Wait, didn't these fries just arrive? How long has Gretel been gone?

But the thought leaves her mind as quickly as it entered.

"Should we order more food?" she asks. She doesn't know why she's saying this. She just polished off a full *döner* kebab and a platter of dumplings. She can't believe how much she's eating. And somehow she's not full—not at all. In fact, she's really, really hungry.

"MUCH MORE FOOD," Alistair agrees.

Something twinges in Filomena's mind when he says this. How long have Jack and Gretel been gone? And where are they? Filomena cranes her neck to look around the room but can't find either of them.

"Hey, let's go find Jack and Gretel," she says to Alistair.

He sighs. "Do we have to?"

Filomena thinks of what might convince him. "There's some food over there that we haven't tried, I think!"

"Oh really? Let's go!"

Believing herself for a moment, Filomena gets excited, too. She feels an unending hunger for this food. The more she eats, the hungrier she becomes. But then she remembers why they're getting up from the table and crossing the dining room toward the arcade game area. Gretel said she was going to play a game. Jack said he was going to "check out this place." Something didn't feel right to him.

They enter through a set of French doors to a large space with psychedelic patterned carpeting in shades of green. Every few steps, there's a vintage-looking arcade game. *Pac-Man. Donkey Kong.* Games from the mortal world that put Filomena at ease to see. But there are others, too, ones she doesn't recognize. The sounds of pinging, music, or artificial voices come from each machine. It's overwhelming, disorienting. Pinpricks of orange, hot-pink, and electric-blue light flash in every direction. As Filomena and Alistair walk through the games, slowly, in a daze, they come across one that tugs on something inside her.

SWORD EXCALIBUR, the arcade game reads. Filomena stops in front of the machine. It looks straight out of the 1980s, like some of the arcade games she's played in Koreatown in Los Angeles. The name of the game flashes in blocky letters. Underneath it, the words CLICK TO PLAY flash, too. On the machine are a joystick and what looks like a sword hilt. She presses a green button to start the game.

More blocky letters fill the screen, telling the player the premise of the game.

Sword Excalibur: Save your mother from certain death by pulling the sword Excalibur from the stone.

Filomena feels a jolt of panic, sickness. Is this a joke?

Then the text disappears. On the left side of the screen is an animation of a large rock with a fancy-looking sword sticking out of it. On the right side of the screen is a woman. She looks sickly. She's holding herself, her arms wrapped around her torso as if to keep standing. Above her is a bar. Above the bar, text reads, *Life-O-Meter*. Filomena stares, frozen, at the game. What is she supposed to do? The life-o-meter starts to drop a little bit, and the woman gets frailer. The woman looks remarkably familiar. Almost like . . . no.

Her own mother.

The image of the rock and the sword starts to pulse. Above, text reads, *Pull the sword!*

Filomena looks at the hilt next to the joystick on the game console in front of her. She puts her hands on it and starts pulling. The more Filomena pulls, the more frantic she feels. It's not budging! She can't let her mother die. The life-o-meter is dropping. Why won't this work? Why can't she just pull the sword out of the stone? Why can't Filomena just be the hero she needs to be?

Suddenly she feels strong hands on her shoulders.

"We need to get out of here *now*," Jack whispers in her ear. "This place isn't right."

"*Noooooo*," Alistair moans when Jack tells him the same thing. "We're having so much fun! We haven't even seen the king-sized beds yet!" he cries.

"I don't think we're ever going to see those beds," says Gretel, who's appeared next to Jack and is looking around anxiously.

Alistair grabs a mini cheeseburger slider off a tray as a waiter walks by, and he pops it into his mouth. "Don't you want any more snacks, Jack?" he says with his mouth stuffed full. "It's a cheeseburger!"

Jack grabs Alistair by the arm and drags him over to where Gretel and Filomena are standing.

"Oh, Fil," Gretel says solemnly, looking at the arcade game Filomena was playing.

You let your mother die! You let your mother die! flashes on the screen in bright green block letters. Filomena is paralyzed. And still hungry.

"You guys . . ." Gretel leans in and whispers very softly to them, "There are images of the Wicked Witch of the East. And there's another woman who looks just like her but with green robes."

Filomena doesn't understand. Her brain feels all fuzzy, and she just wants to see her mom. Is her mom okay? Where *is* her mom? Did she just do something really bad to her mom? Can someone bring her to her mom?

"I want to go home," Filomena says, slumping against the arcade game and down to the floor. Alistair hands her a mini cheeseburger slider sympathetically, and she takes a sad bite.

"How much food have you two had?" Jack asks.

"I don't know, we'll see on the tab! After the *döner* and before the dumplings, there were *bao* . . . ," Alistair says, adding it all up in his head.

"Listen to me right now," Jack says, grabbing Filomena by the shoulders. "We're in danger. We need to leave. NOW!"

The urgency still isn't resonating with Filomena and Alistair. They stay slumped over, leaning against the arcade machines. Why won't Gretel and Jack just hang out? And chill? That's what they said they wanted to do! Plus, Filomena just did so badly in this game about her mom . . . What's happening with her real mom? Does this mean she's going to fail?!

"Okay, this is not working, they're too far gone," Jack says to Gretel. "I think we're going to have to carry them out."

"Wait, the *other one* is looking," Gretel whispers to Jack.

A woman in a green robe has started weaving through the dining tables. She's calmly staring at them.

"Okay," Jack says, coming up with a plan. "We're going to need to pretend we're still under the influence of the food, and then, when she's not looking, we make a run for it."

"You guys are so amazing," Alistair says, putting his chin in his palm. "I love hanging out with you."

Gretel laughs. "Oh, Alistair, I love hanging out with you, too," she says. She's looking at Jack as they pace away from the woman in green, away from the dining room, out of the arcade room, and toward the front door.

"We're laughing, we're laughing, we're hanging out . . . and now she's looking away from us . . . and she's interrupted by some new guests . . . and . . . OKAY, GRAB ALISTAIR, I'LL TAKE FILOMENA, LET'S GO."

Filomena feels her arm be thrown over Gretel's shoulder, and Jack is heaving Alistair over his shoulder, too. Suddenly Filomena is running with Gretel.

"Go! Go! Go!" Jack orders.

"Wait, we never paid the tab!" Alistair cries.

"Too late, honey," Gretel answers. "If we stay any longer,

I don't think we'll be paying with money. More like we'll be paying with our lives!"

Rushing out the front door, Filomena gets one final look over her shoulder at the woman in green. She looks absolutely furious.

The woman starts to run after them, following them through the front doors and out to the stable. "My pretties!" she screams. "My pretties! You can't run from me, my pretties!"

Gretel hops on the magic broomstick and pulls Filomena on behind her. Filomena watches as Jack tosses Alistair onto Toto's back and climbs into the saddle, spurring the horse into a gallop.

"I'll get you!" the woman yells as Gretel and Filomena start to fly away. "And your little horse, too!"

They fly as fast as they can away from the hotel. Galloping wildly behind them are Jack and Alistair on Toto. Thankfully it looks like they lost that strange woman.

After a few moments of intense speed, they arrive at the end of the yellow brick road. It stops cold in front of two mountains. A large set of green doors stands between them. They stop and dismount from broom and horse.

"You two need to chug some water," Jack says, passing Filomena and Alistair a canteen.

They take turns drinking, and Filomena realizes it's bright outside. "Wait a second," she says after gulping down a liter of water. "Is it morning?"

"Where are we?" Alistair echoes. "I feel horrible. What just happened?"

"We were in there *all night*," Gretel says.

"How can that be possible? When we got there, it was evening! It felt like we were there barely an hour!" Alistair says.

"It was the food," Jack says. "As soon as I got away from the table, I realized it was making time pass differently."

"That's when we realized who owns that place," Gretel says. "The Wicked Witch of the West."

They fell for it. Hook, line, and sinker. Filomena chastises herself. She should've noticed that the woman was wearing the same kind of robe as the Wicked Witch of the East!

"Wait a second," Filomena says, "Does that mean Gita led us there? Right into the Wicked Witch of the West's hotel?"

"I should never have trusted her," Jack says through gritted teeth. "I should never have . . ." He can't seem to finish the sentence. But Filomena's starting to understand something. If Jack's the tin man, then the snacks must have made him feel something in his heart. One item on the snack menu was described as *A snack to open your heart*. But what's keeping his heart closed?

Filomena's distracted from this thought when she sees writing on the huge doors in front of them. The doors are as tall as a dragon, but the mountains on either side are taller. Whatever is beyond these green doors is completely obscured. Which means the doors must be guarding something really important. Could it be? Has the group finally arrived at their destination?

"Is this Avalon?" Filomena says, walking toward the doors.

In huge lettering an even darker, deeper green than the doors themselves, letters spell out THE EMERALD CITY.

The Sacred Island

Four heroes from the other side
of Never After
have ventured over
to find their cure.
They've made it through tests,
They've killed a witch,
But have they shown
Their hearts are pure?
Camelot is different now
than it once was,

And that difference is puzzling
to those who know it well.
The Mists of Myth have descended,
Wicked Witches rule the lands,
And is it true that the people are under a spell?
Four heroes seek Avalon
But keep coming up short.
The King of Camelot is missing,
we cannot forget.
Our heroes think they've arrived
At Avalon's doors,
But when they find the island,
Will they be filled with regret?

PART TWO

Wherein . . .

Our four heroes learn what they *really*
want while in The Emerald City.

An Avalonian detour leads to
a surprisingly young
(or really old?) ally.

The League of Seven and their new
friends try their hand at teleportation.

CHAPTER THIRTEEN

THE EMERALD CITY

"If your theory is correct," Gretel says, "and the Emerald City *is* Avalon, then maybe we finally made it."

The four look at one another with grins. But their glee is cut by a piercing laugh coming from somewhere above them.

A little tower in the mountain to the right of the doors echoes with a laugh. A small head pops out of a high window.

"Greetings, travelers!" an old man calls. "I hate to inform you, but you've reached the Emerald City, not Avalon. Avalon is beyond the Emerald City."

Rats, Filomena thinks. Not quite as simple as she'd hoped.

"In that case," Jack calls up to the man, "we seek to pass through the Emerald City! Will you grant us entrance, keeper of the gate?"

Filomena and Gretel smile at each other knowingly. Jack always speaks so formally when he meets new people on their quests. It cracks them up.

"'Keeper of the gate'?" the man says, "Oh, no, no, no, you're mistaken, young man!" The older man seems almost bashful, flustered by Jack's words. "Alas, I am not the famous keeper of the gate. I know, I know, people are always disappointed when they find out. I'm only a security guard. The real keeper of the gate is much more difficult to find. Now *that's* when you'll know you've found Avalon."

"Any idea what he's talking about?" Alistair whispers to Jack.

"No clue. I didn't know 'keeper of the gate' was a formal title, I just thought, *Well, here's a gate, and here's a guy keeping it,*" Jack whispers back.

"What are your intentions in entering the Emerald City?" the man, or security guard, booms. Apparently he's recovered from the mistaken title mishap.

Filomena looks at the other three. Are they really supposed to tell him? How do they know if they can trust him?

"He already heard that we're looking for Avalon," Gretel says quietly. "Should we just say that?"

Jack nods.

"We're in search of Avalon," Gretel booms back.

"And who are you four? What are your titles?"

"I don't think we should say," Filomena adds, "in case the Wicked Witch of the West is on our tail."

"We're a traveling circus!" Alistair blurts out.

Jack looks at him incredulously.

"Oh goodie!" the man in the tower says. "How delightful!"

The man disappears into the tower for a moment, and Filomena can hear a lever being pulled. Slowly, slowly, the giant green doors creak open.

"Welcome to the Emerald City," the guard says. "I'll have to come to one of your shows!"

"We'll get you in for free!" Alistair cries over his shoulder as the group boards their broom and trusty steed and are soon on their way.

The Emerald City is like nothing Filomena has ever seen in her time in Never After. Or her other twelve years in the mortal world, come to think of it. This city is not a village and not like any city she's ever been in. Every building is a different shade of shining opalescent green. Apple greens and evergreens, bright light greens and dark brooding greens, but mostly, of course, emerald. They've found themselves on a main street, and on either side of the road are restaurants and stores, post offices and banks. The buildings are all made of dazzling green glass, and incredibly tall. As the group rides down the center of the street—Gretel and Filomena on the broom, Jack and Alistair on Toto—Filomena is surprised they're not getting more looks from the residents of the Emerald City. Oddly, no one is looking at them. No one is looking at them at all, to the point where it seems almost strange.

"Are you getting a weird vibe?" Gretel says to Filomena.

"Now that you mention it . . ."

She looks around. On both sides of the streets are patios filled with people in fancy green hats, suits, and gowns. Tables and tables filled with adult-age people in elaborate outfits lounging, drinking from tiny green crystal cups, and eating plate after plate of green food. They seem to be either laughing in a screeching, halting manner or showing no emotion at all. There's a sinister tone in the air.

Jack and Alistair dismount Toto. Gretel and Filomena get off the broom, and they all walk side by side.

"Something feels off here," Jack says. "Don't you think?"

Filomena agrees, but she can't place her finger on why exactly. They walk past another restaurant, and she realizes the servers are all children, ones younger than she and her friends by a few years.

"Why are children serving adults at that restaurant?" she says.

The other three glance around with surprise. Everywhere

are children carrying platters of drink and food to the fancy adults lounging and eating.

"Wait a minute," Alistair says to Jack. "Do you remember hearing about the munchkins? Is this where they all went?"

A flash of recognition washes over Jack.

"Munchkins? Like in the movie?" Filomena asks.

"Not sure what they're like in the movie, or what a movie is, but here, they're immortal children," Jack says, still gazing at the waiters. "They live in their own village in Avalon. They're distantly related to the fairies. What are they doing here? And what are they doing working in a restaurant?"

"Super weird vibes, you guys," Gretel says. "Look, I know we're wanting to get to Avalon as quickly as we can, but while we're in a city, do you mind if I stop at a post office to mail my designs to Lillet?"

"Fine by me," Filomena says.

Jack looks around, and his eyes settle on a clock tower in the center of the town square. There are giant spherical emeralds where the numbers usually are on the clockface. Something flies over their heads then, and they all look up. But by the time they've looked, it's gone.

"What was that?" Filomena says, but the others shrug. Probably just a bird.

"Why don't we meet in half an hour in front of the clock tower?" Jack says.

"In that case, I might go walk around by myself for a

bit," Alistair says. He takes Toto's reins and leads the horse off with him.

Filomena is surprised and impressed. She's never seen Alistair go anywhere on his own before.

Gretel tucks the broom under her arm as she and Alistair walk off in separate directions, once again leaving Jack and Filomena together.

As Gretel walks toward a post office, her eye catches on an exquisite-looking shop. The sign above the shop reads COU-TURIER ÉMERAUDE. *Emerald Dressmaker.* The window displays are gorgeous: silks and velvets are arranged in dazzling patterns. Gretel's breath catches in her throat at the sight. It won't be too much of a detour just to take one quick little peek, will it?

A bell rings lightly as she opens the door and enters the dress shop. A woman at a counter looks up from a sketchpad. Gretel thinks the woman looks a bit older than herself but still young, perhaps in her twenties. She must be an apprentice at the shop.

"Hello," Gretel says.

"I'm sorry, miss, I can't sell you any dresses today," the young woman says with a sad smile. She has a sweet face but seems tired.

"That's no problem. I was just hoping to look around," Gretel says.

"Oh, all right then."

Gretel touches the fabrics, taking note of the fine stitching and the ambitious cuts. "Your boss is very talented!" Gretel says, smiling.

The young woman laughs, and Gretel furrows her brows, not understanding.

"I have no boss, miss. I own this shop."

Gretel raises her eyebrows in shock. "But you're so young!"

The young woman shrugs. "It's not so hard, if you're really passionate about it. Well, it didn't used to be so hard, at least."

"What do you mean?"

"Never mind that. Are you interested in dresses?"

"Yes! Dresses, shirts, pants, everything. I make clothes as well."

"*Ah bon, vraiment?*" the young woman says, her face lighting up.

Gretel takes the package for Lillet from her pocket and shows the woman her sketches. Suddenly Gretel wants this person to give approval of her work. She's overwhelmed by the urge for the young woman to like her. The woman riffles through her designs, her eyes flickering with delight.

"You are very talented. Do you know how to translate these designs into clothing?"

"I do," Gretel says. "I love to make clothes."

The young woman considers Gretel for a moment, then

puts out her hand for Gretel to shake. "I'm Céline," she says. Gretel takes her hand.

"Céline, you have an incredible shop. Do you make all this yourself?"

Céline nods.

"You must have a million customers. I've never seen dresses like these."

A sigh escapes Céline's mouth, and the look of tiredness returns to her face. "I once did. But not so much anymore."

"What happened?"

Céline seems hesitant to go on.

"Something strange is happening in Emerald City, isn't it?" Gretel prompts.

"May I ask what you're doing here?" Céline says. "In the Emerald City?"

Now Gretel is the one who hesitates. Both girls are trying to suss out how much they can trust each other. But something about Céline makes Gretel trust her. Perhaps Gretel feels that someone who makes such beautiful clothing must be on the same side as she.

"I'm from Never After. I'm here on a quest. My group and I seek Avalon."

Céline nods slowly, taking this in. "I don't have many customers anymore because I've been banned from selling my wares to anyone except"—she pauses, unsure if she should go on—"except for the Wicked Witch of the East and her sister, the Wicked Witch of the West."

The scene at Exit West reappears in Gretel's mind. The Wicked Witch of the West, wearing her green velvet robes . . .

"How can she ban you from selling to whomever you wish?"

"The witch has quite a hold on the Emerald City these days. More than a hold, really." The words tumble out of Céline's mouth as if she's been waiting for someone to tell. "She has everyone under her spell! The people who laze around, drinking her poisonous drinks all day. All the shopkeepers. And the poor munchkins, ripped from their home and shuttled here to work for no pay. They're trapped by her. We all are. The Emerald City used to be such a vibrant, special place. Now everyone is practically a brainless zombie!"

"How horrible!" Gretel cries. She doesn't tell Céline that she just saw the Wicked Witch of the West nor that her friends killed the Wicked Witch of the East.

"How did all this happen?" she asks.

"It's hard to say, exactly. It's all very secretive, confusing. Camelot used to be much more . . . how do you say . . . *sympathique*. The Emerald City was not so guarded before. People used to travel between different places in Camelot often. Then . . . I am not so sure how to explain it."

Céline looks exasperated. But Gretel urges her to go on.

"A little while ago, things were not so scary in Camelot. The witches, for example, they were not always so wicked.

They were just civilians of Camelot, like the rest of us. This was years ago now. But then rumors started to spread. About the witches, about the munchkins, about everyone. About the knights, even the heroes. Rumors of terrible things everyone had done, evil they had in their hearts. The newspapers were all reporting on it; people wouldn't even look at one another in the street. Gossip everywhere. Everyone started to get very scared."

Céline sighs deeply. "Then, the rumors became true. The witches revealed their true natures, I suppose. They captured the munchkins, made them work for the people of the Emerald City. There is a lot of darkness here now."

Gretel's mind is reeling. "I'm so sorry," she says. "Maybe there's something I can do? I'm here with my friends on a quest, but maybe we can try to help you. To help everyone in the Emerald City."

Céline just shrugs. She seems apathetic. "I don't know that there's much anyone can do these days."

Gretel remembers she has to meet her friends and still has to drop off her designs. "I'm afraid I have to go," she says. "I'm so sorry to leave in such a rush. I hope I can see you again. It was such a true pleasure meeting you. And, of course, I adore your store."

Céline smiles at her. "Judging by these designs," she says, "I think you will have your own someday."

A flare of pride and thrill lights in Gretel's chest. Her own store. Just like this? The beautiful woman places Gretel's package back in her grip and pats her hands goodbye. "Good luck, Gretel. You will do great things."

Rushing out of the store and to the post office, Gretel rides a wave of euphoria. Momentarily, she forgets about all the dangers of Never After, about Olga, about Avalon. All she can think of is owning her own shop filled with her own designs. And conversing with these Frenchwomen—the sophisticated Lillet and the impressive Céline—has shown her exactly where she wants to set up shop: in Paris.

CHAPTER FOURTEEN

THERE'S NO PLACE LIKE HOME, BUT WHERE'S HOME?

Alistair and Gretel going off on their own leaves Jack and Filomena alone. Again. Alistair took Toto with him, and Ira's sleeping at Fil's hip, so it really is just the two of them now. Filomena wonders how they keep ending up alone together. It feels as though the universe is conspiring against her. Although, somewhere deep in her stomach, there is a thrill beneath all the nerves.

"What now?" Filomena asks. They have half an hour to kill before they can move on to Avalon.

"Somehow, even though we ate all night, I still feel hungry," Jack says. "Maybe we can get lunch?"

They go to a fish-and-chips cart, and once they have paper cones of fish and chips, they begin to walk and eat.

"Does this mean there's an ocean nearby?" Filomena asks, munching on a fry dipped in tartar sauce.

"Avalon is an island." Jack laughs. "Maybe these are Avalonian fish."

Filomena takes a bite of the fish.

"Tastes sacred indeed," she jokes.

They walk along the green cobblestones, around a corner and off the main street, and down a quieter lane. There is, as you can imagine, quite a lot of greenery in the Emerald City. Leafy green trees flank either side of the streets. Jack and Filomena are silent for a little while, eating happily. Filomena feels so comfortable, she almost forgets everything that has transpired between them. Almost.

Again a large form swoops overhead. This time Filomena catches a glance of a large spindly wing, like a giant bat's wing. That's all she could see before the thing flew out of view. What kind of birds lived in the Emerald City?

"So that Exit West place was quite bizarre, wasn't it?" Jack says, distracting her from whatever is flying overhead.

"I wonder how many times we're to be under the influence of some strange vision or potion," Filomena says. "Camelot is certainly different from the rest of Never After I know."

"Hey, um," Jack says, squeezing a lemon slice over his fish. "I need to tell you something." He stares at the cone of food in his hands, unable to make eye contact as they walk. "I've been feeling the need to say it since Exit West."

Fil's heart catches in her throat. Or is that a fry? No, it's definitely her heart.

"Yeah? What is it?" she asks.

He nods and sighs. "I really like you. I think that's obvious."

She laughs a hugely loud laugh, louder than she'd meant. "You think it's obvious? We must be living in different realities. Or, you know, different worlds."

He smiles and shakes his head. "I know I'm not great at showing it. I've never really . . . had . . ."

She fills in the blank: "A girlfriend?"

"Yeah."

"Not even Sadie?" Filomena teases, but she immediately regrets it. She doesn't want to talk about Sadie right now.

"Gosh, no. Not Sadie. That whole thing in Snow Country, that was just Alistair being Alistair. Nothing ever happened with Sadie. I just had a little crush on her. But that was before . . ." He trails off, looking at his feet.

"Before what?" Filomena prompts.

He looks up at her, his head cocked sideways. "Before I knew what a real crush feels like."

Filomena feels a sudden lightness in her head. She needs to not be walking right now. "Can we sit down?" she asks.

They walk to a bench under a bright leafy tree and sit in the tree's shade. They sit on opposite ends of the bench. *It's as if we're scared to be near each other,* Filomena thinks. And as for his confession—is this just because he ate a snack that opened his heart? Is this real? Or another enchantment?

Jack takes a deep breath. "All these tests in Camelot," he begins, "they've shown me something about myself. I think I have a hard time letting people in."

Filomena nods, thinking of Jack's vision in the pool. The Vineland fire caused by the ogres, his family burning.

"It was always just me. And then it was me and Alistair. And now it's . . . me and a lot more people. But I can't shake the feeling that, even though I have people around me now, something is going to happen and I'm going to end up alone. Again."

"I understand, Jack," she says softly. "But you won't be alone. I won't ever leave."

Even as she says this, and even though it feels true, her stomach drops. She has a sinking feeling. Can it be true? Will she never leave? Or will she eventually have to make a choice that she can't even fathom?

He moves close to her so that their legs are touching.

"I don't want this fear, this armor around my heart, to run my life."

Filomena nods, her breath catching.

Jack takes her hand in his. He puts her hand on his chest, over where his heart lies.

"Filomena," he says, looking her directly in the eyes. His gaze is so warm. The mischievous glint in his eyes, the cleft in his chin, his sweeping mess of hair, his strong shoulders. Every laugh, every adventure, every glance they've shared— they all flow through her in this moment.

"I love you."

Filomena gasps. She actually gasps hearing this. She's loved Jack for such a long time. Ever since she picked up the first Never After book in her bedroom in North Pasadena and felt both thrilled and safe at once, reading about him. That's it—that's exactly how she feels about Jack. He makes her feel both thrilled and safe.

"Well? What do you think?" he says, sheepish. His shoulders have hunched shyly up toward his ears.

"I love you, too, Jack! I really do." Her face is troubled however, and he notices.

"But?" he asks.

"But are you just saying that because you ate something that made you say it? Remember what was on the menu? *A snack to open your heart.*"

Jack actually laughs. "Maybe it gave me the courage to say it, but that's all it did." He stops laughing and his face is serious. "It didn't make me feel the way I feel. The way I've felt since the moment we met. Without you, I don't see the point of going on."

She is tingling from head to toe, almost dizzy with emotion. "Oh, Jack, I really do love you."

He breathes a sigh of relief. "Thank fairies. It would have been really awkward to be on a quest together if you didn't."

They both laugh, leaning into each other, their shoulders bumping.

"Now I can finally do this again," he says.

Do what? she's thinking as suddenly his hand is on her cheek. This time she sees him lean in. She moves forward and kisses him.

As they pull apart, her head is spinning.

Jack stands quickly, urgently. "I need to do something. For you. Wait here." He grins the widest she's ever seen. "I'll be right back."

He runs away, and she can see him pump his fist in the air a little as he goes.

Filomena stays sitting on the bench and takes it in. Here she is, in the Emerald City and in love. In love! She smiles to herself, her whole body glowing with warmth.

"*Jack and Filomena sitting in a tree . . .*" a voice from her hip sings. "*K-I-S-S-I-N-G!*"

She whips Ira off her hip and holds him in front of her face. She frowns. "How much of that did you hear?"

"Oh, just the end, when he said he had to go do something. He was so forceful, it woke me up!"

With Jack gone and Ira awake, the too-familiar little pinpricks of dread begin to form in her stomach again. They're different from nerves, or even fear. It's like remembering something dreadful. She told Jack she'd never leave him. But is that true? Can it be?

"Ira, can you show me home?"

Ira looks at her, his thick brows furrowed. "And where is home for you, Filomena?"

"You know what I mean. My parents."

"Are you sure you want to see them right now?"

Filomena nods.

Ira sighs, and in a swirl, his face disappears. In his place is an image of Filomena's mother lying in bed. The tree outside her window has lemons, unlike the false vision from Brocéliande Forest. Bettina looks so frail; her skin is thin like tissue paper. Her eyes are closed—she must be asleep—and in her arms she's cuddling one of Filomena's favorite stuffed animals: a little purple dragon. Filomena stifles a sob. Why is she doing this? Why can't she enjoy what just happened between her and Jack? It's like digging a finger into a wound.

Then her father comes into the frame. His shoulders shake, but he's silent. Filomena realizes he's weeping.

"Enough," she says to Ira.

"Oh, Filomena, you're crying," Ira says softly. "I wish I had real hands so I could reach out and wipe your tears."

"It's okay. Thanks, Ira," she says. "I just wanted to check in."

Where did Jack go? she wonders. *Jack.* The boy she told she would never leave. Who told her that he loved her and that without her, he wouldn't know the point of going on. Dramatic, yes. But she understands the feeling completely. And yet . . . she can't deny how torn she feels. She looks down at her feet in despair, then sees she's still wearing the Wicked Witch of the East's ruby-red slippers.

There's no place like home after all.

CHAPTER FIFTEEN

MEETING IN THE TOWN SQUARE

By the time Filomena and Jack reach the town square's clock tower, Alistair, Toto, and Gretel are already there waiting. They're both looking impatient and more than a little freaked out. But Gretel's expression shifts as she realizes Filomena and Jack are holding hands. Her face goes from anxiety to full-blown glee. But since Gretel is the ultimate cool girl and knows far better than to embarrass either Jack or Filomena, she says nothing. As Jack and Filomena reach the clock tower and release hands, Gretel grabs Fil's ear and hisses, "You have so much to tell me!"

"Later," Filomena says, motioning to the necklace she's now wearing.

Gretel's eyes widen like saucers, taking in the emerald heart on the thin gold chain that Filomena's wearing. Jack had run off to buy it for her. Filomena will fill Gretel in later, when they can be alone. For now, it's back to business.

"So here's what we've figured out," Alistair begins. "The munchkins were trapped, brought here from Avalon, and imprisoned by the Wicked Witch of the West. She has somehow gotten power over all of the Emerald City. How, we're still not sure."

Jack nods, taking this in. "All right, well, that's not great, to be sure," he says. "But we can come back and try to figure it out after we make it to Avalon."

"What, and just leave the munchkins here?" Alistair says, taken aback.

"I mean, this is not our quest! We have a lot on our plates. We have to get to Avalon as soon as we can and find Excalibur. For Filomena's mom!"

Alistair starts to nod, conceding. Jack is the leader, and Alistair generally just agrees with what he says. Filomena can see Alistair retreating, passively saying yes, like he always does. But then it looks like something flares up inside him.

"No, Jack, I don't agree. Just because we're on a quest for one thing doesn't mean we can ignore what we come across on the journey. We can't leave a whole people captured and helpless while we go onto our next quest! If we see something unjust happening, like this, it's our duty as heroes to fix it. If we don't, then what are we even doing calling ourselves 'the League of Seven'?"

Gretel and Filomena look at Alistair in surprise. They've never seen him stand up to Jack like this. Not that Jack's ever a bully, but he does usually call the shots. And Alistair rarely has a differing opinion. Alistair turns to Filomena.

"Filomena, of course our number one priority is to get the sword and save your mother, but I just have a feeling about this. I won't be able to live with myself if we leave the Wicked Witch to her own devices. The munchkins will never be able to escape without help."

Filomena nods, impressed. "I'm with you, Alistair. Let's help the munchkins."

"Me too!" says Gretel, pumping her fist.

"All right, all right, I see where you're coming from, Alistair. I'm in, too," Jack says, looking proud.

"Very good, Alistair, very well done!"

That last comment was in a different voice altogether . . . a voice Filomena thinks she recognizes.

They look up. Gita is sitting up high on the tower's clockface, perched on the minute/second hand. She slips off and slowly floats down, her huge skirt acting like a parachute.

"Congratulations, kids. Thanks to Alistair here, you passed," Gita says when she's hovering a few feet above the green cobblestones.

"What do you mean we passed?" Gretel says.

"This was another one of Camelot's tests. Most heroes who pass through the Emerald City are so eager to get to Avalon and on to the next part of their quest that they don't think twice about the munchkins. Or they say they'll come back and save them, but they never do. But you, Alistair? You're clearly brave."

Alistair flares with pride, and Filomena smiles, proud of him and his bravery.

Jack gives Alistair a brotherly slap on the back, then hugs him. "Well done! You were right. I'm a bit ashamed, actually, of my protesting, but I suppose that's why it's good that we work as a team. I'm proud to be on your team."

Alistair smiles wide, warm and lionlike.

"So you mean the munchkins aren't really trapped? That's just part of a test?" Gretel asks.

"Oh no," Gita mutters, clucking her tongue. "They are very much trapped."

Filomena's stomach sinks. Not so simple after all.

"Since you've committed to saving them," Gita continues, "why don't you come back to my lair to recharge and plan?"

"Wait a second," Filomena says. "Last time we saw you, you sent us right into the lair of the Wicked Witch of the West! Why should we trust you now? So much for Gita the Good Witch!"

Gita just sighs and shakes her head. "Filomena, I thought you would have learned by now that good and evil aren't so clear-cut. My job in Camelot is to be neither good nor bad. That's why I am the overseer of these lands. I take no sides; I have no oaths nor commitments made."

As she talks, Gita begins to float around them in a circle, hovering slightly above their heads.

"My only allegiances are to the protection and the harmony of the land. And since you are on the side of Never After, I'm on your side, for the moment. But you heroes can't just be given things; you have to earn them. You all needed to learn from Exit West, and that is why I sent you there. Another test."

Filomena looks at her friends. It's true that she still feels a bit of shame around how she and Alistair behaved at Exit West. They let their guards down, and the greedy spirit of the place overtook them. If it weren't for Gretel and Jack, she and Alistair might still be there, racking up a tab that even Princess Jeanne can't pay.

Just then another one of those flying creatures swoops closer to the ground than Filomena has seen thus far.

"Gita, what are those?"

Gita looks up at the pack headed toward them. "Those are flying monkeys. They surveil the Emerald City. We have to get out of here quickly. Now get on that stolen broom of yours, and let's go."

CHAPTER SIXTEEN

GITA'S LAIR

"This. Place. Is. Amazing!" Gretel yells as she jumps butt-first onto a light pink shell-shaped velvet couch.

Gita's lair is in a tower at the outskirts of the Emerald City, one whose entrance is so high that you can reach it only by flying. Thankfully, with a wave of Gita's silver staff, Toto was levitated right up, which gave him quite a fright but was hilarious to watch.

Gita's lair is pretty much the most glamorous place Filomena's ever been. Everything is gold, silver, and light pink, from the big vanity to the canopy bed, from the fireplace to the rugs to the couch that Gretel jumped on.

"Sit down, all of you," Gita orders. Despite the woman's frilly aesthetics, Filomena is learning that Gita is kind of a drill sergeant. There's certainly no mothering or coddling here.

The four adventurers sit on her pink chaise longue and couches.

"Now listen to me. We have to be quick about all this. First things first, though. I understand you have some experience in killing witches," Gita says, crossing her arms and raising her eyebrows.

Filomena's face gives away her surprise.

Gita points to Filomena's ruby slippers. "You think I don't know who those belonged to?"

"Is this allowed? For me to wear them?" Filomena asks, suddenly worried.

"Those are incredibly powerful, Filomena," Gita says. "They're to be used with extreme caution and extreme care. Whatever you use them for cannot be reversed except under very intense circumstances, so please be careful."

Filomena nods, though she's not quite understanding.

"I'll be frank with you all," Gita says. She's lying on another chaise longue, which starts to levitate. "I don't condone killing witches, not at all. The Witch of the East had a name, you know, and Eeshani was my dear friend, even if we've had differing opinions in recent times. We are very powerful, and I think having differing opinions is good for a healthy society. However, I understand you were under great duress—"

"She was literally trying to kill us with fireballs!" Alistair cries, pulling his hair in frustration.

"Yes, Alistair, that is the *duress* that I was referring to. So I can forgive that under the circumstances. But just know that, in the future, you should never resort to violence as your first choice. I am disappointed to have to tell you that."

As Gita speaks, she levitates the chaise around the room and around them, so that they're forced to stay moving in order to keep their eyes on her. Filomena is humiliated. The guilt she felt about the Wicked Witch of the East has only doubled now. She can tell that Jack, Alistair, and Gretel feel the same.

"Now listen to me. I know you think you know the truth about the Emerald City, but you don't. I don't have time to get into it right now, but just trust me. What you do need to know is that there is only one way to free the munchkins. These immortal children are supposed to live on Avalon. They're being controlled because someone poisoned their immortal flame, the fire on Avalon that keeps them alive. The only way to break their enchantment is to release and purify the immortal flame."

Yet another reason to get to Avalon, Filomena thinks. The four nod, mostly understanding.

"Before I instruct you further, I have to go get something from . . . ah, an old friend, let's say. Make yourselves comfortable, but not too comfortable. Don't eat anything. Don't touch anything. And whatever you do, do *not* leave the tower. I have a feeling the flying monkeys are looking for you."

A chill goes down Filomena's spine as she remembers the flying monkeys that she kept spotting all over the city.

Without further ado, Gita glides off the chaise longue, which drops to the ground. She twinkles and floats right out one of the open windows. Filomena runs after her to close the window. She watches as Gita floats for a few feet, then blinks out with a little spark. It seems like she's altogether disappeared in that burst of light. *She must have her own methods of travel,* Filomena thinks. Filomena looks down and feels her stomach get queasy. They're so high up, she can hardly see the ground. A cloud floats past. At least they're safe up here.

CHAPTER SEVENTEEN

HOW TO MELT A WITCH

"Alone again!" Alistair says, stretching his arms and legs to make himself comfortable on a couch. "Time for a nap maybe!"

"Or how about we start planning for how we're going to deal with this immortal fire thing?" Jack says, standing up and beginning to pace.

Before they can decide what the next few hours or minutes hold (how long Gita will be gone, Filomena has no idea), they hear tapping from the windows.

Gretel screams, and Alistair chokes out a gasp. Jack pulls out his Dragon's Tooth sword.

Filomena whips her head around to see five grotesque-looking creatures hovering outside the windows. Grisly, terrifying, hulking monkeys with thick batlike wings that flap and flap. The monkeys throw themselves against the glass, as if hoping to smash the panes open.

"What's going on?" Alistair cries. "Did Gita set us up? Is this a trap?"

As Filomena considers this, her mind is going a mile a minute from the adrenaline. Could Gita have tricked them into coming here, walked them right into a trap so the Wicked Witch can capture them?

"It seems like they can't get through the glass, at least," Gretel says, shifting her chain mail jumpsuit in place.

The four stand on guard with their swords. They're at a stalemate as the terrifying flying monkeys continue to bash themselves against the glass, to no avail. But then they hear a familiar voice.

"My pretties! My pretties!"

A woman cloaked in a beautiful emerald-green robe floats up on another flying broomstick. Are witches just handed flying broomsticks when they become officially wicked?

Filomena's mind is running at the speed of a train about to fly off the tracks. She can tell the witch is going to break through a window at any second. Racking her brain for options, Filomena remembers the movie *The Wizard of Oz*. How does Dorothy conquer the witch?

Well . . . it's worth a try.

"Alistair, come help me fill buckets with water!" she says, leaving Gretel and Jack to hold down the fort.

But it appears that Gita doesn't spend any time cooking. In the fashion of a true cosmopolitan woman, she keeps high heels in her oven, and there's not a pot to be found! In a panic, Filomena runs to find the bathroom, which holds a golden claw-foot bathtub with an extendable showerhead. *If this can just extend out of the bathroom,* Filomena thinks, *we'll have a chance.*

The showerhead *does* extend, and when Filomena returns to the main room, she gets a jolt at the scene.

Two flying monkeys are holding Jack and Gretel captive, arms behind their backs. The Wicked Witch of the West is pacing the lair with a huge grin on her face.

"Gita never invites me over anymore," she says. "Now it seems I have to break in even to get a glimpse of this place!"

"Maybe if you didn't have the whole city under your command and capture, you'd have more friends," Jack spits out, struggling against the flying monkey's grip.

The Wicked Witch of the West turns around to face him. "City under my command?" She laughs. "I wish!"

"Now, Alistair!" Filomena hisses over her shoulder and toward the bathroom, where Alistair is crouching by the tub. He turns the faucet knobs to full blast, and a strong stream comes out of the showerhead. It's a good thing Gita has excellent water pressure.

When the water hits her, the Wicked Witch of the West starts screaming. But after a few moments, Filomena realizes it's more from annoyance and shock than because the witch is melting, as the mortal world's story goes.

"Turn that thing off! What are you doing?" the witch says, stepping away from the stream. "You're going to ruin Gita's lair!"

They realize this plan is not panning out, so Alistair does as he's told. Filomena grabs her Dragon's Tooth sword. Looks like they're going into battle after all. No loopholes.

She lunges at the wicked witch, who jumps out of the way.

The flying monkeys start attacking Filomena and Alistair. Filomena swings her Dragon's Tooth sword. Once again, she's thankful for such a deadly weapon. The two monkeys who attacked her drop dead, but Alistair isn't having as much luck. He, Jack, and Gretel keep fighting with the three monkeys that remain.

"Honestly, I had no idea *these* were going to be here," the witch says, stepping over the bodies of the two monkeys. "But I guess we're on the same mission. To wreak havoc on you wretched little heroes."

"Why are you coming after us?" Filomena asks, waving her sword.

"Why am I coming after you? You've got to be joking.

She wasn't just my sister. You *killed* my *best friend*." The Wicked Witch of the West stares at them, and tears are brimming in her eyes. Is it possible for Filomena to feel bad for her?

"Oh, Wahida," a warm voice says, "you let the monkeys in?"

Filomena whips her head around. Gita hovers in the gaping hole of a smashed window, then glides through.

"And did you really have to break my window?" she says.

The Wicked Witch of the West shrugs. "Saved time."

"I know you're upset about Eeshani," Gita starts, "but they didn't know what they were doing. They're just kids. They don't know the history of Camelot. They don't understand what's happened here."

"It doesn't matter!" Wahida screeches. "They killed her, Gita. Why are you helping them? They think we're evil, just like the rest of Camelot. They'll kill me without a second thought."

Filomena and Jack make eye contact, confused about what exactly is going on.

"I have to avenge her, Gita," Wahida says. "I don't want to. You know I don't want to do this, but I have to."

"No, you don't have to! They're going to help right things, Wahida. These kids could be the key to making everything right again."

"Why should I believe in them? Why should I believe you?" Wahida is crying now.

"Just trust me," Gita says. She's looking at the Wicked Witch of the West with such intensity that Filomena feels there's a lot she doesn't understand.

"Look, if you don't back off, you're going to have to fight me," Gita says. "I'm not letting you get to them. We need them."

Just then, the flying monkey restraining Jack lurches forward as if to take a bite out of him. But just as quickly, a blast intervenes, sending the monkey flying out the broken window.

"Did you bring them with you?" Gita says, her silver staff cooling from the blast.

"No way. *She* must know the kids are here," Wahida says.

"Can we just get them out of the way before we keep talking?" Gita asks. "They're so annoying."

Wahida and Gita both turn their attention to the remaining flying monkeys. With quick flicks of their wrists, they send them away easily.

"Wait," Jack says, catching his breath after the fight. "Did you just help us?"

Wahida shrugs, looking confused about it herself. "I will never forgive you for what you did to Eeshani, but maybe Gita's right; there are bigger things at stake here than my personal vengeance."

"Truce?" Gita says, looking skeptically at Wahida.

"Witch's honor," Wahida says, touching each of her temples and the middle of her forehead.

"All right then." Gita claps her hands. "Why don't we sit down?"

The once-beautiful apartment is in complete disarray. Gita swooshes the two lifeless flying monkeys out the window and then makes her way over to a couch. A very confused Alistair, Jack, Gretel, and Filomena sit down, too. Jack and Filomena make eye contact. They really don't get what's happening now.

"So those flying monkeys," Alistair begins. "They weren't yours?"

"Fairies, no!" Wahida says, crossing her legs. "Let me guess, you think I'm evil and that I have control of the Emerald City."

Gretel gulps. "Well, yeah."

Wahida shakes her head in disbelief and frustration.

"Come on, Wah," Gita says, "you can't blame them. They only just got to Camelot! Of course they believed the first thing they were told."

"Look, you want the real story?" Wahida says. "I'll tell you. Eeshani, Gita, and I—we've known one another forever. And we are witches, yes. But I'm not wicked. Neither is—was—Eeshani, and Gita here isn't some picture-perfect good girl, all right?"

Gita chuckles and shrugs.

"A while ago, rumors started to spread through Never After. Rumors about lots of people but about us witches in particular. Now, witches have never had a totally spotless public image in the first place, so we're pretty good scape-goats. Easy to blame. People don't trust us for some reason."

Alistair and Gretel look at each other, taking this in.

"Bizarre, horrible things started happening in Camelot. In the Emerald City, too. The munchkins being captured and brought here, for one. And what did all the newspapers say? What did all the rumors claim? That the Wicked Witches of the East and West were taking control of the Emerald City. So untrue!"

Gita turns to the four kids. "And whoever was spreading these rumors painted me as an angel," she says.

"Eventually Eeshani and I got tired of constantly trying to prove that we aren't evil. No one believed us. Whoever started these rumors, whoever really has control of the Emerald City, they were doing a really effective job of put-ting the blame on us. So we thought, *Well if everyone already thinks we're evil, why not run with it?*"

Filomena can't believe it. So the story in the mortal world is wrong, after all. Just like usual. The witches aren't evil, they were forced to be evil by someone else. Her guilt over the Witch of the East doubles again. Though, given how Wahida came here to kill them, Filomena doesn't doubt that Eeshani would have done the same.

"Wait, so whoever was in charge of capturing the munch-kins and taking over the Emerald City—that's who controls the flying monkeys?" Alistair asks.

Gita and Wahida both nod.

"And do you know who it could be?" Jack asks, tentatively.

"That's the thing: We don't know," Wahida says. "That's why we never fully disproved the rumors."

"Camelot used to be so protected by the fairies that no one villainous from other Never After kingdoms could even venture here. So we're a bit out of touch with what's going on in the rest of Never After," Gita explains. "That's why I want to talk to you. You kids know what's happening out there, so I thought you might know who is behind all this."

The four heroes look at one another, chills creeping up their spines.

"I think we know exactly who is behind this," Filomena says.

"Olga," Jack, Gretel, and Alistair say in unison.

"Olga?" Wahida asks.

"Yes, Olga the Ogre Queen," Jack says. "She's been tormenting Never After for years."

"Of course." Gita nods solemnly. "She is who vanquished the fairies, is she not?"

Jack nods.

"I have a hunch, and the more we talk about this, the more I think it's true," Gita says. She rummages around in a drawer until she comes up with an opal case. From this she pulls out a pair of glasses with frames of the same opal.

"The fairies gave us witches these glasses a long time ago," Gita says. "They were meant to allow us access to Avalon even when the fairies had to employ the Mists of Myth for the island's protection."

Jack takes a beat to consider this. If the fairies and the witches were once allies—if the fairies trusted the witches enough to give them these glasses—then shouldn't Jack believe what the witches were telling them now?

Wahida looks at the glasses, clearly fearful that Gita is about to give them away. Wahida looks about to say something, but she stops herself. She sighs, then chuckles. "Say hi to Marlon for me when you get there."

Filomena is confused about what Wahida means by this, but there's so much information to take in right now.

Gita goes on: "I've heard from my allies that the waters of Avalon are shrouded in the Mists of Myth right now. This happens only on rare occasions, when the sacred island is in need of more concealment than usual. The fairies aren't on Avalon, though, so no one knows for sure why it's happened this time. Though I have my own hunch. But the only way you'll see through the Mists of Myth is by using these glasses." Gita passes the glasses to Filomena. "Keep them safe."

"What is your hunch about the Mists of Myth?" Gretel asks.

"My hunch is that whoever caused all this in Camelot and the Emerald City is living in Avalon. Now I believe that it's Olga. Have you ever heard of the Lady of the Lake?"

The four shake their heads.

"She resides in a lake in the center of Avalon. The waters of Avalon hold mystical healing properties. By the waters of Avalon—that's where Excalibur rests. My suspicion is that Olga is living in Avalon and using the waters to regenerate."

Filomena closes her eyes. This quest started out as a way to save her mother. It *is* all about her mother. But when has a quest ever been about just one thing? Olga has done more than curse Filomena's mother; Olga is destroying Never After from the inside out, like a parasite, leaching Avalon's sacred power. She's causing rot and destruction from the center of the fairy world. Olga will stop at nothing until she's destroyed everything good, beautiful, and joyful in all the land. And it looks like, judging by the flying monkeys, Olga already knows that Filomena's on her way.

CHAPTER EIGHTEEN

LANDED OR STRANDED?

"Are we sure this is where Gita told us to go?" Alistair says, stepping over a pile of garbage. "This seems like a bad part of town."

The streets are totally deserted. Storefronts are boarded up on either side of the road, and the only life-forms they see are birds picking at trash heaps.

"'Bad' parts of town only come from neglect!" Gretel says.

The four have left Gita's lair and, upon her instructions,

are walking to an old out-of-service harbor on the edge of the Emerald City. According to Gita, beautiful ferry boats used to usher chosen people—those who made it past all their tests and quests in Camelot—from the Emerald City to Avalon, since Avalon is an island. But ever since the Mists of Myth showed up, which Gita suspects is when Olga took residence on Avalon, the ferries have stopped running. In fact, they've disappeared altogether. Except for one, which Gita rescued.

"I miss Toto." Gretel sighs. "We'd already be there by now if we were riding him!"

Gita had made the four leave Toto and their magic broom at her lair before departing for Avalon. She seemed to think that, on the island, these forms of transportation would be more hindrance than help. *At least we still have Ira,* Filomena thinks, patting her hip.

They walk down an abandoned street toward the harbor. Garbage and newspapers blow in the wind. One newspaper blows straight into Alistair's face. He grabs it off quickly, annoyed, but then looks at what the paper says.

"Hey, guys, check this out!"

The three stop walking for a second and huddle around him. It's a copy of the *Palace Inquirer* from a few weeks ago.

"Fil, it's you!" Gretel shrieks.

And it's true; there's a photograph of Filomena and Jack on the balcony of the Westphalian castle. The headline reads: "Princess Eliana Becomes Queen of Westphalia!"

In the photograph, Filomena is covered in ogre's blood and knighting Jack.

"Jack, you never told me you got knighted," Gretel says, bumping his hip.

"It's true, I am Queen Filomena's loyal servant," he says, giving Gretel a mock bow. "I mean, Queen Eliana."

They laugh and keep walking toward the harbor, which they see down the street.

"It's strange, all this," Filomena says. "When we're on these adventures, I keep forgetting we're, like, public figures. You know what I mean?"

"Oh, Filomena, you'll have to wear something of mine when you host your first Westphalian ball!" Gretel squeals. "That will be so much fun."

Host her first Westphalian ball? Filomena has never given much thought to that or what her duties as queen will look like. All she's been focused on is trying to save her mom. Any ideas around fun and the future all seem so far away. But she smiles and nods at Gretel. She can't get into any of that right now.

The four come to the harbor at the end of the street.

"Do you think that's the ferry?" Alistair says, pointing to a small white ferry boat. On its side is *Avalonian Ferry*.

"Well, that was easier than I thought it'd be!" says Gretel. "Maybe this won't be so hard after all."

"Let's just be careful here," Jack says. "We don't know who runs this boat."

Jack stands on the edge of the dock, holding each of their hands as they climb into the ferry. He gives Filomena's hand a squeeze and smiles at her as she steps on. Then he climbs on, but he leaves the rope docking the boat to the harbor tied, just in case.

"Hello?" Jack calls out. "We seek voyage to Avalon! Who is the captain of this ship?"

As they all walk the deck, there's no reply but a gentle breeze. Filomena notices the rope untying itself from the dock.

"Uh, guys," she says, "I think we're about to set sail."

The boat begins to move swiftly forward. They can see the steering wheel turning on its own.

"It looks like this ferry has no captain," Filomena says, pointing.

"The boat must be enchanted by the fairies," Jack says, leaning over the edge to glance at the water.

"Let's just hope this enchantment has a good sense of direction." Alistair laughs.

The four go to the front of the boat. It feels good to be out on open water. They can see the form of an island in the not-too-far distance. The waters by the Emerald City harbor were a rich green, like lagoons Filomena's seen in the mortal world. But as they sail out, the water shifts colors. The closer they get to Avalon, the more the water turns from an emerald green to a gorgeous pearlescent hue, opalescent and swirled.

"So none of you has ever been to Avalon before?" Filomena asks as she leans over the railing, staring at the water flowing past.

"Nope. Camelot, yes, but never Avalon," Jack says.

"Any idea what to expect?" Gretel says.

"I would think it will be very beautiful, since it's the home of the fairies. But with Olga there, I have no idea," Jack says sadly.

"It's sad that we're going to be seeing it for the first time while it's taken over by Olga." Gretel sighs. "It's like missing the Belle Epoque or the roaring twenties in Paris."

Avalon gets closer and closer until it's no longer a distant image but a large landmass. It's hard to tell what the island looks like exactly, but Filomena sees its edges are all sandy beaches and beyond those are large forests of ancient leafy trees.

The boat, steered by invisible hands, softly pulls up to the sandy shore.

"Looks like we've arrived," Jack says.

It's a tremendous sight to behold. Everything feels still, calm. The sand on the beach is a pure white, with flecks of color glinting in the soft sunlight. The translucent opal water laps against the shore. Trees sway in the breeze just past the beach, and Filomena can see round red apples hanging from branches. It's completely silent, except for the occasional birdsong.

"It's beautiful," she says breathlessly.

Jack jumps out of the boat first and helps each of them climb over the edge. After they've all dismounted, the ferry begins to drift away.

"Hey!" Jack yells. "Where are you going?"

"If that ferry leaves, how are we going to get out of here?" Gretel says, looking worried.

"Come back!" Filomena shouts. "We need a ride home!"

But the ferry doesn't answer; it just keeps floating away, leaving the four standing on the shore.

Alistair sighs. "Looks like we're *stranded* in Avalon."

"Well, what now?" Gretel asks.

Filomena considers their options. Their mission here is to find Excalibur, but as usual, one quest seems to lead to multiple quests. If Olga really is on this island, then what does that mean for their quest? Is retrieving the sword and getting out good enough? Or is a larger quest at hand? For now, Filomena decides to just focus on the agreed-upon quest: finding the sword.

"Ira, what do you know about this sword, Excalibur?" Filomena says, holding Ira up to her face as they all stand on the shore.

"Excalibur is King Arthur's sword," Ira says. "Many, many years ago in Camelot, King Arthur was the only one able to pull it from the stone in which it was fixed. Some say King Arthur is the original hero chosen by the fairies. But Excalibur was not created by the fairies."

Jack nods, considering this. "So Excalibur is somewhere

on Avalon. Gita said it's by the waters of Avalon, but maybe it could be with King Arthur?" he says.

"That I don't know, kid. But it seems likely."

Jack nods again. "Let's get moving; we need to cover as much ground as possible, as soon as possible, and start scouring the island for Olga and King Arthur."

Tired and hungry, Filomena, Alistair, and Gretel agree. Sometimes Filomena forgets just how energetic Jack is when on a quest.

They follow Jack off the beach and into the forest of ancient apple trees. Alistair wants to stop to pick some, but Jack swats away his hand. They walk for a few minutes in near silence. Eventually they come to a clearing where several boulders line the perimeter of the forest. From where she hovers behind trees and brush, Filomena thinks she hears gruff voices. She puts a finger to her lips, motioning for her friends to be silent. She peers over the boulder . . .

It's worse than she feared. Ogres! Ogres everywhere! Suddenly she notices that, all along the border of the forest, there are ogres with machetes, ogres with axes. The place is guarded by an entire ogre army! Dozens and dozens of them! There's no way they're getting through this undiscovered.

Filomena looks at her friends, whose eyes are all wide with shock and fear. Even with their Dragon's Tooth swords, four kids against several dozen ogres . . . They don't stand a chance.

After quietly running back through the forest, the group finds solace on the beach. They decide to hide behind a large boulder down the beach for extra cover as they plan their next move.

"Phew, I haven't been silent for that long since our tests to get the Dragon's Tooth swords," Alistair says from where he's visibly relaxing on the sand.

"And I haven't seen that many ogres since we were at war," Jack says, wiping his forehead.

Gretel sighs. "So much for just walking into Avalon."

"There must be another way for us to get to the center of Avalon," Filomena says. "Don't you think?"

"Hmm," Jack says. "I think we need to raise an army."

"'Raise an army'?!" Filomena repeats, incredulous. "We don't have time to do that! You think that, after all this, we're leaving? When we're so close?"

"I just don't see how else we're going to get past all those ogres. We can't fight them ourselves; we need help."

"But who would even come to fight with us?" Filomena asks.

"You're a queen now. You can call on your citizens and your allies."

Filomena's head is spinning. Going on a quest, sure, she can do that. Fighting an ogre in one-to-one combat, check. But heading an army? That seems impossible! She always forgets just how much happened in Never After before she arrived. Jack and Alistair have fought in several wars against the ogres. To them, maybe this is inevitable. But still, it doesn't feel like the right answer this time.

"It will take too long, Jack," Filomena says, shaking her head. "My mother is in real danger. It would take weeks to get all that organized."

"Uh, guys," Alistair says softly.

While Jack and Filomena tussle over how long it will take to raise an army and bring it to Avalon, Alistair spots some strange creature in the water.

"YOU GUYS!" he yells.

This gets their attention. They whip around to see an ominous shape rising in the water.

"What kinds of sea creatures are in Avalon?" Alistair says, backing away from the shore. "Are they nice or mean?"

The creature rears its head out of the water, gasping for air. It has surprisingly red hair. As it coughs and drags itself to shore, Filomena sees this is no sea creature at all.

CHAPTER NINETEEN

FROM WONDERLAND'S OCEAN TO AVALON'S SHORE

"I am never taking oxygen for granted again!" Rosie yells, gasping and flopping onto Avalon's sandy shore.

Still in shock, Filomena rubs her eyes to make sure she's seeing this right.

"Did you just come out of the water?" Gretel asks, also incredulous.

Rosie holds up a finger while bent over on the sand, coughing up a piece of seaweed. She shakes her hair like a puppy trying to rid itself of rainwater. After Rosie finishes coughing, she opens her eyes and looks at them blearily.

"I have a lot to tell you."

They decide that, since they have no plan and a lot of catching up to do, they'll take a quick pause on the beach to recuperate and plot the next move. Alistair, unbeknownst to anyone, had gone to the market in the Emerald City while Gretel was sending off her parcel and Filomena and Jack were getting fish and chips. He brought his findings with him to Avalon.

"You probably would have made fun of me if you knew I brought this," he says, untying a kerchief filled with a loaf of bread, salami, cheese, tomatoes, and olives. "But aren't you happy now?"

While Alistair begins to prepare sandwiches for everyone, Filomena, Gretel, and Jack sit on the cool sand behind the boulder. Rosie is taking off layers of outer clothing one by one to squeeze free of ocean water.

"I suppose we should start at the beginning," she says.

The other four nod.

"As you know, Beatrice, Byron and I all went back to Wonderland to do damage control."

Rosie explains how Robin Hood has graduated from

simple mischievousness to spreading full-blown lies about Beatrice and Byron throughout Wonderland. He's fully on Olga's side now, after Princess Jeanne rejected him. Beatrice thinks, since Wonderland was under Olga's rule for so long, that Robin thought the kingdom might be susceptible to turning against Beatrice and Byron in their absence. He started spreading lies that they care little for their kingdom, that they want to sell off the best parts of Wonderland to wealthy wolf investors—terrible lies that could turn Wonderland citizens against their king and queen.

"Spreading lies and rumors seems to be a common tactic of Olga's these days," Jack mutters, thinking back to what the witches told them.

"So we held a press conference with media and set the record straight, saying that none of it is true, and we also wanted to use the opportunity to rally support for the League of Seven!" Rosie says.

"Well that's great news!" Jack says. "A great idea. Did it work?"

"The only problem," Rosie says, pulling off her wet socks, "is that in order to prove that we were away for good reason, and to raise some anti-Olga sentiment, we sort of, uh . . ." Rosie looks sheepishly at them, embarrassed, and puts her head in her hands. "We accidentally told the media that you guys are here, on Avalon, searching for Olga."

Everyone is dead silent for a moment.

"WHAT?!" Jack cries furiously, standing up. He immediately begins pacing. "Rosie, come on! Do you realize what you've done?" he says, fuming.

"I know, Jack, I'm so sorry!" she pleads. "It can't be that big a deal, though, right?" Rosie asks hopefully.

"They have all of Avalon on lockdown!" Jack whisper-yells, flinging his arm in the direction of the forest, past which the ogres are all guarding. "Olga must have heard your little speech and decided to treat Avalon like a maximum-security prison!"

"That must be how Olga knew we were in the Emerald City, too," Alistair whispers.

"Oh my fairies," Rosie says, sinking down onto the sand.

"Jack, it's okay," Filomena says, standing up to put her arm around him. "At least now we know why it's being guarded like this. What's done is done. And Olga knew I'd be searching for Excalibur. She'd have figured it out eventually."

"Your mother is waiting for us, Fil! Your mother is waiting for us, and we need to get her that sword," Jack cries. Then his voice turns soft. "We've got to make sure we get it."

Filomena's heart melts a little as she realizes that it's *her* for whom he's so worked up. But she has to calm him down if they're going to get anywhere.

"Maybe we could all use some food now," Alistair says, passing out the thick sandwiches he's assembled.

"So what happened after the press conference, Rosie?" Gretel asks before taking a big bite of her sandwich.

"After that, it didn't seem like I was of much use in Wonderland," she says, wringing out her long red hair, "so I went to the Deep."

Filomena pauses midbite.

"You went to see the dragons? Why?" she says.

"It's something I've wanted to do ever since I first met you guys and saw your Dragon's Tooth swords. I'm working on a new invention and thought they might be helpful."

Jack has finally calmed a little and sits to eat his sandwich. Nothing like hearing about the dragons to calm him down.

"What invention, Rosie? Jack and I have a few ideas—" Alistair starts before Jack nudges him in the ribs.

"I've been working on a teleportation device, and in my many, many months of reading in Snow Country, I discovered that dragon wings have magical transportation properties. I thought, maybe, that might be the missing piece."

The four are glued to Rosie, listening and eating. Rosie pulls something from her pocket. It looks like an extremely shiny black stone. "After I passed the dragons' tests, they gave me this. It's a scale from a dragon's wing." The scale is very beautiful and about the size of a deck of cards. "Also, get this!" she says excitedly, putting the scale back in her pocket. "The dragons stole a talking mirror from the ogres!"

"No way!" Filomena yells, shocked.

"Yes way! Apparently they heard about our animating one and thought they should have one of their own! Isn't that great? A talking mirror back on our side!"

"I wouldn't say the dragons are exactly on our side, Rosie," Jack says. "But I suppose they're neutral, at least."

"Wait, you still haven't explained how you washed up on the shore," Alistair says quizzically.

"Oh right!" Rosie laughs, slapping her knee. "That was the dragons, too! They told me there's a hidden shortcut between Avalon and Wonderland in Wonderland's ocean. If you follow the seabirds and walk down the stone steps into the ocean."

Jack looks rapt at this development.

"It's rather frightening"—Rosie giggles—"because, of course, you have no idea if it's going to work! I still wasn't sure if I should trust the dragons at first. But I made it all in one piece. If a bit damp."

"Incredible," Jack says. He looks puzzled. "A shortcut. I never knew of such a thing. It's not a swoop hole?"

"No, I believe it's something else altogether," Rosie says. "But it certainly works!"

"So what about Bea and Byron?" Filomena asks. "Are they coming, too?"

Rosie shakes her head. "They said to tell you they are sorry and that they wish they could come, but there's still too much to do in Wonderland. One press conference isn't enough to completely fix the damage Robin Hood has done. Bea thinks they need to be present as rulers for a while."

Filomena nods, understanding completely. She feels a little guilty that she isn't doing the same for her kingdom. *Her* kingdom. It's still unbelievable. But what can she do? This quest is hers.

With stories told, clothes dried, and food eaten, all that's left to do is plan. Jack stands up and resumes his pacing.

"So what we're thinking," he says to Rosie, "is that we have to raise an army of our allies from Never After to fight the ogres guarding Avalon."

"No," Filomena says from where she's leaning against the boulder, "we're not thinking that. That was one option Jack came up with."

Jack looks at her, and Filomena raises her eyebrows, daring him to challenge her.

"Okay, yes, that was my idea," he concedes, "but I don't hear anyone else coming up with any better ones."

"The gate . . . ," Rosie says softly.

Gretel turns. "What was that, Rosie?"

"As a thank-you for their gift of the scale, I gave the dragons a small vial of truth serum. You remember the truth serum the Winter Witch gave me?"

Filomena nods, remembering how that serum helped create Ira.

"Well, I gave them that, and in return, they told me that, when I return to Avalon, it might be worth looking for a gate. Perhaps that can be helpful to us now?"

"The dragons do not like to be in debt." Jack chuckles. "They match every gift with another gift."

Gretel's head snaps up. "The keeper of the gate!" she cries.

"What's that?" Rosie asks.

"When we arrived at the doors to the Emerald City. Remember, everyone?" Gretel looks to Alistair, Filomena, and Jack.

"Oh yeah," says Jack. "The guy in the little tower on the mountainside who let us in? Alistair told him we were a traveling circus?"

"Right!" Alistair giggles. "I wonder if he ever looked for our show."

"Jack," Gretel goes on, "you called him the keeper of the gate, to be formal, remember? And he got really flustered and said, 'Oh no, I'm not the famous keeper of the gate.' He said when you find the famous keeper of the gate, that's when you'll know you've really found Avalon."

The memory dawns on Filomena, and she knows Gretel's right. "You genius girl!" Filomena jumps on her. Gretel laughs shyly.

Jack nods, considering this. "Gretel, Rosie, this is wonderful. We're lucky to be on the same side as you two."

Gretel blushes. She's still getting used to her newfound confidence in her intelligence. Rosie shrugs like, *Yeah, I know.*

"Now the only question is," Filomena says, "where is the keeper of the gate?"

CHAPTER TWENTY

THE KEEPER OF THE GATE

"I wonder what he'll be like," Gretel says to Filomena. "The keeper of the gate. Do you think he'll be like the wise old Wizard in *The Wizard of Oz?*"

The League of Seven (minus two) has decided to walk the perimeter of the island to search for the keeper of the gate. Alistair said it makes sense for a gate entrance to be along a perimeter, but mostly they're trying to avoid the ogres and their machetes. Rosie and Alistair are leading the way, with Jack just behind them; Gretel and Filomena are bringing up the rear of the group.

Filomena laughs. "Didn't the Wizard of Oz turn out to be a phony?"

"Oh right." Gretel frowns. "But since mortal stories are always wrong, maybe in this version, he actually isn't!"

"Either way, if he is a wizard, I think we should look for him in the hollows of trees," Jack says. "I've heard that's where wizards like to live."

The forest here is beautiful. Afternoon light dapples the trees, and those apples hang, bright red and shiny, from every branch. Filomena remembers what Ira said about enchanted forests versus mystical forests.

"Hey, Ira," she says, unhooking him from her hip. "Is this forest enchanted or mystical?"

"Mystical, definitely mystical. The magic is built right into the biological makeup of the forest itself. There's a great amount of power in this forest."

"Ira," Alistair calls from the front of the pack, "can we eat these apples?"

Ira seems to consider this. Apples seem to carry a lot of significance in stories. There are Eve's apples, Snow White's apples . . . and Avalon's apples.

"I'd say it's safe enough to try one, but be careful with them, Alistair. They're mystical as well, and we don't know what they might be capable of."

"Why don't you hold off until we don't have a life-or-death mission to accomplish?" Jack urges.

"But, *Jaaack*," Alistair whines, "we always have a life-or-death mission to accomplish!"

Filomena laughs, thinking Alistair has a point. But then she stops laughing, remembering the mission. She wonders how her poor mother is doing. Once again, Filomena is thankful that, though days have passed since this quest began, for her mother it will have been only minutes, hours. Still, the very thought of Bettina makes Filomena speed up her walking, urge herself to go fast, get moving. As she moves quickly, she and Jack seem to switch spots in their lineup, and he falls back with Gretel. Filomena overhears them behind her.

"Did you get that package sent off, Gretel?" Jack asks.

"I did! You know, when I was doing that, I stopped in quickly at this amazing dress shop."

"Oh really? What was it like?"

Filomena is surprised to hear this. Jack's not annoyed at Gretel for dillydallying, and he seems genuinely interested.

"There was this fabulous woman, Céline, who owns it. She's so young! And the shop was gorgeous. It really made me think about some things."

"Like what?"

Gretel pauses. All in the League of Seven have fallen silent and are eavesdropping on this conversation.

"Well, I didn't really want to get into it until we'd finished our quest," Gretel says softly, "but I guess I'll just tell you. I'm thinking of opening my own store."

Filomena whips her head around, no longer pretending she's not listening.

"What?!" she says. "That's incredible, Gretel!"

The League of Seven are all in a tizzy with this news.

"Oh my gosh," Rosie says excitedly, "I bet Bea and Hori and Filomena will want to get all their royal outfits there! Bea was talking about all the work you'll have when you get back. Tea parties, alliance and council meetings, civilian greetings, balls and town halls! Wow, I can't believe I just got excited about tea parties and balls. Bea must be rubbing off on me." She skips away merrily.

Filomena only nods blankly, overwhelmed by all the tasks that apparently await her.

"Where is it going to be, Gretel?" Alistair asks. "Eastphalia? Westphalia? *Northphalia?* Wait, don't tell me you're thinking of Snow Country. That's way too far. Wonderland could be cool . . . but I think Westphalia will be best, since that's where we'll be living when this is over."

Filomena looks at Alistair, puzzled. They will? Alistair starts to look a little insecure.

"Well, won't we? Right, Jack? We'll all be in Westphalia together when Filomena goes back to be queen? Isn't that what we talked about?"

There's a sudden silence—an awkward silence. Jack looks at Filomena with a sheepish smile and shrugs. He looks so open, so vulnerable. He and Alistair talked about this? About moving to Westphalia, to be near Filomena? Filomena realizes she has no idea what she's planning on doing when, as Alistair said, "this is over." Suddenly she hopes this quest will last forever so she never has to figure out what to do when it's done. She can't respond to any of this right now; she has no idea what she's going to do once her mom is saved, so she just smiles at Jack and takes his hand. They entwine their fingers and walk, holding hands.

"Actually, Alistair, I've been thinking of a different place," Gretel says softly. "I've been thinking I want to open up a shop . . . in Paris."

"Paris? What's Paris? Is that a neighborhood? Is it like a nickname? Sounds like a name Princess Jeanne would like. Is it in Northphalia?" Alistair's so nervous, he's talking a mile a minute.

"Actually, it's in the mortal world."

Filomena's heart, strangely, lights up at the idea of Gretel in the mortal world. Does *she* want to be in the mortal world? Even if Gretel is in Paris and Filomena's in California, country to country is a lot closer than world to world.

"Oh" is all Alistair says in response.

Everyone's quiet following this admission. Alistair has gotten sulky, and Filomena thinks she hears him sniffle.

"So what do you guys think this old wizard looks like?" Gretel says in a joking tone, hoping to change the topic and the energy.

No one answers her. Filomena realizes none of them has been looking in any tree hollows as they walk; they've been too caught up in this conversation. Except . . . Where's Rosie?

A burst of red hair is running toward them. Rosie must have gone up ahead.

"I think I found something," she says as she gets closer. "Come on!"

The five adventurers jog to follow Rosie deep into the forest, along a series of twists and turns that lead to the biggest tree Filomena's seen yet. Rosie motions for quiet and mimes sleeping, putting her palms together under her cheek. Then she points to a small opening in a tree trunk. Could the Wizard be in this tree? Like Jack suspected?

Filomena steps forward and peeks in. There is someone in there, but it's not an old wizard, not at all. It's a young boy.

Chapter Twenty-One

Talking Mirror, Meet Talking Owl

"So you found a kid sleeping in a tree hollow?" Jack whispers to Rosie. They're a few paces away from the huge ancient tree.

"Didn't you say wizards like to live in trees?" Rosie asks, shrugging.

"Yes, but apparently so do small children!" Jack hisses.

"Don't you think this could be a wizard?" Rosie responds.

"No way. Wizards aren't kids."

"Have you met the keeper of the gate before?" Rosie asks Jack. The rest of them stand, unsure what to do.

"Well, no—"

"So you have no idea what he looks like. This could be him."

"Or it could be an angry little sprite that will bite and hex us."

"Is Jack the Giant Stalker really afraid of a little kid?" Rosie says, crossing her arms and smirking.

Jack rolls his eyes.

"Fil, what do you think?" he says, turning to Filomena.

Filomena is not sure what she thinks of this, of any of it! Of Gretel setting up a dress shop in Paris, of Alistair and Jack moving to Westphalia, of the many tasks awaiting them back in their respective kingdoms. But she tries to focus on the task at hand. What does she think of this kid sleeping in the tree?

She shrugs. "May as well give it a try?"

"So, what, do we just knock?" Alistair asks.

Rosie steps forward and sticks her head in the hollow. "Hello?" she yells, and the yell echoes out of the tree.

She steps back. They hear a yawn. The child stands and rubs his eyes. He's a Black boy of about eleven with a sweet cherubic face. But his youthful features soon form the expression of a disgruntled old man.

"What's all this?" he says in a high soprano voice.

"Hi, I'm Rosie," Rosie says. "We're the League of Seven.

Well, most of the League of Seven. We're down two members at the moment." She motions to her four friends who each wave.

"Okay . . . ," the boy says, still rubbing his eyes from sleepiness.

"We're looking for the keeper of the gate," Alistair says, taking a step forward.

The boy narrows his eyes. "I thought I hid my tree better. My enchantment must have worn off." He looks cross with himself, lost in thought, but then comes back to the present. "All right, so here I am."

"*You* are the keeper of the gate?" Jack says, shocked.

"That depends," the boy says. "What do you want?"

Now Filomena knows it's her time to step forward. "I'm Filomena Jefferson-Cho of North Pasadena, otherwise known as Eliana, Queen of Westphalia."

She waits for a look of recognition to form on his face, but he remains impassive.

"Look, I don't get out much these days," he says, "so titles, names—these things mean nothing to me."

"Fair enough." Filomena nods. "The long and short of it is that we're looking for Excalibur. My mother, she was cursed by Queen Olga and is very, very sick, and we've been told that the only solution is to find the sword."

The keeper of the gate nods. "And so you want to use my gate to get to the sword."

"Precisely." The kid rubs his eyes again. It seems like he's just woken up from a very deep slumber. He looks at them but doesn't make a move.

"What's your name?" Rosie says.

"He's the keeper of the gate," Jack replies.

"Yes, but that can't be his name," she says. "What's your real name?"

"Merlin," he mumbles.

"Merlin! Like Merlin the wizard of Camelot?" Filomena gets a flutter in her stomach, connecting the pieces. Merlin was the most powerful wizard in Camelot! He was a friend of King Arthur's! At least, he was in the stories she's heard.

"No, not *Merlin*. Man, why do people always pronounce it wrong?"

The boy's face disappears into the tree. For a moment Filomena worries that she's bungled it all, that they've lost their chance. But then the tree opens. The front of the tree swings on invisible hinges in the shape of a door.

"Come on in," the boy says. "You might as well!"

Slowly, the five file in. At first Filomena wonders how they'll all fit into this tree, but as she steps inside, she finds it's enormous! It's a circular room with a hardwood floor with hundreds of tree rings on its smooth surface. The curved walls are covered in bookshelves with books, and there's a table with all kinds of notebooks, feather pens, beakers, cauldrons, and gizmos. Filomena looks up—there's no ceiling. The room seems to go forever upward, up, up, into the tree.

"Close the door behind you, please," the boy says to Gretel, who's last to enter. "First of all, it's Marlon, not Merlin," he continues, sitting in a rocking chair. "I don't know why everyone pronounces it *Merlin*," he says crossly. "You five are interesting to me. It's been a while since anyone's come to visit."

"Since Olga took over Avalon, you mean?" Alistair says.

Marlon sighs deeply. "Yes, that timeline probably aligns." He rocks in his chair, frowning at them skeptically. His short legs don't meet the floor, and he looks at once like an old man and a young boy.

"*Hoooo, hooooooo.*" A hooting comes from far above them. "*Whooooo* is here?"

"I'm not sure, Archimedes," Marlon says as a small brown owl lands on his shoulder. "I'm still trying to figure out who they are."

Filomena hears Rosie say, "Wow." She's surveying the tableful of books, papers, notes, and calculations. "I've never even heard of some of these books!" she exclaims.

"That might be because I've written a few of them," Marlon says, rocking, "and others are out of print."

Rosie holds up a volume on the history of Snow Country's giant community. "I lived with these giants!" she says, smiling.

"How fascinating. What were they like?"

"Horrible taste in décor," she says, and immediately Filomena's brought back to the giants' lace doilies and floral curtains. Seems like a lifetime away, right now, though it was only a few weeks ago.

"I like this much better," Rosie continues, waving at the bookshelves, which go as high as the eye can see.

The other four adventurers are frozen, watching Marlon and Rosie interact. Filomena is still processing the fact that Marlon seems to be friends with a talking owl.

Rosie excitedly points to a book with a dark green spine. Silver lettering reads, *An Oral History of Dragon Powers.* "I was just in the Deep," she says, plucking the book from its shelf.

"Rosie! Don't touch anything," Gretel says.

"No, it's okay," Marlon says. "What were you doing there?"

"Trying to get this," Rosie says, and pulls the smooth black dragon scale out of her pocket.

"Why could you possibly be looking for a dragon scale?" Marlon asks, eyes wide.

"I'm trying to invent something," Rosie replies. "But I don't know how much I should tell you. Can we trust you?"

Marlon rocks in the chair, then stands. Archimedes, the talking owl, flutters off him and lands on Alistair's head.

"Owl! Owl on my head!" Alistair cries.

"Apologies," the owl says, "you just looked like a good resting spot."

"Your claws are actually giving me sort of a good head massage," Alistair says, trying to look up at the owl without tipping the bird off his head.

"Are you really a wizard?" Gretel asks Marlon.

Marlon turns around to look at her and blushes. Filomena wonders if she's the only one who's caught it. Gretel does look particularly beautiful in her sleek chain mail jumpsuit.

"Uh, yes, I am," Marlon says.

"I didn't know kids can be wizards," Gretel replies.

"I'm not a kid; I'm eleven!" Marlon says. "Eleven hundred years old, give or take an eon or two."

Filomena gasps at his age. Can they trust him, this wizard? She has a good feeling about him, but once again she remembers Lance and Gwen's words. Things are not what they seem in Camelot, now more than ever. But wait—Marlon. Why does that name sound familiar?

"Do you know the Wicked—er, sorry. The Witch of the West?" Filomena asks Marlon.

His eyes light up at the title. "Miss Wahida? Yes of course! Wait, do you?" he asks, now suspicious himself.

"We were just in the Emerald City," Filomena explains. "We met Wahida and Gita."

Marlon sighs deeply. "What horrors are going on there these days? Do people still hate Miss Wahida and Miss Eeshani?"

Filomena gulps. She didn't think this through. She brought up the Witch of the West; naturally the Witch of the East would come up, too. Maybe she'll save the news about Eeshani for when they know Marlon better. She tries to send that message to the others.

"We learned all about what's happening in the Emerald City," Filomena continues. "Wahida asked us to say hello to you, I think."

Marlon softens at this. "Did she now? Well, in that case, I suppose if my old friend Miss Wahida is passing a message through you, you must be safe enough."

"So what do you say?" Rosie asks, trying to bring them back to the matter at hand. "Will you show us the way to the gate?"

"Not so fast," Marlon says, turning to Rosie. "I'm curious. First prove that you're actually an inventor and not just a poser."

Rosie squints. She doesn't like to be questioned. "Filomena, show him Ira."

"Ira?" Marlon asks.

"Ira Glassman. The talking mirror Filomena and I created."

Filomena does as she's told and holds up Ira. She taps the back of the mirror to wake him up from his slumber.

"Oh, uh, hello!" Ira says as his face appears in a swirl of mist.

"Ira, this is Marlon the wizard," Filomena says, "also known as the keeper of the gate."

"Ah, so we're on the right track," Ira says.

Filomena shakes her head, annoyed once again by Ira's limited capacity to just tell them what to do. But she is slightly assured that he said they're on the right track.

"Amazing," Marlon says, taking a step toward Filomena. "May I?"

Filomena hands over Ira, and Marlon peers deep into the mirror's face.

Ira laughs. "Back it up there, kiddo. Getting a little too close."

"Okay," Marlon says, handing Ira back to Filomena. "You made this? That's pretty neat. Okay, I believe you're an inventor . . . What was your name?"

"Rose Red. But my friends call me Rosie." She smiles.

"Rosie. I'll show you the way through the gate. I'll even come with you through it myself. But on one condition."

"What's that?" she asks.

"I want to know what you're inventing with that dragon scale."

CHAPTER TWENTY-TWO

A Bunch of Roots

The gate that the keeper of the gate keeps is not the kind of gate Filomena was expecting. She was expecting something grand, like the entryway to the Emerald City: an enormous set of doors between two mountains. After all, they are getting deeper into Avalon, the most sacred place in all of Never After. But for that reason, maybe this way actually makes more sense.

The five adventurers followed Marlon and Archimedes, the boy wizard and the talking owl, out of Marlon's home in the trunk of a tree and through the forest. Marlon's now stopped the group at a thick tangle of roots between two ancient trees.

"Here we are," Marlon says. Archimedes lands on his shoulder. Marlon motions to the roots.

"*This* is the gate?" Jack says, incredulous. "A bunch of roots?"

"Careful what you say, Jack Stalker," Marlon says, crossing his small arms. "They might hear you."

"Who might? The ogres?" Alistair asks.

"No, no," Marlon responds. "There are no ogres on this part of the island. The trees."

Filomena looks around. They are surrounded by trees, the same types of beautiful apple trees that cover the rest of the island. These trees can hear them?

"Go on, Marlon," Jack says, looking around quizzically.

"The gate I guard is not necessarily mine to invite people through. I do guard it, yes, and sometimes, when I choose, I lead people to it. Well, theoretically. It's been a long, long time since I've actually done this. But anyway, my gate is a way to travel through Avalon belowground, where you'll be uninterrupted by ogres."

"That's perfect!" Filomena says, hope rising in her chest. "But how?"

"Via an underground tree system. All trees are connected through their roots. They speak to one another, and they allow for travel. This 'bunch of roots,' as you called it, Jack, is the gateway to that system."

"I'm sorry, Marlon, I didn't mean offense," Jack says.

"It's not me you have to worry about offending," Marlon says. "You're going to have to plead your case to the nature spirits."

Filomena feels a tingling sensation on her skin when Marlon says this. The nature spirits? Thoughts of Snow Country and the giants' kitchen come back to her. Jack explaining the nature spirits and how they're an older force than even the fairies. How they're neutral, like the dragons—apparently like witches, too—and their only mission is to keep the harmony in Never After.

"We . . . ," Filomena starts softly, "we have to talk to the nature spirits?" It seems like an overwhelmingly daunting task.

"You'll have to plead your case for entrance," Marlon says.

"Where are they?" Gretel asks quietly.

Marlon smiles, and for a moment he looks like the kid he appears to be. "They're everywhere!" he says. He jumps into the air, his arms above his head and a crack-of-sunshine smile on his face. He floats there for a few moments before softly descending.

"Whoa. Can you teach me how to do that?" Rosie says, eyes sparkling.

"We'll talk," Marlon says. "Now, Filomena, why don't you speak on behalf of the group. You sort of seem like the leader here, right?"

Everyone nods. Filomena's a bit taken aback. Things

always feel so equal between them that she doesn't think of herself as the leader. But it appears everyone else does.

"Well, Filomena *and* Jack," Rosie says. "They're sort of a dynamic duo."

Jack squeezes Filomena's hand, and she looks at him. He smiles confidently. "You can do this."

Filomena Jefferson-Cho from North Pasadena has never in her life made a plea to nature spirits on a sacred island with a wizard present. But for Eliana, Queen of Westphalia? Filomena supposes this is just another day in Never After. She takes a deep breath and gets on her knees. Is that the right thing to do? It seems like the right thing to do, out of respect. She turns on her mark of Carabosse, which sometimes gives her extra confidence in these kinds of situations. The mark reminds Filomena that she is a gift from the fairies, and though so many of the fairies are dead—all but Sabine—she still feels them protecting her.

"Do I have to speak out loud?" she says, looking up to Marlon.

"Hmm. Good question. I've never asked. But I'd think not," he says.

Filomena nods. She'd rather do this privately. She closes her eyes.

Hello, nature spirits, she says in her head. *I've heard a lot about you. I'm so happy to be on this beautiful island that you live on. Avalon is the most special place I've ever been. Well, maybe except my home in North Pasadena. That place is pretty special,* too. It's not as beautiful—it doesn't have opal ocean tides or red apples or emerald buildings or anything—but it does have my parents, who are the most important people in the world to me. There really is no place like home, right? Which is why I'm here, so far away from home. I need to find Excalibur to save my mom. Olga, evil ogre queen Olga, cursed my mother as a way to get back at me for trying to protect Never After. And I suppose I was born in the fairy world, and Bettina, my mortal world mom, is my adopted mom, but she's my real mom to me. So please, please let us through the gate. We are really good people, and we're just trying to save my mom.

Filomena hears a collective gasp from the group behind her. She opens her eyes. The tangle of roots has opened up, revealing a wooden staircase that leads underground. Filomena stands.

"Looks like the nature spirits are letting you pass," Marlon says. "Good job, Filomena."

Filomena feels an overwhelming sense of love for the trees all around her, as if she is protected by them. She touches the bark of a tree next to her and internally says, *Thank you.*

"Well, good luck, you guys. It was nice to meet you."

Filomena takes her hand off the tree and sees Marlon looking at the ground sadly. She's confused. She thought Marlon was coming with them.

"You're not coming?" Rosie says.

"You don't need me anymore. I'm just the keeper of the gate. I led you to the gate, so that's it, right? You don't have any more use for me."

He keeps looking at the ground with his head hung low. It strikes Filomena just how lonely he must be, an immortal boy wizard alone in a tree with only his books to keep him company. Well, and Archimedes. Thank goodness the owl can talk.

"But I have so many more questions for you!" Rosie says, running over to Marlon. "Please come with us. We have so much more to talk about."

"Really?" Marlon says, looking up shyly.

"I've never met anyone as interested in the same things as me. We could have a lot of fun together, I think." Rosie smiles.

An answering smile creeps onto Marlon's face. "Well, okay, I guess I do have a few things I could teach you."

"That's the spirit," Rosie says, slapping Marlon's back. "Just don't get too boastful, or I'll make Archimedes like me more than you."

Chapter Twenty-Three
Underground Invasion

The underground tree network has a feel sort of similar to the cavern of crystals in Camelot, except the tunnels are all smooth wood. It's a tunnel network, really, or sort of like a maze. Smooth wooden floors curve up to become smooth wooden walls and smooth wooden ceilings. It seems like it's lit from the inside, too. Something to do with photosynthesis, maybe? Filomena makes a note to ask Marlon about it, but he's busy talking to Rosie at the moment.

Every so often a fork in the path arises or a new hallway presents itself. Even Marlon is unsure of which path to take, but Jack's Seeing Eye comes in handy yet again, for this reason.

Jack and Filomena walk several yards in front of the others. The tightish tunnels make it difficult for more than two people to walk next to one another. As they walk, Jack tosses his arm over Filomena's shoulder. His other hand holds the Seeing Eye to his face.

"You did great back there, Fil," he says.

Jack's touch on her shoulders feels somehow both comforting and stomach fizzing.

"Hey," she says, and stops walking, forcing him to stop, too.

She puts her hand on his face and looks at him. She tries to really look at him, to see not just Jack Stalker the hero, but Jack the boy. He leans in and kisses her, one arm still around her shoulders, the other now behind her back and pulling her closer. Stars, sparkflies, peony punch, opal waves—none of it even comes close.

"UGH!" a voice says, and they pull apart instinctively.

"You guys are, like, in love?" the voice says. The voice is Marlon's. "Gross!"

Filomena and Jack burst into laughter. Filomena remembers when she first saw Beatrice and Byron kiss and how gross she thought it was. But now she sort of gets the appeal.

"Come on, let's keep moving," Jack says, smiling and grabbing Fil's hand.

But just as soon as he grabs it, he drops it. He puts both

hands on his Seeing Eye, peering through and looking confused and concerned.

Filomena takes this as an opportunity to ask Marlon something that's been on her mind. "Marlon, I was wondering. How did Olga get through Camelot? How did she pass all the tests meant to keep out those who don't have a pure heart?"

"The fairy magic was weakened," he says sadly.

"So not even the tests of Camelot could keep Olga out? Not even the nature spirits?"

"I heard that two more fairies died recently. When that happened, Olga took her chance to pounce. With only one fairy left, the protective powers of Camelot and Avalon dimmed. That's when Olga tromped her way through. She timed it perfectly, and then, once she took up residence on Avalon, she convinced the Emerald City and the rest of Camelot that the witches of East and West were the ones terrorizing the land."

"Oh, that we know," says Gretel.

"You know that? How? No one seems to know that."

"Wahida and Gita told us," Gretel replies.

He nods. "Right, right."

Filomena feels a pinch in her stomach. Guilt.

"Marlon, how do you know the witches?" Gretel asks.

"They were my mentors when I started out as a wizard, a long, long time ago. Miss Wahida especially. She was my teacher, my guide. She taught me almost everything I know,"

Marlon says sadly. Then he laughs. "Or at least she likes to think so."

"What did you do when the rumors about them started?" Filomena asks.

"I was already here, working as keeper of the gate by that point. The fairies assigned me the role when I became advanced enough. But I was disappointed in Miss Wahida and Miss Eeshani. They gave in to the rumors. They figured that if people already thought badly of them, then they may as well live up to the expectations, the stereotypes, out of spite." Marlon shrugs. "I didn't agree. We haven't spoken in a long time," he says.

"Marlon, I feel like we have to tell you something," Filomena says.

She looks at Alistair and Gretel. She looks at Jack, but he's still peering through his Seeing Eye as they walk.

"We sort of . . . It was almost an accident, but we were defending ourselves . . . ," Filomena starts.

"We pushed a house onto the Witch of the East during a battle with her," Alistair jumps in. "She was trying to kill us, or at least that's what it seemed like."

Marlon is quiet for a few minutes as they walk.

"I knew they would get themselves in danger if they kept acting so antagonistically," he says softly.

"We're so, so sorry, Marlon. We had no idea at the time of who she was or what her history was," Gretel says.

"Miss Wahida, though? She's okay?"

Gretel, Alistair, and Filomena nod.

"STOP!" Jack says. He's just a few feet ahead of them and thrusting his right arm out sideways to prevent anyone from passing him. "EVERYONE, STOP!"

"What's going on, Jack?" Filomena asks worriedly.

"I see something up ahead. I'm not sure what, but . . ."

A click-clacking sound fills the air in the tunnel. Like a hundred scuttling feet. Or a few pairs of eight feet.

"GIANT SP-SP-SPIDERS!" Alistair screams.

It all happens so fast. The group turns around and starts running back down the tunnel as massive, hairy, ugly, spindly spiders crawl toward them at warp speed, teeth gnashing.

"This way!" Marlon directs them, turning down a tunnel.

"Ah!" Rosie screams as a spider grazes her ankle. Alistair lifts her onto his back, and they keep running.

The group follows Marlon down a series of ever-twisting tunnels, hoping to lose the spiders, but it's to no avail. The spiders are right on their tails.

Jack is taking up the rear of the group, trying to fend off the spiders while running. *This boy, this hero, what is he doing?!* Filomena thinks. He's being too risky. He's running backward, slashing at spiders with his Dragon's Tooth sword. Filomena looks over her shoulder and notices another one crawling swiftly on the ceiling above Jack. It's about to land on him, and he can't see it!

Without thinking, she whips around and stabs it through the head, though she has to stop running to do so and, as a result, collides with Jack. She yanks the sword from the spider's head as Jack grabs her, and they turn around and keep running.

"What just . . . ?" he says.

She pants. "Spider—ceiling—"

"And you . . . ?"

"Stabbed."

"Amazing!"

Filomena's starting to get out of breath. She's not sure how long they can keep running. Eventually they come to what seems like the meeting point of several tunnels. It's a circular area, with four tunnel entryways. The ceiling is taller. Filomena knows what they have to do.

"Quick, draw your swords. We have to fight them!" she yells at the others. "We can't keep running forever."

Everyone's heaving for air, and in their few blissful seconds of reprieve, Fil, Alistair, Jack, and Gretel pull their Dragon's Tooth swords. Marlon has a wand at the ready. Rosie appears unarmed, but Filomena sees she has her silver net, the one she used to capture Queen Christina, the one woven by Rumpelstiltskin's sister.

One deep breath—and then six giant teeth-gnashing spiders fill the cavern. Filomena slices the air with her sword, daring them to come near.

Jack leaps to get closer to one, but Marlon yells out a warning: "Careful! Their hair might be venomous! Don't get too close."

They're at a standstill. The four with the Dragon's Tooth swords keep slashing the air, and the six giant spiders keep gnashing their teeth menacingly. One gets dangerously close to Rosie, and Filomena cries out, "No!"

But in a flash, Rosie's gone. Then she appears on the other side of the tunnel. What the . . . ?

"You figured it out?" Gretel yells.

"Just testing it!" Rosie says, holding up the dragon scale. "Figure a crisis is as good a time as any!"

Rosie keeps doing this, disappearing and reappearing in new places around the cavern. The spiders are getting confused. The four keep slashing their swords, but Filomena wonders how long the spiders' patience will last. She looks over at Marlon and notices he's whispering something. His wand is waving; his other hand is moving in time with it.

The spiders begin to levitate, ever so slightly. Filomena gets an idea.

"Rosie!" she shouts. She desperately hopes in this moment that giant Avalonian spiders don't understand English.

Rosie grips the dragon scale and pops into existence right next to Fil.

"How far does that silver net stretch?" Filomena asks.

Rosie gets a ferocious smile on her face. She pops over to Marlon, who nods.

He keeps whispering, and the spiders levitate farther. This confuses them even more, though they continue to gnash. Then, when they're a good two feet off the floor,

Rosie teleports right next to the spiders and tosses the silver net over all six. The net contracts tightly, binding the beasts together in a horrifying, thrashing pile of black ooze.

As soon as the spiders are tied up, Marlon collapses to the floor.

Rosie runs over to him. "Marlon! Marlon! Are you alive?" she cries.

"He's all right, child," Archimedes says from where he's fluttering above them. "Spells are extremely exhausting to cast. He just needs to rest."

Rosie nods, touching Marlon's forehead. But it seems like she's extremely exhausted, too. Teleporting yourself around a room, disappearing and reappearing . . . Filomena is sure it can't be easy on the body.

Archimedes grabs Marlon by the shoulders of his robe, and Marlon, seemingly asleep, lifts into the air.

They all take a deep breath, but it's hard to breathe properly when there's a pile of giant spiders screeching right next to you.

"Let's get out here," Filomena says.

"The farther away from those things, the better," Alistair says, looking over his shoulder and shuddering.

CHAPTER TWENTY-FOUR

FILOMENA AND THE OGRE QUEEN

The League of Five plus Marlon and Archimedes are looking worse for wear. Not only are they exhausted from the fight, there's a new sense of terror at what could be around each corner. Jack is still at the front of the group and using his Seeing Eye to navigate. The Seeing Eye gave them a little warning against the spiders, but not much.

And then what happens when they reach Excalibur?

Filomena has to escape Avalon with the sword; somehow cross over the water back to the Emerald City, even though they don't have a ferry ride home; and then go back through the Emerald City, back through Camelot, and back through the Brocéliande? Is that how it works? And not to mention that, after she reaches Never After, she'll have to travel all the way back to the mortal world. And *then*, once she gets to her mom, what will she do with the sword? Will just being near Excalibur heal her mother? Swords are meant for stabbing. How can this one heal?

The whole prospect exhausts her. She's so, so tired. What she wouldn't give to be napping fireside at Gwen and Lance's Bed-and-Breakfast for Questing Heroes. *They should really expand their business*, she thinks. *Make it a chain throughout Never After.* Although, she supposes that, outside Camelot, they won't get a lot of business. It seems like the League of Seven are the only heroes beyond Camelot after all.

Filomena thinks all this while she brings up the rear of the group, walking arm in arm with Gretel.

"How's it going?" Filomena asks her.

"Eh, you know, escaped certain death again, so I have that to be thankful for." Gretel laughs. "But seriously," she goes on. "Alistair is not taking me leaving for Paris well."

"Were you guys talking about it?" Filomena asks.

"Yeah. When we entered the tunnels, he was asking me about it. Do you think I'm a bad friend, Fil?"

Gretel looks at her so earnestly, so openly. Gretel is the

most brazen person Filomena knows, but she's also the kindest.

"First of all, of course not. But why do you want to go to Paris?" Filomena asks.

"Ever since I was a little girl, I've dreamed of Paris," Gretel says. "When I worked for my dad, when you guys found me in Los Angeles, I was falling asleep every night dreaming of owning my own shop there. It just feels like home to me. I can't explain it."

Filomena thinks of Gretel strolling along the Seine, eating pretty pastries at cafés, wearing her sophisticated creations while admiring art in beautiful museums. Of course it makes sense. Paris is glamor, and Gretel is glamor.

"When I joined you guys," Gretel goes on, "I sort of forgot all that. Suddenly there was this whole new world to explore, all these missions to go on. But I've never felt at home anywhere in Never After, not really. I've felt at home with you, Jack, and Alistair, but not in any place. I don't belong to a kingdom; I don't have a community here. If it weren't for the importance of our quests, I wouldn't be here! I wouldn't be important to Never After at all."

For a moment Gretel looks saddened, but Filomena is certain that what she's saying is not true. "Gretel, you'll always be important no matter where you are, because you're so uniquely wonderful," Filomena says.

"Thanks. But you know what I mean. I'm not a knight,

not part of a prophecy, not a gift from the fairies. I'm not a queen or a princess or anything like that. I'm not like the rest of you. I'm just Gretel the cobbler's daughter. Swept up in a great adventure." She smiles, but tears form in the corners of her eyes. "And I'm so happy that I've had that, I've loved it, even if it's been terrifying. It's challenged me; it's made me realize who I am. But working with Lillet, and then seeing that woman Céline in her own shop—they just reminded me that I've always known what I'm meant to do. And it's not in Never After."

Filomena feels her heart aching a great, deep ache. The kind of ache you get when you know an ending is coming.

But as it turns out, there's not much time for feeling right now.

"So my minions didn't finish what they started, I see."

This voice is one that used to send chills down Filomena's spine but now sends a bolt of fire down it instead. Olga. They can't see her, but they'd recognize that voice anywhere. She must be just around the bend.

Filomena and Gretel tense up, pulling their swords from their sheaths. In front of them, Jack, Alistair, and Rosie prepare for battle. Marlon is still being carried by Archimedes. Filomena walks through the group so she's standing at the front. Jack tries to get in front of her, but she motions for everyone to stand back. She needs to be the first person Olga sees.

Finally, twenty feet away from where the group stands, Olga turns a corner, emerging from a tunnel passageway. She's even more grotesque than Filomena remembers, with a sickening smirk on her face. Filomena wants to wipe that smirk right off. All the evil Olga's done, all the creatures she's slain, the villages she's razed, the suffering she's caused—it all rises in Filomena's chest. But most of all, Filomena thinks of her mother. Her mother, who's teetering on the edge between life and death, all because of this horrible ogre queen.

"Rose Red!" Queen Olga shouts down the tunnel. Ogre minions trail behind her. "Thank you so much for warning us that your friends were going to be here. It would have been so much more difficult if we were taken by surprise," she says in a voice dripping with mockery.

"Oh, Filomena," Olga continues, "look at you standing there, so brave. Your search for the sword has been a bit difficult, I hear. I'm honestly impressed you made it this far."

"You wretched, despicable—" Filomena says as she moves to charge, but Jack catches her arm and holds her back.

"Don't ambush. Not yet," he whispers.

"You will never find what you seek, however," Olga says as she slowly paces toward them. "The sword is kept in the most secret part of Avalon, a part that I will personally ensure you never reach!"

"I'm glad to see you're finally confronting us face-to-face, Olga!" Filomena spits at her. "You're usually too much of a coward! Although I suppose, this time, it's only because we've come to get you."

"'Too much of a coward'? For five kids? I think not. I can't believe this world lets children run kingdoms. That kind of thing only happens in stupid fairy tales! Perhaps I should be thankful that none of you have actually done anything with your positions so far. Speaking of which, have any of you stopped to think about how vulnerable you've left your kingdoms in your absence?"

Olga sneers at them, and Filomena tries to put out of her mind whatever games Olga is playing. Mary Contrary, who's quite contrary and the reigning regent of Westphalia, is watching over the kingdom. Filomena knows this. She doesn't have to worry.

"And, meanwhile, your poor, poor mother. Yes, she'll be left to rot from the inside out."

Flames lick Filomena's insides at this. A rage she's never felt bubbles and boils, and it's like *she's* burning from the inside out. Before Jack can stop her, before she knows what she's doing, Filomena sprints forward and attempts to stab Olga. But Olga jumps, having had a bit of time to react thanks to Filomena's having to cross so much tunnel, and Filomena only catches her in the leg. Still, a leg wound from a Dragon's Tooth sword can be fatal; Filomena knows this much. She tries to swing again, but her arms are pulled back by two ogre minions.

Olga backs away, her leg streaming and oozing black blood, and sits awkwardly on the floor.

"You foolish girl! You think you can win just because you have a Dragon's Tooth sword, just because you have some friends fighting with you? I have an entire army of cutthroat ogres, and I don't care if every single one of them dies; I will never let you win!"

The ogres holding Filomena turn toward Olga in shock at hearing this, and their surprise loosens their grips enough for Filomena to slip out.

"Get them!" Olga shrieks from her place on the ground, where she's holding her gashed leg.

In the time since the adventurers' journey to the Deep, many ogres have been vanquished by the Dragon's Tooth swords. Filomena, Jack, Alistair and Gretel fight, and the ogres by Olga watch several of their brethren fall dead at one swipe. The ogres grow hesitant to attack.

"You cowards!" Olga screeches to the ogres. "Get them! Get them!"

But the ogres are afraid, and, after hearing that Olga would see them all die, perhaps they're also questioning what they're doing here. Filomena has injured Olga badly enough that she's useless, and eventually Olga calls for the ogres to carry her off.

"You'd better get out of these tunnels," Olga seethes as she's carried away. "You have no idea what creatures of the night I have on my side. I'll send more spiders after you. I'll send worse! Get out of these tunnels, or I'll send everything I have against you!"

And just like that, Queen Olga retreats from sight yet again.

CHAPTER TWENTY-FIVE

THE TEENAGE KING

Filomena's whole body is pounding with adrenaline as she heaves for air in the bowels of the tree network.

"That was so badass, Fil!" Alistair yelps, pumping his fist into the air.

"Let's get out of here quickly," Jack says, never one to linger after a victory.

But Filomena needs a moment. She's seething. One slash wasn't enough. She wants to kill Olga. Filomena's scared by the power of her own rage right now. She wants to stab her sword into the wooden floor, and she raises it up to do so.

"No!" Marlon says. He's finally awake, having recovered from casting the spell on the spiders. "Stop! You'll hurt the trees."

Filomena looks at her hands in shock. She was about to stab the root system for no reason! Her hands look foreign to her suddenly. Archimedes lands on her shoulder and nuzzles her neck. Marlon puts a hand on her other shoulder.

"Think of the trees, Filomena, think of the creatures. Think of the land you're protecting by fighting Olga. Don't let the rage overtake you. Breathe in, breathe out."

Filomena does as he says, dropping the sword, and she begins to come back to herself.

"I understand your anger, but anger has no final outlet. It will never bring peace. You could stab a thousand Olgas, and it would never release this anger from you," Marlon says.

"Gosh, you're smart, are you a wizard or something," Gretel says, leaning against a wall.

Filomena opens her eyes and sees her four friends plus two new friends looking at her.

"You're doing a great job, Filomena," Ira says from her hip.

"Am I, though? Somehow we're no closer to finding Excalibur than when we arrived on Avalon!" she shouts. She wants to punch something, but then she looks at her friends. They seem worried for her.

"I'm sorry. I just—my mom," Filomena says uselessly.

"I think we should get some air," Marlon says. "Let's get aboveground."

They all nod, and Jack, with his Seeing Eye, leads the way.

As they walk, Filomena keeps to the back of the group, her head hung low. She's upset, but she's also embarrassed about her outburst.

Rosie hangs back with her. "Hey," she says softly. "You okay?"

"Not really." Filomena sighs.

"I get it." Rosie nods. "When my mom died, I felt so angry, I wanted to make Queen Christina suffer. I wanted to invent something horrible to make her castle explode. I was furious."

Filomena feels a wave of guilt wash over her. She hasn't even asked Rosie how she's doing, about all of it.

"I'm sorry, Rosie. I've been so caught up in myself, I haven't even checked in with you lately."

"It's okay, we all have our own things going on."

"How are you feeling these days?" Filomena asks, putting a hand on Rosie's shoulder.

"Pretty awful. I miss my mom so much. Every time I think about her, it feels like I'm being hit with a tidal wave all over again. I barely even got to see her after we found her." Rosie starts to tear up, her breath hitching slightly. She shuts her eyes and breathes, willing herself to be calm. "It's why I've thrown myself into my inventions so much, I guess. They're the only things that really take my mind off her. And being with you guys—that helps, too."

Filomena stops for a moment and gives Rosie a bear hug.

"Thanks, Fil," Rosie says, patting Filomena's back.

They start walking again.

"Look, we're going to save your mom," Rosie says then. "I know it. We won't let anything happen to her."

Filomena just nods. She admires Rosie so much.

"I have some stuff I want to talk to Gretel about, so I'm going to head up front," Rosie says, "but thanks for listening."

"Always," Filomena says. "We can always talk."

Rosie smiles and walks to the front of the group. Marlon hangs back a few paces to walk in line with Filomena.

"Nice shoes," he says.

"Oh right, I sort of forgot I was wearing them." She laughs, admiring the sparkling ruby-red slippers. "They're surprisingly comfortable for high heels."

Marlon smiles. "I'm glad. Looks like my designs paid off."

Filomena gapes at him in shock. "*Your* designs?" she says. "You made these?"

Marlon nods. "One of my earlier projects. I made them for Miss Wahida a long time ago. I heard Miss Eeshani liked to borrow them."

They both laugh, Filomena shaking her head in disbelief. She's just coming to terms with the fact that Marlon truly is a great wizard. It's a funny thing, these immortal boys in young bodies. They are all both wise and naive, in turns.

"Just be careful with them," Marlon says. "They're very

powerful, if I do say so myself. Do you know how to use them?"

"Well, in the world I come from, they're actually in a very famous story, though Merlin from Camelot doesn't make them. But in the mortal world's story, Dorothy clicks her heels together and says, 'There's no place like home, there's no place like home,' and the shoes take her from Oz to her home in Kansas."

"Hmm, that's a lot catchier, actually. When I told Miss Wahida how to use them, I made her say, 'Home, there's no place like it,' but your way rolls off the tongue a lot better." Marlon laughs.

"It's so strange," Filomena says. "The stories of Camelot and Oz are two separate stories in the mortal world. Usually the versions in the mortal world are opposite of Never After stories, not divided."

"Stories have a lot of power." Marlon says. "How did the stories get to, as you call it, the mortal world?"

"Olga." Filomena sighs. "She's spread lies to my world in order to take over power in this world."

"Then maybe the story of Oz and Camelot, together as they are in this world, is simply too powerful," Marlon ventures. "Maybe by splitting them into two different stories in your world, she drains them of their power here."

Filomena is struck by this idea. It makes a lot of sense to her.

Archimedes swoops through the tunnel and lands on

Marlon's shoulder. "Marlon, there's great news," he whispers.

"News? What news could you have uncovered here?" Marlon says, brow furrowed.

At the front of the group, Alistair pauses. He's found a hallway that branches off to the left of the main tunnel. "What the—?" Alistair says, tensing and reaching for his dragon sword.

The rest of the group catches up with him.

A boy in his late teens is standing in the mouth of the tunnel, frozen. He's brown and lanky, with a light pink buzz cut and a look of shock on his face, like a deer who's just been spotted. Marlon pushes through the five adventurers to get to the front of the pack.

"Marlon?" the teenage boy's face lights up with confusion and surprise.

Marlon runs toward him and jumps into his arms, and the boy lifts up the younger wizard.

"So this is where you've been hiding!" Marlon says when the boy puts him down. "Have you been here the whole time?"

The boy looks embarrassed. "I've been getting to know the nature spirits, you could say."

Marlon turns around to face the rest of the puzzled group, each of whom has been silently watching what appears to be a reunion.

"Everyone! I present to you King Arthur of Camelot,"

Marlon says, bowing with his arms outstretched. "Or you can call him by his real name, Arturo."

The five collectively gasp. They've each heard about King Arthur; he's the stuff of legend in both the fairy and mortal worlds.

"Hola," he says, looking uncertainly at the group. "Marlon, who are these people?" he says quietly.

"These are the League of Seven. Well, minus two," Marlon says, introducing each adventurer by name. Each nods in turn, bowing slightly.

"And how do you know them?" Arturo asks Marlon.

"They came to ask for my help on their quest."

"Ah, of course. Always a quest here in Camelot." Arturo rolls his eyes. "Well, it was nice to meet you all—nice to see you again, Marlon—but I'd best be going."

"Wait a second," Filomena chimes in. "What are you doing underground?"

"I'm sure you can understand how that's really none of your business," Arturo says as he starts to walk away.

"Actually, it is!" Filomena says. Arturo pauses. "Camelot is in total disarray, your friends are looking for you because they have no idea where you are, Olga has taken over your sacred Avalon, and you're, what, hiding underground?" Filomena takes a deep breath, reminding herself of the things Marlon told her to focus on earlier. Clearly some of that rage from her fight with Olga is still within her.

"Excuse me?" Arturo says, cocking his head to the side

and crossing his arms. "Who are you to be questioning me, the king of Camelot?"

"She's the queen of Westphalia," Alistair pipes up. "So you better show some respect."

"Alistair!" Gretel elbows him in the ribs. But then she smiles. Filomena knows Gretel loves when Alistair gets feisty.

"Okay, this just got interesting," Arturo says. "But still, this is none of your business. We're on my turf."

"Sure doesn't seem like it's your turf if you're hiding when it needs you," Rosie mumbles, looking at the ceiling.

"What was that?" Arturo says, squinting, arms still crossed.

Rosie just looks at him and shrugs, knowing he heard her the first time.

Arturo sighs. "You say my friends are looking for me," he says to Filomena. "What are you talking about?"

"We stayed with Gwen and Lance at their bed-and-breakfast," she says. "They specifically asked us to keep an eye out for you, because they're worried about you and have no idea where you are."

A look of shame falls over the young king's face. Hearing about Gwen and Lance seems to get to him.

"All right, well, if you see them again, you can tell them that I'm safe. I just needed a break, okay? I needed a break from being the king of this place. Do you know how exhausting it is, all these tests, and heroes, and quests . . . ?"

"And ogres," Filomena finishes.

"Yes. And ogres." He sighs.

"So you admit that you went into hiding when Olga came to Camelot?" Jack says.

"Who are you again? You look familiar," Arturo says.

"Jack the Giant Stalker, of Vineland."

Arturo snaps his fingers. "Vineland, of course! I knew I recognized you. Okay, I get it. You're a big hero, and you've come to chastise me. Well, too bad, I've already made myself feel as bad as I possibly can about this decision, but I was scared, okay?! I was scared."

Filomena's impressed that Arturo's actually admitting this. She softens toward him. "I understand that, King Arturo. Of course we all understand that. We're scared all the time! So I get it. You've had to be in charge of Camelot for a long, long time. I'm sure it can get tiring."

"You have no idea how intense running a kingdom is," he says, running his hands over the soft pink fuzz of his buzz cut. "Or, maybe you do, Queen Filomena."

She doesn't correct him that it's *Queen Eliana*. "No, I don't. I've barely had time to step foot in Westphalia. And you know why? Because Olga is terrorizing my family; she's cursed my mother and has taken over this whole island." An idea pops into Filomena's head. Of course! "Actually, it's your sword that I need to save her. Excalibur. You wouldn't happen to have it on you, would you?"

Arturo laughs. "I wish. No. Olga took over the center of the island, where it rests in a stone."

Jack steps forward. "Arturo, I'll venture to say that I probably understand your situation more than almost anyone in Never After. The fairies swore to protect me, and as a result, almost all of them have died. I've known the weight of responsibility my whole life. All my life has been one quest after another. Nowhere to call home, nowhere to rest. I understand the appeal of hiding in here, away from all your responsibilities. But Camelot needs you right now, maybe more than ever."

Filomena watches Arturo's face change as Jack talks. His rigid, guarded expression is starting to fall, to reveal something like recognition, softness.

"We need to stop Olga. If she holds on to Avalon, the most sacred place in the fairy world, there's no telling what damage she'll do. She's one step closer to taking over the whole of Never After by drawing on Avalon's power. The End could be near. We need to get Filomena Excalibur to save her mother, but we also need to get Olga out of Avalon. I don't think we can do that without you. You do officially rule over Avalon in the absence of the fairies, don't you?"

Arturo considers all this. There's a long pause before he speaks. The tunnels are dead silent.

"What do you think of all this, Marlon?" Arturo says. "Do you think I'm a coward for hiding?"

"Are you kidding? What do you think I was doing before these five came and dragged me from my tree hollow? No.

I don't think you're a coward. But I do think that Jack is right. We need your help."

Arturo nods, taking in the group. "*Está bien,*" he says. "I'll come with you. Now let's get out of here. I need some fresh air, anyway."

Chapter Twenty-Six

The King's Summer Castle

A rturo's castle is smaller than Filomena would have expected, but he explains that this isn't his real castle.

"More like a summer cottage," he says as they enter the front doorway.

The castle looks to be made of marble or perhaps opal. Everything in Avalon seems to have an iridescent sheen. The castle is one massive room with tall windows. Outside, it's surrounded by wild apple trees. Sparkling chandeliers float under the ceiling, and the couches by the tall fireplace, the chairs, and the kitchen table all seem to float as well. Filomena gets a bit dizzy, looking at it all, but then it starts to have a dreamy effect that's quite pleasant.

Marlon stands outside the castle's front doors, casting another spell.

"He's putting an enchantment on the castle and our tree," Archimedes explains to Filomena once they're inside Arturo's home. "So the ogres can't find them."

Filomena nods, relieved they'll have a moment of reprieve from worrying where the ogres are. But when Marlon finishes and walks in, he has the same look on his face as after casting that spell on the spiders. Like all energy has been drained from him. He collapses on a hovering chaise longue and closes his eyes.

"Is it just me," Alistair says, circling the grand dining table, "or is everything in here floating?"

Arturo laughs. "You're not hallucinating, Alistair, don't worry. Or did you eat an apple here in Avalon? In that case, you might be hallucinating. But you're right: Everything is floating." Arturo sits down in one of the kitchen chairs, and it begins to rise. "The fairies created this place for me when I became king of Camelot," he says. "I usually live in Camelot, but they wanted me to have somewhere to stay when I came to visit Avalon."

"How did you become king, anyway?" Rosie asks.

"That's a long story, but it does have something to do

with the sword Filomena's looking for. Excalibur." He shrugs. "Tulip tea, anyone?"

They all nod, and he jumps off the chair and walks over to the kitchen to put a kettle on.

"Speaking of the fairies," Arturo says as he gets seven porcelain teacups and saucers from a cupboard, "how are Zera, Sabine, and Colette? I haven't heard from any of them in a while."

The group grows quiet as they settle into chairs and couches around the room. They all look at one another, not wanting to be the one to break the news.

Finally Gretel speaks up. "Zera and Colette have left us, Arturo," she says.

"'Left us'? What do you mean, 'left us'?"

Gretel looks at Rosie, who has walked over to a window that looks out onto the apple trees. Filomena gives her a hug.

"They're dead," Gretel clarifies.

Arturo looks shocked, putting down the teacups and staring into the middle distance. A thousand thoughts seem to be running through his mind.

"Oh, no. No, no, no."

"Rosie is Colette's daughter," Gretel adds softly.

"Oh, Rosie, I'm so sorry," Arturo says, snapping out of his daze and looking over to her.

She nods, saying nothing. Her face is buried in Filomena's shoulder.

"This all makes so much more sense now," Arturo says.

He's back to staring into the middle distance. "How Queen Olga made it through Camelot, how she took over Avalon. But what of Sabine?"

"The last time we saw her was in Vineland," Jack says. "We believe she's still alive. We would have felt it, or been sent word, if she died. Remember what the prophecy said.

Thirteen fairies born to the Fairy King and Queen;
When none live, so shall Never After die with them.
And that is the End of the Story.

And we're still here, aren't we?"

Arturo agrees, looking only the smallest bit relieved. Arturo is on the same page as the rest of them now; he knows what's at stake.

Rosie pulls herself from Filomena's shoulder and wipes her eyes. "I'm okay. Thanks, Fil," she sniffs.

"You sure? Do you want to go for a walk? Get some air?"

"That might be a good idea," she says.

"I'll come with you."

"No, it's okay. I think I just need some time alone."

Filomena nods, understanding that need.

"Just make sure you stay within the gardens, Rosie," Arturo says. "That's as far as Marlon's enchantment reaches."

Rosie says she will and slips out a back door in the kitchen, out to the apple trees and the rest of the castle's gardens.

The rest gather around on floating chairs for tulip tea.

Arturo pours with surprising grace for a king. Filomena's getting the idea that the brutal, brisk warrior he seems to be painted as in the mortal world is not exactly the truth of the real Arturo. He passes out cups to each of them except Marlon, who's still recovering on the chaise longue.

"So," Arturo says, sipping from his teacup, "what's the plan?"

Filomena laughs. "We don't really have one yet. We've sort of been making things up as we go along, on this adventure."

"That seems to usually be our style." Jack smiles.

"Have you all known one another a long time?" Arturo inquires.

"It definitely feels that way," Alistair says.

"You're making me miss my friends." Arturo smiles. "I should go visit Gwen and Lance. When this is all over, of course. Or I guess I should really move back to Camelot."

"Your friends seem to really love you," Filomena says.

Arturo sighs. "We've been through a lot, the three of us. Many quests, many adventures. But before Olga came barreling through, things were starting to settle down a bit. It was nice. It felt like we were passing the torch on. To the likes of you, I suppose!"

"Well, we're more the other side of Never After types." Jack smiles, running his hand through his hair and pushing it out of his face. It's a move that always makes Filomena feel a bit weak in the knees. In a good way.

"Fair enough." Arturo grins. "Seems like they need you over there."

Something itches in Filomena's mind with them talking like this. About one side of Never After and the other.

"Speaking of Never After," Filomena says, "where do you think Brocéliande Forest is now?"

Arturo smiles. "It's anyone's guess, really. That thing is so unpredictable. It just moves anywhere it needs to be."

The idea is forming more concretely now.

"Is Brocéliande Forest the only place that can do that?" she says.

"What do you mean? Move around at will?" Arturo frowns. "I believe so. It was the fairies who created that, too, after all. I've never heard of anything else like it."

"Well, we have some experience creating versions of things that the fairies created," Filomena says, a smile covering her face. "I think I have an idea."

CHAPTER TWENTY-SEVEN

MARLON'S CAULDRON

I t's a crazy idea, it's true. She has no idea if it will work, or if it's even worth trying. But at this point, Filomena isn't sure what else to do. The crazier, the better is what she's thinking. They've spent all this time trying to get into the heart of Avalon, where the sword in the stone, Excalibur, lies. And they've come so far, only to be rebuffed at the very edge of their goal. So if they can't get into Avalon, then they'll just have to move Avalon to someplace where they *can* get to Excalibur. It would take way too long to bring an army into

Avalon to fight Olga and her ogres. But perhaps they can bring Avalon to a place where they have backup.

At first, everyone is resistant. Arturo is worried the whole idea is sacrilegious, that the fairies would never have approved. Jack is concerned that it will disrupt something in Never After's ecosystem. Alistair wonders if anyone will get hurt in the process, and Gretel doesn't understand how exactly it will even work. That last concern Filomena especially understands. She's not quite sure yet, either. But still, something about this idea makes sense to her. If they can't get into Avalon, then they have to transport Avalon to Westphalia. Then Filomena will have home-court advantage and finally be able to get the sword and rescue her mother.

"But what about the consequences of such a large action?" Arturo says. "Do we know how it could alter the very fabric of Never After? All the things the fairies put in place?"

"The fairies aren't here to protect us anymore," comes a voice from the chaise longue. Marlon has woken up. He stands up and walks over to the table. Arturo passes him a cup of tea.

"Only one fairy is left, and who knows what she's doing, or where she is?" Marlon says. "Yes, something might shift in the fabric of Never After. But if we don't do something drastic, and soon, then something will shift anyway. With Avalon under her power, it's only a matter of time before Olga starts overtaking other kingdoms. We need to act now."

Everyone has grown increasingly impressed with Marlon's

power despite his eleven-year-old form. It's clear that he's a powerful wizard, a confidant of the king of Camelot.

"Okay, Filomena, I'm interested. How do you think we can do such a thing?" Arturo asks.

"Well, I think there are two major factors we'd need for this. Or more like major *people*. Marlon, of course, and Rosie."

"What about me?" a voice says from the kitchen's back door. Rosie joins them at the dining table.

"Filomena's just telling us about her plan to save the world," Alistair says. "And you play an integral role, apparently."

After much discussion and many more cups of tulip tea, everyone is finally on the same page. They walked back to Marlon's tree to start, because if they're going to cast a spell this strong, they'll need every trick and ingredient he has to offer and then some, or so Marlon says. Rosie and Marlon sit at his table, poring over a cauldron, with several books out for reference. Everyone else lounges around the large sitting room in the tree hollow.

"I've never heard of anyone attempting anything like this, Filomena," Marlon says, shaking his head and flipping through a book of enchantments.

"Well, no one's had to!" she replies, leaning in the doorframe.

"We're going to need your dragon scale, for sure," Marlon says to Rosie, who places the smooth object on the table. "Plus . . ." He trails off, flipping between books. It seems that Marlon is improvising heavily here, using methods from a variety of spellbooks.

"Looks like we'll also need an Avalonian apple, some soil, a leaf from the highest branch in the kingdom—which luckily is this very tree—and also your blood." Marlon points to Arturo, who's been rocking in Marlon's rocking chair.

"My *blood*?" he says.

"Yep. Quite a decent amount actually. 'Blood of the rightful ruler,' it says here," Marlon says, still looking at his spellbook.

"You're being so casual about that ask, Marlon," Arturo says, standing up.

"For the good of Never After?" Jack offers, smiling weakly.

"Indeed." Arturo sighs.

Marlon finally looks up at Arturo. "Actually, this will be great. I think your blood will be even more powerful, since you are not only the rightful ruler but also have claim to Excalibur."

"In theory," Arturo says. "It's been so long since I've even been able to get near my lovely sword. I do have several dozen other swords, of course, but none of them is like Excalibur." Arturo looks wistful for a moment, fantasizing about his swords. "Jack, speaking of swords, I'm thinking you and I should get to planning," Arturo says, turning to Jack.

"Planning?" Jack asks.

"Yes. We'll need to raise an army to fight with us in Westphalia."

Jack nods, agreeing, and thinking.

"An army?" Filomena asks.

"Yes, to fight the ogres," Arturo says, as if it's obvious.

This was part of the original plan, but hearing it out loud, Filomena's just realizing the reality of it.

"And who would you get to form an army in Westphalia?" Filomena says, getting a sickening feeling in her stomach.

"The citizens, of course." Arturo shrugs. "I figure with you, me, and Jack all there, heaps of people will want to sign up for battle. I mean, look at us. We're quite a charming trio, are we not?"

Arturo smiles a dazzling smile, and Filomena is sure he's right, that people in Westphalia would be happy to fight on their behalf and for the good of Never After. But the idea makes her sick, the idea of more bloodshed in the kingdoms, more death, more destruction.

"Isn't there another way to get rid of Olga without so many people having to risk their lives?"

Arturo shakes his head. "Sometimes war is just what is necessary, Filomena. You'll understand this the longer you're queen."

"Now, for the spell, we'll also need something potent to represent Westphalia," Marlon says, tapping his chin. He starts pacing around Filomena, sizing her up.

"I feel like a prized calf at the fair," she says, laughing.

"Shhh," Marlon says. "I'm thinking."

He looks at her shoes, considering, then shakes his head. He leans in toward her and sniffs. Then he picks up a lock of her hair.

"This could do the trick," he says. "Rosie, pass me that knife."

Rosie tosses Marlon a knife that's lying on the table.

"Wait a second, you want to cut my hair?!" Filomena screeches.

Jack laughs softly. "For the good of Never After?"

"Just wait till it's your turn, Jack." Arturo chuckles, rocking again.

"Fine, fine, for the good of Never After," Filomena says, closing her eyes. "Just make it quick."

In a swift motion, Marlon grips all of her hair and swipes the blade across it so that several inches of glossy black locks fall right into his hand. She thinks the hair looks like a small animal, so separate from her.

"Perfect," Marlon says, and drops it into the cauldron.

"Did you really need to take that much?" Filomena says, self-consciously touching her neck, which is now exposed.

"The more we have, the more effective the spell will be." Marlon shrugs. His eyes are already glued to his books again.

Jack walks over to Filomena, and she shyly turns away from him.

"Wow" is all he says.

"Yeah?"

"Yeah. Wow." He touches her hair, which is slippery now from the fresh cut. He runs his fingers over the ends, and then along her jawline, smiling at her. "You look beautiful," he says, so softly that only she can hear.

Maybe the cut is worth it after all. She'll get used to it. And she could get used to this. She smiles back at Jack with the warmth of a thousand sparkflies.

"You know," Gretel says as they're climbing, "I think it really suits you."

The outside of Marlon's enormous tree has a staircase winding around its trunk. Each step is a piece of wood, and they emerge one after another, round and round, leading to a branch at the top that's flattened to form a lookout tower. Gretel, Alistair, and Filomena are climbing the staircase now in order to get an Avalonian apple and a leaf from the tallest tree, for the spell.

"You think so?" Filomena says, shaking her head, feeling the bounce of hair that's now cut so short, it sits just below her cheekbones.

"Totally. You look like a chic starlet," Gretel says.

Alistair's smile fades a little at the mention of something chic. The great elephant in the room among them all, still, is Gretel's eventual departure to Paris.

"I'm just glad I don't have to offer up any blood," Filomena says, trying to brighten Alistair.

They come to the top of the tree and stand at the lookout. From this vantage point, they can see almost all of Avalon. The island spreads out in front of them, vast and lush. There's a haze at the edges, so it's hard to tell exactly where the island ends and the water begins. But it's a gorgeous sight. Filomena wishes she could have seen more of Avalon. If only the ogres weren't occupying so much territory. Somewhere out there lies the cure to her mother's sickness. If only she knew where it was.

"I wish I could fly over this island," Alistair says, looking out dreamily at Avalon. "It's so beautiful. I wish I could just swoop over the whole thing. Like a dragon, you know?"

Like a dragon . . . like a dragon! Filomena swells with an idea.

"Alistair, you're a genius!" she says. "Now, Gretel, grab a leaf; Alistair, grab an apple but *don't* eat it; and let's get back down there. I have an idea. Again."

Chapter Twenty-Eight
A Dragon–Sized Favor

The idea for the spell is simple, though the execution certainly is not. Filomena's idea is that if they can't get Excalibur out of Avalon, then they'll bring Avalon someplace where they'll have backup, where they'll have a better chance of fighting all the ogres guarding Excalibur, and then Filomena can quickly take a portal to the mortal world. If Brocéliande Forest can move, Filomena figures, why can't Avalon? Marlon's still not sure if this will work, but it makes complete sense to Filomena. The only problem is that, once they land in Westphalia, Jack and Arturo want to raise a Westphalian army to fight the ogres. And Filomena can't bear the thought of her citizens risking their lives for this. She won't bear more bloodshed if she can help it.

And so, thanks to Alistair's wild imagination, she has another idea. But this one isn't proving to be so popular, either.

"Are you serious?" Arturo says.

The seven kids, plus Ira the talking mirror and Archimedes the talking owl, sit staring at her in Marlon's tree hollow. They each have an expression of disbelief on their face. If they thought moving Avalon to Westphalia was a crazy idea, apparently asking the dragons for help is on a whole other level.

"The dragons don't just help anyone," Jack says. "They bargain, sure. They trade. They reward those who pass their tests, okay. But help? Out of the goodness of their hearts? I'm sorry, Fil, but no way. I'm not even sure dragons have hearts."

But Filomena isn't dissuaded.

"You guys, you have to remember that desperate times call for desperate measures. This isn't a normal time in Never After. We'll be on the verge of another interkingdom war if Olga tries to take over. Do the dragons really want that?"

"I'm sure they wouldn't prefer it. They're pretty lazy creatures," Jack says. "But they're in the Deep. They're safe there. There's no risk of Olga ever going down into the Deep. It's far too protected."

"But isn't that what you would have said about Avalon before all this?" Filomena counters. Jack is silent. She knows she's right. No one could have seen this coming with Avalon. With the number of protections Camelot had in place to protect Avalon, how could anyone have thought someone as evil as Olga capable of not only getting into Avalon but taking it over?

"You might be right about that, Filomena," Arturo says, "but even if they do end up wanting to help, how will we talk to them and plead our case? It would take ages to get all the way to the Deep from Avalon."

Filomena's already thought this one through. "Rosie, didn't you say the dragons stole back one of the talking mirrors?"

Rosie nods, her face glowing with excitement. She knows what Filomena's getting at.

"Lucky for us, we have Never After's fourteenth talking mirror." Filomena smiles, waving Ira around by his handle.

"Careful there, Fil!" Ira shouts, flying left to right. "You're making me queasy!"

"Sorry, Ira," she says, looking into his mirror face. Then she looks at Jack and Arturo. "Look, the idea of Westphalian citizens fighting the ogres just doesn't sit well with me. But I do understand it. I just want to try something else first. If the dragons say no, then we'll do it your way. But this could save a lot of bloodshed."

Filomena explains that if the dragons chase Olga and her ogre army out of Avalon and into the ocean, then when Rosie and Marlon magically transport Avalon to Westphalia, they'll be able to get Excalibur safely, without having to deal with the ogres at all!

"If this works," Arturo says, "and the dragons agree, then I see your point, Filomena. I agree with you that there's no use starting a war if it can be avoided."

"Wonderful. Rosie, Jack, why don't you two help me talk to the dragons. They seem to like you both."

Jack, Filomena, and Rosie sit on a brocade red velvet couch upstairs at Marlon's. Filomena was surprised when Marlon pointed them to a spiral staircase that she hadn't noticed in a corner of the main room. The spiral staircase leads up the inside of the tree to what seems like an endless set of rooms. Marlon instructed them to stop off in the third room, which is a small sitting room where Marlon usually hosts people for tea. It is partway up the tree and filled with more books, as well as beautiful couches and a large globe. The surface of the globe is constantly shifting, so quickly that it's impossible to get a good look at the landmasses or which world they reference.

Filomena sits between Jack and Rosie, and Gretel and Alistair volunteer to take turns holding Ira in front of them, switching off when one of their arms gets tired. Who knows how long it will take to convince the dragons?

"So, Ira, how does this work exactly?" Filomena asks. "How do we call the dragons' talking mirror?"

"Everyone ready?" Ira says.

The three nod.

"Jack, straighten out your hair a bit. It looks wild," Ira suggests.

Filomena turns and does it for Jack, and Jack watches her the whole time with a light smile on his face.

"Okay, here we go . . . Let's see if they pick up . . . Three, two . . ."

Then Ira's misty face disappears, and a vortex of color swirls on the surface of the mirror. The color clears, and then a dark cave appears.

"Is that their cave?" Rosie says, confused.

"Hello?" a gruff voice says through the mirror.

"Hi! Dragons?" Filomena says. "Your majesties?"

All of a sudden, the cave seems to shift, as if the mirror were flying backward through space, the cave getting farther and farther away. But then Filomena realizes that the cave is attached to a head. The cave is actually a dragon's nostril. The mirror reveals two enormous dragons sitting next to each other. Their eyes glow a bright green, though the cave they sit in is almost pitch-black.

"Is this thing on?" one dragon says, squinting at the mirror.

"Hello, your dragon highnesses! This is Filomena!"

"Filomena? Eliana of Westphalia?"

"Yes! I'm here with Jack Stalker and Rosie—Rose Red—who you met recently, I believe."

"Is that the girl we gave a scale to?" the other dragon says. The first dragon grunts in response.

"What are you calling us for?"

"Well, you see," Filomena says, "we have a rather large favor to ask . . ."

The next day, Filomena is sitting alone on top of Marlon's tree. Looking out over the whole of Avalon, she thinks of how far she's come since that first day in Never After, when everything baffled and stunned her. She still feels baffled and stunned pretty often, but now she also feels like she's capable enough to manipulate the world around her, to contribute to it, to bring her expertise and ideas to it. Sometimes, when she's alone, she thinks of herself in her bedroom in North Pasadena, reading the Never After book series under her bedcovers. She wishes she could tell that version of herself everything that's happened. She'd never believe it. Or maybe she would believe it. Somewhere inside her, she's always known the stories felt real. She just never knew *how* real.

And now, here she is. Sitting on top of Marlon the wizard's tree home, waiting for the dragons to arrive. In love with Jack Stalker, in Avalon, having orchestrated this whole endeavor to save her mother and Never After. She never realized she was capable of this much. But somehow bravery doesn't feel so terrifying when friends are with her.

"You've done very well, Filomena," Ira says from her hip. She lifts him up so she's looking at him and so he can see Avalon.

"Thanks, Ira. But it's not done yet." She sighs.

A pair of huge spiky wings appear in the distance. Then three more pairs appear. Four more. Eight enormous dragons zigzag across the Avalonian sky. Jack was shocked, during their talk yesterday, that the dragons were game for such a thing. But it turns out that the dragons loathe Olga as much as they do change. They were willing to fight on Never After's behalf, so long as this is the only time they're called upon. And if it puts an end to a longer, more boring (in their words) war.

"They came!" she says gleefully.

Ira chuckles. "You knew they were going to."

"I know, but, I mean, just look at them coming to rescue us."

And here they are, as promised. Filomena hopes that Olga's still a bit injured from their fight yesterday, but, based on what Gita said about Olga living in some sort of healing waters, Filomena isn't so sure. Regardless, a surprise attack always has the upper hand. Especially when it can fly in and attack from the sky.

Filomena watches as the dragons shoot fire far away, on the other side of the island. Their hot fiery breaths are no doubt eviscerating Olga and her evil ogres' camp! Filomena doesn't delight in violence, by any means, but there is something satisfying about this. Because if Olga is vanquished here and now, then that means all the fretting and fighting are over and Filomena can finally slip back and forth between Never After and North Pasadena, living her very best biportal life.

She'd asked the dragons to either kill Olga and her ogres or run them out of Avalon and into the ocean. Then the group can do the spell and move Avalon. But now it seems like one of the dragons is falling.

"Ira," she asks, "can you let me see what's happening over there?"

Ira's face disappears, and in its place is a zoomed-in version of what Filomena can see from the tree.

The dragon's wing seems hurt. The dragon is faltering, flying in a choppy, broken manner. Are the dragons getting hurt? This isn't part of the plan!

Another dragon seems to drop. How is Olga doing this? Is she shooting them? Filomena can't bear the idea of her causing the demise of the dragons. No, this simply can't happen.

From her perch, she sees the other six dragons herding the ogres out toward the ocean. They're on a beach now, pushed by the dragon's fire breath. Olga is flailing, falling back into the water.

Filomena knows she has to act fast now. They don't have much time If they want this to work—moving Avalon without the ogres and without the dragons getting fatally injured—it has to happen now.

Chapter Twenty-Nine

Home: There's No Place like It

"We have to act now!" Filomena says, rushing to the entrance of Marlon's tree.

"Have the dragons arrived? What's happening, Fil?" Jack says, rushing to meet her.

"They're here, and they have the ogres on the edge of a beach."

"Okay, this is good," Marlon says.

"I'm worried the dragons are getting hurt!" Filomena cries.

"We knew that was a possibility," Arturo says, standing up.

"We need to do the spell now, Marlon," Filomena says, ignoring Arturo. "Are we ready?"

Marlon looks around the room. Alistair comes down from the upstairs sitting room. Rosie is at the table, reading. Gretel's sitting next to her.

"Let's do it," Marlon says. "Everyone, gather around the cauldron."

Marlon lifts the cauldron from the table and places it in the center of the room. He motions for everyone to form a circle around it.

"A spell like this has never been cast before," Marlon explains. "In order for it to work, we're all going to need to pour our collective power into it."

The seven form a circle around the cauldron, and Marlon motions for them to hold hands. Standing between Jack and Gretel, Filomena takes a deep breath and focuses all her energy on making this spell work.

"This is a homeward-bound spell," Marlon explains. "The draw of home is powerful enough that I think this should work. Just picture your home, Filomena, and everyone else, picture that, too. With the right ingredients and intentions, plus my enchantment, I think this should work."

"With any luck," Jack whispers in Filomena's ear, "when you open your eyes, we'll be in Westphalia."

"Filomena," Marlon says, "make sure that, while I recount the incantation, you click your heels, okay? We need all the power we can get. Use those shoes!"

Filomena nods, looking down at her ruby-red slippers. Home, there's no place like it.

"Here we go," Marlon says.

He begins to speak in a language Filomena's never heard before. It sounds like it could be Latin, but it has a more slippery, less clunky quality to it. It must be an ancient wizard language, Filomena thinks. She takes one last look around at the faces of her friends, some of whom she's known for so long now, and some of whom she's just met. Rose Red, Arturo, Marlon, Gretel, Alistair, Jack, Archimedes even. All of them have come together now to pull off such an enormous task. Somehow she feels a pang of sadness, a longing in her heart, though she's not sure what for or what it means. She ignores it, closes her eyes, and lets Marlon's spell wash over her.

A sweeping sensation starts in her chest. Her hands are clutching one of Jack's, one of Gretel's, but she can feel, all of a sudden, a chain of energy through all their hands, like a current running through their circle, around and around. She remembers to click her heels together, thinking about home, and when she does, the sweeping sensation turns into a humming, lifting sensation. She doesn't dare open her eyes, though she can see light pooling and flashing in front of her closed eyelids. She keeps clicking her heels together, and each time, she gets a little shock wave, like sparkflies are colliding in her feet. Then it feels as though she's levitating, as if she were one of the chairs in Arturo's summer cottage.

Home. There's no place like it. *Home.*

With a thud, she falls backward, forced to let go of her friends' hands to catch herself. When she opens her eyes, she's still in Marlon's tree hollow. She's sitting on the ground next to the cauldron with the others, who all are also on the ground. She blinks several times and rubs her eyes, trying to orient herself.

"Hey," Jack leans over to her. "You okay?"

"I think so. Is the spell done?"

She looks up to see Marlon lying unconscious on the floor.

"Marlon!" she cries.

Arturo kneels beside Marlon and checks his pulse. "He's all right. Right, Archimedes?"

Archimedes nods.

"Spells are typically exhausting, but this one was a tremendous feat of wizardry. He'll just need a few moments to recover."

Arturo picks Marlon up and puts him on a couch.

"Well, that was quite a feeling!" Gretel says, stretching.

"I'm feeling a bit faint," Rosie says, swaying. She swoons,

luckily, right into Alistair's arms. He lays her on a couch, too.

"Did it work?" Filomena says to Jack, eyes wide and bright.

"I think there's only one way to find out."

Jack, Alistair, Gretel, and Filomena leave Marlon's tree hollow and climb the swirling staircase to look from his treetop.

"That felt so strange," Alistair says. "Nothing like a swoop hole."

"Did you guys feel like you were . . . floating?" Gretel says, climbing.

"Yes!" they all say at once, then laugh.

The whole thing felt so powerful, Filomena's certain it must have worked. So far she's not seeing any dragons in the distance, which she thinks is a good sign—the dragons must have pushed the ogres into the water, and since they were in the air and not on Avalonian soil, most of them didn't get swept up in the spell. As they climb higher, rising above the treetops of the island, she keeps her eyes peeled for signs of Westphalia in the distance, a sign to indicate they made it. She looks for her castle, where Mary Contrary is waiting for her.

But when they reach the top, it's not the Westphalian castle they see.

It's the Hollywood sign.

"Wait a second," Alistair says, squinting. "Isn't that . . . ?"

Filomena gasps. "Oh my fairies."

The four heroes are silent for a moment, taking in the hills and the highways in the distance.

"Well, Filomena," Jack says, a look of terror on his face, "it seems like it worked. You brought Avalon home."

Two Worlds

The original quest
is almost conquered,
But quests are never
as simple as they seem.
Excalibur may be out
of Olga's clutches,
But there's a new disaster
that our heroes must redeem.
Casting a spell
is not so easy;

There are always consequences
to balance it out.
The wizard and his friends
have moved the sacred island.
Something is altered
Without a doubt.
Filomena's two worlds
have now collided.
From Never After to West Hollywood
Our heroes roam,
But collisions are short;
They don't last forever.
Now Filomena will have to decide
Where she calls home.

Part Three

Wherein . . .

The gang finally meets the Lady of
the Lake . . .

Filomena pulls the Sword from the
Stone . . .

Marlon's spell works . . . or does it?

CHAPTER THIRTY

WESTPHALIA OR WEST HOLLYWOOD?

At first, there's total calm. The seven have just success-fully transported the sacred island of Avalon into one of the least sacred places of all time: Hollywood. Specifically, West Hollywood, in the mortal world. Westphalia, West Hollywood—what's the difference, really? An abundance of trendy nightclubs?

Filomena feels like her brain is glitching as she stares over the Avalonian landscape—serene, tranquil, sacred—and, just past it, at the Chateau Marmont, the Hollywood sign, and LA traffic. Jack, Alistair, Gretel, and Filomena are silent, taking in the gravity of what they've just done. What this means for them, for Never After, for Olga, for the mortal world . . . none of them has any idea. Can they enter the mortal world from here? Can the mortal world see Avalon? So many questions, and absolutely no answers. So they're calm, silent. But then the freak-out starts.

"Uh, what did we just do?" Gretel says quietly.

"Are we . . . ? We're here. And Avalon? It's . . . we're . . . magic, mortal . . . the fairies! And Hollywood? And Never After—" Alistair stutters.

"I think we broke Alistair," Jack says, putting his arm around his best friend.

"WHAT ARE WE GOING TO DO?!" Filomena suddenly screams. Her heart is pounding like the feet of a thousand chippermunks.

This snaps Jack out of his daze. "We need to tell Marlon."

They run down the tree's outer staircase as fast as their legs can possibly take them, the weight of their actions pushing them down, down, down. They burst in the front door, and Marlon, thankfully, seems to have roused from his spell-induced nap.

"I messed up," Filomena says at the same time that Jack yells, "We're in Hollywood!" and as Gretel screams, "How did this go so wrong?" and as Alistair goes, "No, no, no."

"Whoa, whoa, back up," Marlon says, standing. "What's going on?"

"I accidentally moved Avalon to West Hollywood," Filomena says, her face now in her hands.

"West Hollywood?" Marlon squints. "Is that a neighborhood in Westphalia?"

"No, Marlon," Gretel says, putting a hand on his shoulder. "We messed up real bad. West Hollywood isn't in Never After."

Marlon's eyes widen. "You mean . . . ?"

"Yep. Welcome to the mortal world."

Immediately Marlon runs up the spiral staircase to another floor in the tree home.

Gretel jokes. "Was it something I said?"

Jack is pacing. Filomena still hasn't looked up, and Alistair runs to the kitchen to grab the batch of cookies he made earlier.

"Thank fairies these transported across the worlds, too," he says, stress eating.

"It was the shoes!" a voice from upstairs screeches.

Marlon runs at light speed down the spiral staircase, carrying a thick spellbook.

"It was the shoes," he says, pacing and shaking his head, pointing at Filomena's ruby-red slippers. "They're too powerful." Then Marlon stops and looks up at Filomena. He pulls her hands from her face with one hand; the other holds the giant spellbook.

"Filomena, what does home mean to you?"

She pauses for a moment. She knew her mistake the moment she saw the Hollywood sign.

"I guess home means North Pasadena."

"This was my fault, Filomena. I shouldn't have done a spell that left something up to chance, to emotion, to something that we couldn't be certain of!"

He starts shaking his head and pacing around the room.

"Rosie." Marlon points at her where she's sitting on the couch. "Take note of this. Never, ever assume anything about the people you're working spells with. I assumed Filomena's home was Westphalia, and that was my mistake. So I tailored the spell to take us 'home,' and that's why we're . . . in the mortal world."

"What do we do now?" Alistair says.

Jack clenches his jaw. "For starters, we do what we set out to do on this mission. We get Excalibur to save Filomena's mother. Then, after that's done, and only after that's done, we figure out what in the worlds to do about the rest of this."

They decide it makes the most sense for Jack, Gretel, Alistair, Filomena, and Arturo to go find Excalibur. Rosie and Marlon will remain at Marlon's tree hollow, where they'll be researching in his books and trying to figure out if there's a way to rectify this, to reverse the spell and put Avalon back into Camelot. Before Filomena and the others left, Rosie placed the dragon scale in Filomena's hand. The last thing Filomena wants at this point is to do any more teleporting, but Rosie insisted.

"So where is Excalibur, exactly?" Gretel asks Arturo as they walk through the Avalonian forest outside Marlon's tree.

"It's in the center of the island. Not far from here, actually," Arturo says, stepping over a fallen log. "The reason it has healing powers—the ones I'm assuming you need for your mother, Filomena—is because it rests by the waters of Avalon."

Filomena nods, but she's not really taking in any of this. She's distracted. Her worlds are suddenly colliding, and she doesn't know how she feels about it, exactly.

Arturo, who's been leading them through the trees, starts stumbling a little as though confused. "I'm sorry, guys, this is weird, but I'm having a hard time finding my way."

"What do you mean?" Gretel asks.

"I mean, I've made this trip dozens of times, to the waters of Avalon. But right now, each time I think I know what direction we're going, everything gets . . ."

Something clicks in Filomena's mind. "Misty?" she asks.

"Yes!" Arturo looks at her with wide eyes. "Exactly! Misty."

"The Mists of Myth must still be here, even if Olga's gone," Filomena says, and a look of recognition dawns on Jack's, Gretel's, and Alistair's faces.

"Do you still have the glasses?" Jack says urgently.

Filomena nods and pulls the opal glasses Gita gave her from her pocket. "Try these on, Arturo."

"Whoa," Arturo says, looking at the frames and putting them on. "These are rad. Where did you get these?"

"Ever heard of Gita?" Alistair says.

Arturo looks confused for a moment.

"Wait, you're not talking about Morgana, are you? Morgan le Fay? She's my godmother! Of course she has something this cool." He chuckles. "Have you guys seen her apartment?"

The glasses work, and soon Arturo is no longer lost in the mist. He leads them along a series of twists and turns through the trees and over multicolored rock formations. Eventually, after clearing away shrubs and branches, they come to the edge of a lagoon. Without ogres blocking their every path, Avalon seems a lot smaller. But its beauty is still shocking. The lagoon is a glistening dark turquoise in a cove surrounded by lavender-colored rocks. The water glints like it's liquid gemstone. Filomena jumps back when she sees scaled forms swimming beneath the translucent surface.

"Are those sharks?" Alistair says nervously.

Arturo laughs. "No! Oh no, they're very nice."

A beautiful girl's head and shoulders emerge from the water, and she starts giggling wildly. "Hi, Arturo," she coos, waving.

Another one pops up. "Heyyyy, Artie."

"You know them?" Filomena asks.

Without another word, the girls giggle to each other, then dive under the water. Filomena sees a large tail, like a pink-and-blue fish tail, flip out behind them.

"Yeah, I like to hang out with the mermaids." Arturo laughs. "They're a lot of fun. They helped me out the first time I came to find Excalibur."

Filomena's amazed at what she's just seen, but before she can take it all in, Arturo leads them around the edge of the lagoon, past the lavender rocks, and to another body of water.

Arturo elbows Filomena. "My guess is this is where Olga set up camp before you got the dragons to kick her out."

"What is this place?"

"These are what's known as the waters of Avalon."

A lake lies before them, crystal clear, with a pink sandy bottom. The surface of the water is covered in mist, and on either side of the shore is a waterfall pouring itself into the lake.

As the five adventurers watch, a woman appears at the bottom of the lake and slowly rises toward them.

A woman who asks, "And who do I have to thank for this pleasure?"

CHAPTER THIRTY-ONE

THE OPAL BLADE

Her melodic voice seems to echo from the lake itself. She continues to rise through the water, as if walking up a set of stairs. Actually, she *is* walking up a set of stairs— stairs formed by the pink sand at the bottom of the lake. Her head and shoulders, then the rest of her, step out of the water and onto the shore. The woman looks to be in her twenties, Filomena observes. Her dress is the same turquoise as the mermaids' lagoon, and though at first Filomena thinks the woman is covered in seaweed all over her shoulders and arms, she then sees that they're intricate and delicate tattoos.

"Auntie Vilma!" Arturo says, running to hug the woman who emerged from the lake.

Arturo and the woman embrace like the family members they are.

"You've been bad, Art," she says, pulling back. "You never come to visit anymore."

"I know, I'm sorry, Auntie Vil."

"Plus you didn't even *try* to rescue me when those *grande malvados* took over my lake! I grace you with Excalibur, and that's what I get?" She pouts. "It still smells like ogres! Pew!"

"I'm so sorry. I know I failed you."

The woman sighs and rubs her hand over Arturo's pink buzzed hair. "*Muy bien*, teenagers are allowed to be delinquents sometimes. Even kings. Thank fairies my castle is under the lake, where at least I could hide. I caught up on my beauty rest. Developed some great seaweed facials!"

"You do look very beautiful." Arturo smiles, turning up the charm.

Vilma just laughs. "Flattery will get you everywhere, *querido*. But luckily, it seems like someone arranged some dragon interference," she continues. "I'm assuming you four had something to do with that?"

"That was all Filomena here," Jack says, motioning to her.

"Pleasure to meet you," Filomena says. "I'm Filomena, or Queen Eliana of Westphalia."

"Oh! A girl queen! So cute, you're so cute," Vilma says.

"I'm Vilma Alvarez, or, officially, the Lady of the Lake. Welcome!"

"Sorry, but did you say your castle is under the lake?" Alistair chimes in.

"I did, cutie. You want a tour?"

Alistair nods enthusiastically, but Jack intervenes. "Maybe after we ask you for help," he says. "Filomena here is the one who called the dragons to chase Olga out of Avalon, and we have a favor to ask of you in return."

"Yes, you're a total lifesaver," Vilma says to Filomena. "Olga is a horrible creature. She was sucking up all my healing powers!"

"We happen to be in need of some of those healing powers," Filomena says. "Olga cursed my mother, and a mirror prophecy told me that the only way to heal her is with Excalibur."

"Oh, totally!" Vilma says, twirling her hair. "You want me to lead you there?"

Filomena nods, relief flooding her chest.

Vilma brings them over to one of the waterfalls. "Just through here." She points to a cave entrance covered by the waterfall. "Artie, be a good boy and take her in."

They walk over, and Arturo puts his arm out, parting the stream of water as if it were a curtain. Filomena steps through and into the cave. There, in the center of the space, is a boulder with a sword stuck in it. *Just like the story*, she thinks.

"This is your sword?" she says to Arturo.

"Yeah, technically, but it's a sword for whoever needs it. Right now, that's you."

"Will you pull it out for me?" Filomena asks him, staring at the opal blade, the shining silver hilt.

"No," he says.

"What?" She looks at him, shocked.

"You have to pull it yourself, Filomena," he says, laughing. "This is your quest, after all."

Her quest. Right. Her heart pounds in the presence of such a powerful object. Slowly, Filomena walks up to the sword. Finally, she's face-to-face with the thing she's been searching for all this time. She puts her hand on the hilt, and a strip of light like moonlight shines onto the blade. With one swift motion, she pulls it, and . . . nothing.

"What's wrong?" she says. "It won't budge!"

She starts to feel panic, thinking back to the arcade game at the Witch of the West's emporium. The feeling of helplessness.

"I thought this might happen," Arturo says. "Camelot does love a test."

"Am I not supposed to get the sword?" Filomena says nervously.

"Don't worry, this happened to me, too, when I first discovered Excalibur. We're at the very heart of Avalon now," Arturo explains. "You know how Camelot is always testing you? Well, those tests have become perverted since Olga took over. But Olga's gone now. And the obstacles were originally to weigh the purity of heart of a person entering Camelot."

Arturo points to the large stone in which Excalibur is stuck.

Filomena glances down, removing her hand from the sword hilt. The rock is inscribed with glowing letters, as if it's burning inside.

Do not turn your back on those you've met along the way.
A selfless deed to complete your quest.
Find the fire.

At first, Filomena is confused. Jack, Alistair, and Gretel are waiting for her on the other side of the waterfall. *A selfless deed to complete your quest. Those you've met along the way. Find the fire* . . . It rings a bell, but she doesn't quite know to what this is alluding.

"So I have to complete one more test in order to get the sword?" she asks.

Arturo nods. "Any idea what the stone is referring to?"

Filomena thinks about those she's met along the way. Gwen and Lance, the witches. It strikes her: They moved on from the Emerald City so quickly that she forgot all about the munchkins!

"We left the munchkins, the immortal children. We left them in the Emerald City under Olga's spell!" she cries.

She motions for Arturo to follow her, and they cross the waterfall to where the other three are waiting.

"Well?" Jack says hopefully.

Filomena shakes her head. "We have one last test."

Filomena isn't quite sure how this dragon scale works, but she's throwing all caution to the wind at this point. She's already transplanted the most sacred place in Never After to Hollywood. How much worse can it get?

Jack, Alistair, and Gretel were all ashamed when they realized they'd left the munchkins in the dust. Especially Alistair, who argued to save them in the first place! Filomena remembered what Gita said: The only way to save the munchkins is to release and purify the immortal flame.

The four heroes plus Arturo and the Lady of the Lake each put a finger on the dragon scale. Filomena prays this will work. She closes her eyes and imagines the immortal flame. When she opens her eyes again, the group is on a completely different part of the island.

"Wow!" Alistair yelps, looking at a forest the color of candy. "This place is amazing!"

"Ah, the city of the immortal children." Vilma smiles.

"It's so empty," Gretel whispers.

Now they've landed in what appears to be a town square. In its center, a fire roars in a circular stone fireplace. The fire has green and black tinges to its flames. *It looks poisonous,* Filomena thinks.

"Lady Vilma," Filomena asks, "it's time to use your healing powers!"

"Oh, okay!"

"We need to purify this fire to break the enchantment on the munchkins!"

Vilma motions for Filomena and the group to follow her, and they walk toward the ugly gaseous fire.

"I always carry some travel-sized potions with me." The Lady of the Lake winks. "Consider this a favor, Filomena. You'll pay me back someday, I'm sure."

Vilma passes out several vials of a light blue potion and instructs each of them to pour the vials' contents on the fire on her count. When they pour, the fire sputters, and a black cloud puffs from it. They all jump back. Filomena's worried that the potions are just making it worse. But it appears that the fire is ridding itself of toxins. Soon it becomes a light blue, calm and lovely. Pure. Filomena just hopes that it worked.

Back behind the waterfall, Filomena returns to the blade. There are no glowing words this time. Just her, Arturo, and Excalibur.

"Go ahead, Fil. You can do it," Arturo encourages.

Excalibur slides out of the stone like a knife out of butter.

Filomena breathes a deep sigh of relief, tears welling up in her eyes.

Arturo stands with his arms crossed, beaming. "I always thought you were special," he says. "I was right. That blade doesn't come out of the stone for just anyone. Now let's go save your mom."

As they exit the cave, Jack, Alistair, and Gretel beam at her.

"Brava!" Vilma claps. "Well done, you!"

"You're a sight to behold, Filomena," Jack says.

Standing there with her new short hair and Excalibur in her hand, Filomena is ready. She's ready to end this quest.

CHAPTER THIRTY-TWO

THE END OF THE QUEST

Before leaving Avalon for West Hollywood, they stop at Marlon's tree again. Arturo thinks just Fil, Jack, Alistair, and Gretel should go to Filomena's house for now, so as not to overwhelm Filomena's mother. They give Marlon the address in case of an emergency and explain the concept of taxi cabs to the Never After gang.

"It's kind of like a carriage," Alistair says. He's proud to use the expertise he learned from the other times he'd visited the mortal realm. "Except you pay with a little magical card, and the carriage is like a weird metallic thing with wheels instead of horses and a wagon."

Luckily, Gretel, biportal queen she is, still has her dad's credit card on her, so the four squeeze into a cab, trying their best to conceal Excalibur from the driver through distraction. Gretel chats with him the whole way so that he doesn't turn around to see a giant opalescent blade.

How strange, to be riding down these streets again. Filomena's heart is in her throat, thinking of her mother. She tries to steady her breathing, to not be too impatient, but this is the moment she's been waiting for! Jack keeps her tethered to her body by squeezing her hand every minute or so. She feels comforted by the pressure, by his touch.

Finally they pull up to her house. North Pasadena. As always when she returns from Never After, there's an uncanny feeling. So much has changed, and so much hasn't. They get out of the cab, Gretel taps her dad's credit card, and they catch only a glimpse of the baffled driver as he pulls out of the driveway. It looks like he just now noticed Excalibur, and his jaw dropped.

"At least he'll have a good story!" Gretel laughs.

"For some reason, I feel so nervous," Filomena admits.

"That makes sense," Alistair says. "I always get nervous before the end of a quest."

Jack nods in agreement.

"Yeah, it's everything you've been working for, leading up to this moment. Now we see what happens."

"Hey, before we go in . . . ," Alistair says, then wordlessly pulls them in together for a group hug.

Filomena starts to tear up a bit in the arms of her three best friends. Why does this feel like an ending? Shouldn't she be excited that she's saving her mother? It's a beginning, not an ending! Still, something nags at her.

They pull apart, and she walks up and opens the front door.

"Mum? Dad?" she calls to the empty living room and kitchen.

"Filomena!" her dad cries, running down the stairs. "What are you—?" he pauses, taking in the sight of his daughter in ruby-red slippers, her hair chopped off to chin-length, carrying Excalibur, holding hands with Jack Stalker, and walking next to Alistair and Gretel.

"Hi, Mr. Cho," Jack says, stepping forward and putting out his hand to shake Carter's. "It's great to see you again."

"Hi, Jack." Carter smiles. "So . . ."

"Dad, I know how to save Mum," Filomena says, stepping forward.

"Oh, honey," he says, looking skeptical. "You're so sweet, but I don't know if that's a good idea."

"Why not?"

"She's so weak right now, I'm not sure getting her hopes up is a good idea."

"No, Dad, you don't understand!" Filomena takes a deep

breath. Her parents have come to terms with the idea of Never After, the magic, the history, but she gets it. When her mother's health is at stake, believing in magic is a whole other thing. "Please. Just trust me."

Carter Cho looks at his daughter. Filomena's sure this isn't how he expected his day to go. He's hesitant, scared of getting his own hopes up, probably. But he gives in. "All right. Go ahead, honey."

"Do you want us to come with you?" Gretel asks Filomena.

"I think I have to do this alone," she says.

The three nod.

Filomena started this alone, and she'll finish it alone. She walks up the stairs of her own house—stairs she's walked thousands of times in her life—but they feel different to her now. This is the last staircase of a quest, not just stairs to the second floor of her childhood home. As she reaches the doorway to her parents' room, she braces herself for what she'll find. And then she enters.

Her mother is lying in bed looking frailer than ever. She's pale, her skin paper-thin. Her eyes are closed, and her breathing is ragged. She must be asleep.

No one ever told Filomena what exactly to do with the sword to save her mother. But then she remembers that she's actually not alone.

"Ira?" she says, lifting him up from the strap on her hip.

"You've done it, Fil." Ira smiles, his face appearing in the mist of the mirror's surface.

"Well, almost. What do I do now?"

"Just lay the sword on her. That should be enough."

So she does. She lifts the mighty sword Excalibur, the sword that made Arturo king of Camelot, the sword she traveled across worlds to find, that pushed the limits of what she knew was possible, and she lays it on top of her mother so that it's vertical and so the opal blade rests on Bettina's chest, stomach, and legs.

Filomena takes a step back and hopes.

A mist begins to rise off the bed, off her mother, and off the sword. A light, bright but milky, like a combination of moonlight and sunlight, glows from the bed. There's a gasp, and her mother sits up.

"Filomena!" she cries. Color has returned to her cheeks. Her skin, no longer pale and thin, is flushed with life, pumping with blood.

"Mum!"

Filomena runs to her, pushing the sword aside, and hugs her mother like she's never hugged her before.

"You changed your hair!" Bettina says. Both of their eyes fill with tears, and the tears drip onto their grinning, laughing faces.

To feel her mother's heart pumping, to feel her warm skin, her thick hair, her scent like an English rose garden, Filomena knows that finally, finally, she's home. And truly, there's no place like it.

CHAPTER THIRTY-THREE

ONE LAST TWIST

The scene downstairs is a knot of anxiety. Jack, with his arms crossed, is tapping his foot restlessly in a rhythm that Gretel finds unsettling. She keeps swatting at him to stop, but he can't, and seconds after she swats, he unconsciously starts up again. Gretel is trying to distract herself by reading the spines of all the books on Filomena's parents' shelves, and Alistair is chatting with Carter, Filomena's dad, attempting to distract him. But they all snap out of their dazes instantly when they see the two beaming women rush down the staircase.

"Bettina!"

Carter immediately breaks into tears and a face-splitting, open-mouthed smile as Bettina jumps, like a full force of energy, into his arms. He lifts her, turns, marveling at her, then brings her into his arms, and they hug, gripping each other.

"Wow. So this is what true love looks like, huh?" Gretel says, smiling, head tilted in awe.

"Filomena, how . . . ?" Carter says, pulling away for a second to bring Filomena into the fold. He's wiping continuously pooling tears from his eyes.

Jack, Alistair, and Gretel look at Filomena being embraced by her parents and the joy on their faces, and for the first time, they realize the force of Filomena's family's love. Filomena thinks she sees Jack's smile falter for a moment, but he composes himself quickly.

After a few minutes of disbelieving reconciliation, Bettina pulls away from Filomena and Carter and looks at Jack, Gretel, and Alistair with awe. "Thank you so much, you three. I owe you, quite literally, my life."

"I want to hear everything!" Carter shouts. "Let's have dinner—my treat. I want to hear all about the adventure, and we have to CELEBRATE! Your mother is back! My wife is back!"

Filomena can't believe her luck. Her heart is levitating with a golden joy. The thought of their spell-induced mix-up is the furthest thing from Filomena's mind now.

She forgets about Marlon, about Avalon, about Never After, about everything outside this living room. This night, this evening—nothing can ruin it. Her parents and her best friends are in her home, in her favorite place.

"Let's order takeout!" Bettina says. She runs to the record player to put on music for them.

"I'll get the menus!" Carter runs to the kitchen to fetch their favorite takeout menus.

"You guys want to stay for a while?" Filomena asks sheepishly.

"Duh!" Gretel says, hugging Filomena. "I'll stay forever!"

"I'm so happy for you, Fil," Jack says.

"Another quest accomplished!" Alistair leaps up. "Together, what can't we do?"

They're several songs deep when a knock on the door sounds.

The night has been perfect. Jack and Filomena, Alistair and Gretel, Carter and Bettina—all are dancing wildly to Fil's parents' records, their stomachs full from an extravagant feast. It wasn't the kind of feast they'd have had in Never After, but Filomena thinks this one is much better: They ordered from their favorite Chinese restaurant. Heaps of noodles, lush saucy chicken dishes, slick crunchy vegetables, fried rice. The night has been perfect. But then, just when Filomena is dancing with her mother, still in disbelief that Bettina can jump and twirl around again—then comes the knock. Filomena feels a sinking feeling in her stomach, though she doesn't know why.

Her dad opens the door. It's just Marlon! Thank goodness.

"Marlon!" Filomena runs over and hugs him, welcoming him inside. Behind him are the others: Arturo, Rosie, even Archimedes.

"Mum, Dad, these are my other friends from Never After!" Filomena smiles, naming them all. She's so excited to see them that she doesn't clock their grim faces.

"Pleasure to meet you!" Bettina says, smiling with her arm around her husband. "It's so wonderful to meet all of Filomena's friends. These four have been telling us so much about you. I can't thank you enough for saving my life."

"Don't thank us yet," Marlon mutters, walking past Filomena's parents and into the house. Gretel's smile, Filomena notes, is fading. She looks confused. There's a strange energy in the air. Filomena doesn't get it. Everything worked out!

Archimedes swoops in and lands on Marlon's shoulder. "Lovely house you have," he says to Bettina.

"A talking owl!" Carter says. His eyes are wide in disbelief, and he has a big smile on his face. "This Never After world just keeps getting more and more interesting."

"Rosie, is everything okay?" Filomena whispers as her friends file into the house.

"Uh, we're not sure," Rosie says quietly, shrugging. "I think it's better for Marlon to explain. He knows the details."

At first Filomena feels anger. How dare they come in here and ruin this night? Things have just started to fall perfectly into place! Her mother is healed, her best friends are here, why can't Never After just let her have this one? Just one night of calm?

Rose Red, Marlon, and Arturo sit on the couches and the carpeted floor of Filomena's parents' living room and look around.

"Wow, nice record collection," Arturo says to Carter.

"Thanks, man." Carter nods. "Cool hair. Do you think that would look good on me?"

"Is something wrong, honey?" Bettina asks, seeing Filomena's expression change.

"I'm not sure, Mum, but I think they might be here to tell us something."

"Is this the boy wizard you told us about?" Bettina whispers and giggles, nodding to Marlon in deep red robes whose eyebrows are furrowed. He's stood up and is pacing. It's a funny combination, but Filomena's suddenly in no laughing mood.

Marlon sighs deeply. "Filomena, everyone, we have some bad news."

They knew the spell went wrong, but they didn't know just how wrong. While Filomena and the others left to get Excalibur, Marlon, Rosie, and Archimedes spent the whole time in Marlon's library, researching the consequences of such a spell. It was difficult to piece together at first, but the more they read, the more they realized just how badly they'd messed up the spell. There is a whole chapter about cross-world travel in one of Marlon's ancient texts. It's incredibly dangerous to move a whole place between worlds, let alone a place as sacred as Avalon. The magical shock wave from such an enchantment caused a rift in the portal system, making it extremely problematic to travel between worlds.

"We have a twenty-four-hour window," Marlon explains, "before the portal between the worlds closes."

Everyone is silent, taking in what this means, the weight of this statement.

"What do you mean, 'closes'?" Jack says, standing.

His face is flushed, and he looks panicky. Filomena does not like seeing him like this. It doesn't bode well.

"I mean that after this time window closes, attempting to go through a portal will mean risking your life. If you're incredibly, incredibly lucky, you might make it through. But it's far more likely that the results are disastrous—that you will die in the process. There will no longer be a safe passage between Never After and the mortal world. We've destroyed it by bringing the most sacred place in Never After into the mortal world. It distorted the portal beyond repair."

Filomena feels like she's going to throw up.

"What this means," Arturo says, "is that being biportal won't work anymore."

Filomena looks to Gretel, who has paled tremendously. Gretel was ready to move to Paris, but Filomena knows her friend planned to visit Never After whenever she wanted. But now?

"In short, everyone is going to have to choose what world they want to stay in," Marlon says grimly. "And once you choose, that's it. Forever."

CHAPTER THIRTY-FOUR

UNDER THE JACARANDA TREE

Filomena is too shocked to cry. To speak. To move. She always knew that, one way or another, she'd have to choose to spend most of her time in one world over the other. Whether she decided to be queen of Westphalia and come visit her parents on weekends, or whether she decided to stay in the mortal world and go to Never After on weekends—that was already going to be a difficult, nearly impossible, choice to make. But this? The sinking feeling she's been trying to ignore since this quest started has finally descended on her at full force.

"Filomena," Bettina says, walking over to where Filomena sits in shock on the couch, "why don't you and your friends take some time to talk about this? I'm sure this is a real shock. Your father and I will be upstairs if you need anything."

Carter turns to Marlon.

"You said there's twenty-four hours left?"

"There were twenty-four hours from when we did the spell. That was probably about twelve hours ago now."

"Looks like we're having an all-nighter," Alistair says with the smallest amount of enthusiasm anyone has ever expressed about the prospect of an all-nighter.

Usually Filomena's parents would never allow her to walk around the neighborhood alone at night, let alone with a *boy* at night. But these are, they know, special circumstances. When Marlon dropped this news, all Filomena wanted was to be alone with Jack. To talk to him, to figure this out. Her most trusted confidant, her hero, the love of her life.

So now, here she and Jack are, walking around her suburban North Pasadena neighborhood in the warm California night air. Under any other circumstances, this would be one of the most exciting moments of her young life, to be alone with Jack under the jacaranda trees in their full purple bloom.

"I just want to say," Jack says, breaking the silence they've been walking in, "that no matter what you choose, I support you. I don't want to affect your choice."

She nods. She appreciates that sentiment. Never After holds so much more for her than just Jack, of course. But there's no denying that she has two choices, and one way means she sees him; the other way means she doesn't.

"So this is where you grew up?" Jack says after another silence.

"It is." She smiles softly.

"It's so peaceful," he says.

"It's been pretty great. Sometimes it's too peaceful, but after everything in Never After, it does feel pretty nice. Though school wasn't great."

"But that was before, right? When Olga's trolls were there. I'm sure now . . ." He trails off. They haven't broached the real subject of why they're out here. After Filomena's parents retreated to their room to let the kids talk, Filomena announced she needed some air. And she asked Jack to come with her. He, of course, always the gentleman, obliged. She wonders what everyone else is talking about, back at the house.

"I never fit in here," she says. "I mean, at home, of course I did. But with other kids, I never felt like I fit in . . . until I met you."

"I felt the same," Jack says quietly. "It was different when it was just me and Alistair. You, Gretel, everyone we met afterward . . . that was a different kind of feeling than when it was just me and him. A feeling like we weren't just lost kids, outcasts on a journey. We had a place we belonged. With you."

Filomena stops walking and closes her eyes for a moment. "What are we going to do, Jack?" she says.

She opens her eyes, and they keep walking. She touches her necklace without realizing.

"Do you like it?" Jack asks.

"I love it. I'm going to wear it every day, forever."

"I hope that's true," he says, looking at his feet as they walk.

They come to a large lawn shaded by a jacaranda tree. Purple petals have fallen all over the lawn. Filomena sits down under the tree and motions for Jack to sit, too.

"I guess the mortal world is pretty after all." He smiles.

Filomena lies backward on the petals. Jack lies backward, too. They're both staring up at the sky, at the stars that peek between the tree branches. A breeze blows over them. Now that they're not looking at each other, Filomena feels like she can say something she's been working up the courage to say.

"When we were at Exit West . . . ," she starts.

She hears him inhale sharply.

"You said . . . I don't know if you remember . . . You said

that if you ever lost me, you don't even know what the point of anything would be."

"I remember," he says softly.

"Do you still feel that way?"

He's silent for a moment.

"I've met a lot of people in my life, Filomena. Through moving around a lot, traveling, questing. You just meet a lot of people. But I've never met anyone I've connected with the way I have with you. You make me feel like, every day, there's something to look forward to. Even just going for a walk, if it's with you, is exciting to me."

She feels her heart swelling and breaking at the same time. It's such a strange sensation.

"So yes, I still feel that way. But also, no. As in, sure, maybe life would have less of a point without you in it, but also, no matter what happens now, we'll always have known each other. So life will always have a point, because of that."

She feels tears rising and tries to fight them, the hot feeling at the back of her throat.

"Could you stay with me?" she asks, quietly. "In this world?"

Jack sighs. He turns on his side, so he's looking at her now, not the stars. She's scared to do the same, but she does. They lie face-to-face.

"I wish I could," he says, and her heart sinks. "I wish I could grow up with you. We could go on dates—I don't even know what that means! I only learned that word from Gretel."

Filomena laughs. "You talked about dates with Gretel?"

"Yeah, after the Emerald City, she told me I need to ask you on a date soon, but I didn't know what she meant. I don't think we have that word in Never After."

Filomena covers her eyes with her hands out of delight, embarrassment, excitement, all of it. "You were going to ask me on a date?"

"Of course! As soon as we got your mom healed. Although I don't really know what it means. What do people do on dates? Go on walks?"

"We could go to the movies, go roller-skating . . . When we turn sixteen, we could get our driver's licenses and then drive anywhere we want."

"I don't even know what any of those things are!" Jack laughs.

"Wow, I guess I never really understood how much you don't know about the mortal world." Filomena smiles sadly. "You don't even know what a movie is! But you're right, a walk can definitely count as a date."

"Does that mean we're on a date right now?"

She smiles wider. "Yeah, let's say we are."

"At least then we'll have been on one date."

Filomena starts to cry a little bit at this. "You really can't stay with me?" she says, tears spilling gently onto her cheeks.

Jack looks at her like he's in pain. Like her being in pain is paining him. "Where would I live? With your parents? I don't have parents to live with."

"I guess you don't have any money, either," she sniffs.

"Even if there were some place for me to go, you know I have to stay in Never After. Without me . . . I just can't leave it. It's part of being a gift from the fairies. You're different, you weren't raised there. I'm not biportal like you and Gretel. Never After needs me. I can't let it down."

"But," she starts, wiping away her tears, "what does that mean for us?"

"Well, do you want to stay in Never After?" Jack sits up, getting excited suddenly. "Alistair and I will move to Westphalia with you! We can help you figure out what it means to be queen. We can go on quests together. But also, we can actually just hang out!" Filomena sits up, too, putting her hands under her chin, her elbows on her knees. Jack goes on. "After all this craziness, we can just have fun," he says, grinning.

"And if I stay in Never After," she asks, "would I stay this age forever? Like you?"

She thinks of ruling Westphalia, of living there with Jack, with Alistair. Mary Contrary could rule the kingdom in Filomena's place, but Filo is the true and rightful ruler in the end.

"I think so, yes. We'll both be immortal! We can make the kingdoms better places for everybody. Every creature. You can even learn how to use your magic more."

"My magic?" she says, a thrill rising in her chest.

"Yeah, you know. It's obvious that you have fairy magic in you; you animated a talking mirror, for goodness' sake! Think of everything Marlon can teach you and Rosie. You could do such amazing things together!"

Hearing him say all this makes it so tempting. It's like Filomena's dreams have come true, the dreams she had back when she'd fall asleep with her reading lamp on, halfway through a Never After book. Dreaming that she was a part of it. And now she is, and Jack, her forever crush, is in love with her. And she has all these best friends. And is capable of magic, maybe. And now she might have to give it all up? Why would she give it up?

But something else occurs to her.

"I think I have to write the thirteenth book, Jack."

"What?"

"Remember? The fairy Carabosse, my aunt. She wrote the first twelve Never After books but died before she could write the thirteenth. And we lived the thirteenth book."

"Is that it, then? Is the thirteenth book over? Have we lived it all?" he says. His face is falling with sadness.

"I don't know. Maybe?"

"So does that mean you want to stay in the mortal world?"

"I wish I didn't have to choose."

Jack pauses and sighs. "Even if you didn't have to choose now, you'd eventually get tired of going back and forth. And

I don't know how it would work, with you growing up. If you'd get older or not. No one can have two lives."

Filomena knows he's right. But why not? Why can't she just split herself in two, have one life with her parents in North Pasadena and another in Never After with Jack, Alistair, Rosie, everyone?

Finally he looks at her. His eyes are full of tears, but he smiles through them, ignoring them, brushing them aside. "I get it," he says. "I'd choose my parents, too, if I could. Especially if I had parents like yours. I don't think I could ever give that up. But I don't have to make that choice. I can't."

"I'm never going to forget you, Jack," Filomena says, holding on to her emerald heart pendant.

"You might," he says, looking away.

"No, I won't," she says, the tears coming more heavily now. She stifles a sob. "I'm going to wear this necklace every day until the day I die. And I'll think of you every single day."

"The day you die," he says, suddenly rigid. "Whoa. I guess that's inevitable for mortals, huh?"

They're quiet for another moment.

"I love you, Jack," she says.

She grips him suddenly in a tight hug, so tight that she feels they might fuse together, like an ancient statue. A statue of two best friends, two people in love, forced to choose between worlds. Jack's arms are wound fast around her, and she tries to commit this feeling to memory. When they kiss, it's like time doesn't exist, just for a moment.

Eventually, they just look at each other.

"Should we go back?" he asks.

"Let's walk around for just a bit longer," she says, standing up. She grabs his hand and helps him to his feet. "I don't want to leave you just yet."

CHAPTER THIRTY-FIVE

THE LAST GOODBYE

Filomena hoped Gretel would choose to stay on this mortal side of the portal, but she wasn't sure. She's relieved when it's confirmed. When she and Jack returned to her parents' house, there was an intense sadness in the air. Everyone had guessed what Filomena's plans were, and they were right. Carter and Bettina drove everyone up to the portal in the Hollywood Hills. Now Filomena's parents wait in their cars while Filomena and Gretel say goodbye.

Filomena and Gretel stand facing Jack, Alistair, Rosie,

Marlon, Archimedes, and Arturo. What is there to say? Too much. So much. Nothing.

"Even though I just met you recently," Arturo says, "this feels like a deep tragedy. You're both such wonderful people."

"I'll miss you both," Marlon says. "I hope somehow, some way, we can meet again."

Arturo, Marlon, and Archimedes step into the portal, and just like that, they're gone.

Rosie, Filomena, and Gretel huddle together in a tearful hug.

"I-I-I . . . ," Rosie stutters, attempting to speak between sobs.

"I love you guys so much," Gretel cries.

Filomena gives them both deep hugs. "I'm always so impressed by you, Rosie," she says. "You're a genius. You're going to do amazing things; I wish I could be there to see them all."

"I'm going to find a way to fix this," Rosie says, wiping away her snot and tears. "I can fix it, I promise."

Filomena doesn't believe she can, not even someone as smart as Rosie, but the sentiment eases things a little bit. Just a smidge.

Rosie steps through the portal.

Watching Gretel and Alistair say goodbye is almost as hard as saying goodbye to Alistair herself will be, Filomena thinks.

"You're my soul mate," Alistair says to Gretel, his eyes like a puppy dog's, his tears overflowing. "Not romantically, but cosmically."

"Oh, Alistair," Gretel says, "I love you so much!" The two of them embrace tightly.

Meanwhile, Filomena can hardly bring herself to look at Jack.

When Filomena says goodbye to Alistair, it feels like being ripped from a brother, though she's never had one.

"I know, somehow, we'll find one another again," Alistair says. "You two are my family."

With final kisses and hugs, he steps through the portal, too.

At last, there's Jack. Gretel hugs him tightly, and he whispers in her ear. She smiles through the tears. Then Gretel takes a few paces away, letting Jack and Filomena have their last moments together.

"You're with me forever, Jack," Filomena says.

"You're the love of my life, Filomena."

Jack looks into her eyes, and a thousand lifetimes flash before her. Is she making the right choice? Is this the life she's meant to have? Why does she have to make such a life-altering choice when she's so young? How is she to know what's right? What does the mortal world hold for her? What does Never After hold? She doesn't know, she doesn't know; all she knows is that she loves Jack, and she loves Never After, and she loves her friends. And yet . . .

One last kiss.

When they pull apart, Jack touches her necklace's pendant. "Think of me," he says. "You'll always be the only one."

And then he's gone.

Gretel walks over to where Filomena is, now dropped to the ground, crying. They hug each other for a few minutes, letting each other cry at everything they've lost. But then, eventually, their bodies tire from crying, and they have no tears left.

Gretel puts her arm around Filomena as they look out at the Los Angeles sunrise.

"I guess it's time for the rest of our lives," Gretel says.

The girls walk arm in arm toward their futures.

Of Choices and Consequences

A choice is made,
A love is lost,
A life is started,
But at what cost?
Filomena and Gretel
In the mortal sphere;
They're growing up,
But change is near.

As kids they had two worlds,
And now they have one.
Their Never After past
Is not something they can outrun.
Do they remember
Their mystical life from before?
And what happens if Never After
Comes knocking on their doors?

Part Four

Wherein . . .

The Queen of Westphalia is all grown
up . . .

A knock on the door is a portal to the
past . . .

Old friends are reunited once
more . . .

CHAPTER THIRTY-SIX

BACK TO THE FUTURE

"Thanks so much!" Filomena says to the delivery-person, taking the bag of takeout into her bunga-low and closing the front door. She's lived here for a few months already, but she still can't believe it. Her own home!

After living with her parents in college, Filomena finally branched out when she graduated and has lived in apart-ments in Los Angeles for the past few years. None have felt quite right, felt quite like home, but this one is starting to. Finally, at twenty-five, she feels like she really has a place of her own. She figures that eventually the feeling of home will catch up to her.

"Woo! It's here?" Calvin says from the couch, pausing the movie.

Filomena smiles indulgently at him. Calvin is tall and dark haired and kind and so very smart. "Come help me grab plates?" Filomena calls, walking into her kitchen. On the kitchen table, her cat is rolling on his back.

"How's my cute Phalia, huh?" Filomena says, scratching Phalia's stomach.

"So are we having dinner with your parents tomorrow?" Calvin asks, walking into the kitchen and grabbing plates.

"Uh-huh, before Mum's book launch, remember?" Filomena responds. She's opening all the little boxes of *banchan* and transferring the contents to small ceramic bowls.

"Sounds great! I just have to get my applications in beforehand," Calvin says, moving the food to the dining table.

"How are they going?" Filomena asks.

"Eh, you know. Really close to being done, but I always feel underqualified when applying for things. It's hard to know what chance you stand. And graduate school applications are especially intimidating."

"I totally feel the same about my applications," Filomena says.

"Oh, come on," Calvin says, playfully rolling his eyes.

"What?"

"You have the most solid grad school application of

anyone we know! Your grades were the best in your under-grad classes, plus all your extracurriculars. You don't need to be worried, Mena."

"All right, all right, stop flattering me." She swats at him. "I don't want to talk about the future anymore right now. Let's just relax tonight, okay? We'll both get in big workdays tomorrow, then dinner with my parents, then we can go out dancing with everyone tomorrow night, after we submit the applications."

"A perfect day," Calvin says, leaning over to kiss her nose. "You know, you've done a great job decorating this place."

Filomena surveys her Silver Lake bungalow, nodding in agreement at her thriving houseplants and framed posters. She's pleased with herself.

Filomena sits on the couch next to her sweet boyfriend and kisses him on the cheek. Their weekly ritual of takeout and a movie has been going strong for three years now, ever since they got together. It's nice, comfortable. He's lovely. They met in a fourth-year political science class but didn't get together until they met again through mutual friends after finishing school. Is it true love? Filomena doesn't know if she believes in that, exactly. True love, that is. Sure, her parents definitely seem to have it. But it just doesn't seem like something everyone gets. Sometimes, when she dreams, she gets flashes of that feeling. But it always disappears by the time she wakes up.

The movie continues. They've seen this one before, but

Calvin loves it. After she finishes eating, Filomena lets her mind drift off. Even though it's early, she's really tired after a hard day of work plus working on her applications. She starts to slip into a light sleep. Strange images always come up in her dreams. But, funnily enough, they always feel comforting, no matter how strange. Opal water, riding on horseback through a field. Talking to a small handheld mirror. Fighting with swords. She has a recurring dream of being stuck in a gingerbread house—that might be the weirdest one. In another, she's locked in a beast's castle. The dream she likes best is one in which she just walks around a beautiful city all colored emerald. There's always another person in that one, but she can never see them clearly; it's more a feeling than an actual person. She always wakes up from these dreams a bit sad.

This evening, she doesn't dream; she just slips into a light sleep. Her head falls on Calvin's shoulder, and she wakes up to him giving her a shake.

"Do you want me to get that?" he says.

Someone's knocking on the door. Pounding, more like it.

"No, I'll get it," she says.

She looks through the peephole and sees two figures. One's glancing around in a panic, and the other has their arm slung over the panicked one's shoulders and seems . . . unconscious?

"Filomena!" the panicked one yells.

This person knows her name? She opens the door. But it's

not a person. Well, it is, but it's not an adult person. It's a kid! A thirteen-year-old kid.

"Filomena! Thank fairies I found you," the kid says. "It is you, right? I mean, you look different. Why are you so tall?"

"Who . . . What?" she says, her brows furrowed.

"No, come on, don't tell me, please don't tell me . . . ! Marlon said this might've happened, but I never thought you'd forget us. Come on! It's me!"

The boy looks really panicked now. He's short for a thirteen-year-old. Wait, how does she know he's thirteen?

"Who's there?" Calvin calls. He walks to the door.

"Oh my god!" he says, seeing the unconscious figure slung over the boy's shoulder. "Is he okay? What's going on?"

"I'm a friend of Filomena's," the boy says. "We need to come in."

Before Filomena can do anything, the boy walks past them, dragging the unconscious one with him. They go into the living room, where the movie is paused on the TV screen.

"Jack's really hurt, Fil. It's bad this time, even for an immortal."

The boy lays the other boy down on the couch. *Fil.* No one calls her that except Gretel.

"Well, say something!" the boy says.

"Who are you?" Filomena asks.

"Mena, you don't know these boys?" Calvin asks.

"Mena? Who's Mena? Oh, that's what people call you now?" the boy asks, crossing his arms.

"Who?" is all she can get out. Her brain feels so strange, like she's in a dream. Like her brain is covered in . . . "Mist," she says, frowning.

"It's Alistair! I'm Alistair, from Never After?" the boy pleads with her. "Oh fairies, I really hoped Marlon would be wrong about this one . . ."

Alistair . . . Alistair . . . and this other boy. Who is he? She touches her emerald pendant absentmindedly, like she always does when she's thinking.

"You're still wearing the necklace!" the boy, apparently named Alistair, says excitedly. "Think, Fil. Where did you get that necklace? Who gave you the necklace?"

She hasn't thought about the origin of the necklace in so long. Maybe ever. Was it from her parents? No, that doesn't feel right. She touches it. Feels the pendant's smooth texture. She wears it every day. She doesn't really know why; she just does. She doesn't feel like herself without it. But why? Where did it come from? The necklace feels so personal, it's almost like it came from her. From inside her. Or like it came from a dream. Like the dream of the emerald city. Those buildings, the walking, that feeling of love. It's almost like the necklace came from that dream. A wave of intense emotion washes over Filomena. The emerald city. The Emerald City!

Faces flash in her mind. The face of this boy, this sweet stout boy, laughing with her over a wooden dinner table. Trapped in a gingerbread house. At a ball. In a desert. In a large castle with a unicorn tapestry. In a tavern being served by a white rabbit.

Sword fights. Giant spiders. A crown. Standing on a balcony over a kingdom.

"Oh! Alistair! Oh my god!" It all comes rushing back to her, her memory opening like floodgates. Her eyes fill with tears. "Oh, you're here!" She runs and hugs him tightly, only having to bend down a little to reach his height. She hasn't grown *that* much since she was thirteen, after all.

"You remember," Alistair says, burying his face in her shoulder. "I knew you'd remember."

And then she remembers the unconscious boy on her couch. Riding horseback with him. Jumping through a swoop hole with him. Swiping at ogres with him. Kissing him. Walking through the Emerald City with him. Saying goodbye to him.

"Jack!" she cries. "What's happened? Is he okay? How did you get here? Isn't that impossible? Oh fairies, Alistair, oh, you're here, and Jack—he's hurt? Is everything okay over there? Well, of course it's not, why would Jack be hurt if it were, and—oh, he's hurt! We need to call an ambulance!" She turns to Calvin. "Call 911!" she yells.

Baffled, Calvin reaches for his cell phone.

"What's nine one one?" Alistair says, confused. "Fil, I don't know what you're thinking, but nothing mortal can help Jack."

Of course. Of course he's right. Oh, she can't have 911

coming to her house with two magical immortal boys in here!

"Don't call 911! Never mind, Calvin!"

Calvin wordlessly puts down the cell phone and raises his hands in surrender. "Mena, can you tell me what's going on here? Who are these boys?"

Filomena kneels on her couch next to an unconscious Jack the Giant Stalker. She can see he's breathing, thank fairies. And he doesn't appear to be hurt—no blood, no cuts, no bruises. But Filomena knows that if Alistair's here, something must be really wrong. She puts her hand on Jack's forehead, feeling his temperature. She leaves her hand there and can't take her eyes off him.

"Calvin, these are some old friends of mine," she says, still looking at Jack. "This"—she points to Alistair—"is Alistair. And this is Jack."

"Old friends? Like, as in you used to babysit them when you were in high school?" Calvin says, tremendously confused.

"And who are you?" Alistair says, arms crossed.

"I'm Filomena's boyfriend, Calvin."

"Boyfriend?! Fil, this guy's your boyfriend?"

She peels her eyes away from Jack for a moment, still stunned by the whole situation. Seeing Jack and Calvin in the same room is like seeing a high school boyfriend next to a college boyfriend. Except the high school boyfriend hasn't aged a day since she last saw him.

"Yes, Alistair, he is. We met at school. He's a wonderful guy."

"Hmm. I'll be the judge of that," Alistair says, circling Calvin and sizing him up.

Filomena is reeling. She feels a mixture of grief, loss, and profound joy. To remember Never After, Jack, and Alistair . . . It makes her heart leap with such an intensity of feeling. But it also makes her ache, thinking of how she's forgotten them. She promised she never would. How could she have? How has she been living her life without them? Without the memory of their adventures and love? There are so many questions. But she starts with the most obvious.

"Alistair, please tell me what's going on," Filomena says. "I thought we couldn't cross between worlds anymore? I thought the portal was closed forever. How are you here right now?"

"Right, the portal. Well, you see, that's sort of the whole reason we're here."

CHAPTER THIRTY-SEVEN

FROM PARIS WITH LOVE

Before Filomena lets Alistair say any more, she knows she has to do something first.

"Wait, Alistair. Before we get into whatever this is, I'm calling Gretel."

At this, Alistair glows with delight, like someone just turned on the sun. "Yes! Tell her to come over! I need to see her. I miss her so much. How long until she can get here?"

"Well, it'll probably be a while," Filomena says, looking around the room for her cell phone. "She's in Paris."

"How far is that from here? Are we talking, like, Vineland to Northphalia, or Snow Country to Eastphalia?"

"What is this guy talking about?" Calvin says. "I feel like I just stepped into an alternate universe. And wait, how does he know Gretel?"

"Just give me a second, honey, and I'll explain," Filomena says.

Though, she doesn't know how to explain, exactly, because she's still piecing this together herself. Her brain is running a mile a minute, and she can barely keep up with what's happening in real life, what with all the memories flooding her.

Never After. Jack. Alistair. Gretel's a shoemaker's daughter? The gingerbread house was real . . . Oh my fairies, where is Ira? Her talking mirror! Rosie! And her inventions! The beast in her dreams is Byron. Byron and Bea, ruling Wonderland, Wonderland's ball, Cinderella! Robin Hood, Princess Jeanne, Northphalia Castle. Northphalia. Wait, Filomena is queen of Westphalia! Phalia . . . Is that why she named her cat Phalia? Did some part of her remember and long for that place? Do her parents remember? Does Gretel remember?

Deep breath, Filomena, deep breath, she says to herself. She uses meditation tactics to calm herself down. She counts backward from ten, eyes closed, while Calvin and Alistair stare each other down skeptically.

"Okay, I need to call Gretel now. Calvin, I promise I'll

explain everything. Please just be nice to each other until I get back," she says, running to her bedroom and closing the door.

Her cell phone is on her bed, and she picks it up and calls Gretel immediately. It's 7:00 p.m. in California, so it's 4:00 a.m. in Paris. She just prays that Gretel's phone isn't on silent and that she picks up.

Filomena and Gretel have stayed close over the years. But come to think of it, they never really talk about *how* they met. But now Filomena remembers. She remembers it all. They met on a quest! Their meeting just sort of faded from Filomena's memory, in the same way inside jokes from middle school fade away as one experiences more and more things with friends, or the way imaginary games fade away when one becomes a teenager. But their time in Never After wasn't an imaginary game; it was real. Filomena feels so confused, like she's betrayed a deep part of herself by pushing the memories aside. Will Gretel remember? Why did they forget? Is it because, in the mortal world, magic is so nonexistent that it pushes the very notion from the mind?

When Filomena studied abroad in Paris during her third year of undergrad, she lived with Gretel, who by that time was already a darling in the Paris fashion scene. It had been a magical year, going to art shows together, walking through the town, Gretel showing Filomena all her favorite places around the city. Now, Gretel is a full-blown fashion icon. She's even had a collection in Paris Fashion Week. But they're both busy in their own lives, and it has been too long since Filomena's seen her, especially since Filomena's been dating Calvin. Calvin hasn't met Gretel, but Filomena talks about her all the time. And ever since Filomena decided to apply to grad school for political science, she's been even less in touch with Gretel.

"Please pick up . . . ," Filomena says while the phone rings. "Please wake up, Gretel!"

And Gretel does pick up.

"Hello? Fil? That you?"

There's tons of noise in the background of the phone call. Gretel definitely was not sleeping. Someone yells Gretel's name, and there's the sound of loud music.

"Just a second!" Gretel yells in response to the person who called for her. Then, it gets quiet, except for the sounds of cars beeping.

"Hi! Sorry, I'm just at a party; that's why it's so noisy. I just stepped out onto the street, so it should be better now. What's up? How are you? I miss you so much! I wish you were here with me right now. You'd love this party!"

Filomena instantly feels calmed by the sound of her best friend's voice. She's about to launch into a story about something funny Calvin said earlier that day and how she's almost finished her grad school application, when she remembers the reason she actually called. Then the feeling of calm vanishes.

"Gretel, I have something kind of crazy to ask you about."

"Go ahead! You know nothing's too crazy for me. You can ask me anything."

"Okay, well, do you remember Alistair?"

There's a pause on the other end of the line.

"Wait . . . Yeah, I do."

Filomena's breath catches.

"Is that that guy we were friends with when you did your year abroad here? The guy with the motorbike?"

Filomena's heart sinks. "No, no, it's someone we knew when we were younger. When we were twelve and fourteen . . . Does that ring a bell for you?"

"Oh, you know, that time is so blurry in my memory for some reason. Can you remind me?"

"We were friends with him, Alistair, and Jack. And your cousin Rosie, and Beatrice and Byron. And we went on quests."

"Quests?" Gretel giggles. "What are you talking about?"

"Do you remember the first designs you did, Gretel? When you made a bunch of clothes in Princess Jeanne's castle? Then when you and Alistair hitched a ride in that carriage to Eastphalia and you met Lillet? Remember that?"

Filomena's trying to use fashion to jog Gretel's memory, hoping that something connecting to her present moment will make her remember the past. Their buried past.

"Remember the ruby-red slippers? The Wicked Witch of the East?"

"Wait, Mena, what kind of gibberish are you . . . ?"

Gretel trails off for a second, and then Filomena can't

hear whether she's laughing or crying. "Are you okay, Gretel? Are you laughing? Crying?"

"Oh my gosh, I'm doing both. I'm . . . Did you just remember all that?"

"Tonight, yeah."

"Never After," Gretel says in awe. "I completely forgot. I completely forgot! Is it real, Filomena? Was it all real? Me, you, Jack, Alistair. Avalon? Dragons? Oh, so many things are coming back to me. Wait, are ogres real? Did we kill ogres? With swords?" The laughing-crying noise comes back again. "How did we forget that?" she says. "How did you remember?"

"Well, hold on to your beret, my darling," Filomena says, "because, uh, Alistair is here."

"WHAT?!"

"Yeah." Filomena bursts out laughing at the absurdity of it all. "He's in my living room. With Jack."

"*What.*"

"Yes."

"Wait a second, Filomena. You and Jack were so in love! How could we have forgotten about that? Wait, Jack's with you now? Is Calvin there?"

"Yes, he is."

"And is Jack totally freaking that you have a boyfriend? Are you freaking out? Is Calvin jealous?"

"Well, Jack's still thirteen, first of all, and second of all, he's unconscious."

"What? Why?!"

"I don't know yet. As soon as they showed up and I remembered everything, I called you, because I don't know what to do and I need you here, now!"

There's a pause.

"Okay, you know what? I can get my friend to cover for me in the shop this weekend. I'm coming to California. Let me look up flights right now."

There's a pause as Gretel checks flights on her phone. "There's a flight from Paris to Los Angeles that leaves in a couple hours. I'm coming, Fil—hey, remember I used to call you that? Hold tight. I'll be there by morning. Don't let anything too exciting happen without me, okay?!"

"I love you, Gretel. Thank fairies for you."

"'Thank fairies'! Oh, I forgot about 'thank fairies'! Wow, we have a *lot* of catching up to do."

Chapter Thirty-Eight

Pastries and Portals

When Filomena comes out of the bedroom, Calvin is pointing to the TV and explaining what a movie is to Alistair. "Are you sure you're not punking me?" Calvin says. "You've never seen a movie?"

"We don't have movies where I come from," Alistair says, shrugging.

"Mena, thank goodness you're back," Calvin says, looking relieved and confused.

"Okay," Filomena says, "Gretel is on her way. She's catching a plane right now, so she should be here by morning."

"It takes that long to get here?" Alistair says, looking disappointed. "You know, since you've been gone, Fil, Rosie has done amazing things with dragon scales. Teleportation via dragon scale is totally commonplace now! Used more often even than swoop holes. We could really use a dragon scale right about now."

"What is he talking about?" Calvin says, looking incredulous.

Filomena ignores her boyfriend for now.

"Alistair, is Jack in immediate danger?" she asks.

"Yes and no. Yes, as in that's why I'm here, we need your help to heal him as soon as possible, but no, as in he's not going to die overnight. Marlon said we have a fortnight. But, Fil, he *is* dying."

This is a lot to process. She takes a deep breath. "Gretel's going to be here in the morning," she says. "Can we wait for her to get here and then you can tell me everything? With her? So we can all figure it out together?"

Alistair seems pleased with this idea. "Sounds good to me! By the way, do you have anything to eat?"

Filomena tries to explain everything she can to Calvin, but it's hard for him to believe it. She understands—it's hard for *her* to believe it, in some ways—but it's harder to believe that she's forgotten about it for all these years. Eventually Calvin says he is too overwhelmed by the whole thing and doesn't want to stay overnight. Filomena isn't sure how she feels about that, but she just chalks it up to stress about the grad school applications. Plus, she supposes it would seem strange for a twenty-five-year-old girlfriend to have a storied past with two thirteen-year-olds. Especially when that past took place in a different world. So, seeming baffled after many attempts by Filomena to explain it all, Calvin says he'll call her later and leaves around midnight.

When she wakes the next morning, it's from the same dreams she's been having for years. Except now she realizes they're not just dreams. They're memories.

She walks out into the kitchen, where Alistair's already cooked an elaborate breakfast.

"Did you also forget my amazing cooking skills?" he says, placing a plate of croissants in front of her. "Calvin said they're French pastries, so I thought they would make Gretel feel more at home."

"I have ingredients for croissants in my kitchen?" Filomena laughs, taking a bite from a flaky pastry.

"You know," Alistair says, "I've been working as a touring chef for the past while. I've been cooking all over the kingdoms."

Filomena shakes her head in amazement. "We have so much to catch up on."

There's a pounding at the door.

"Gretel!" they both cry out, and run to answer.

When Filomena opens the door, Gretel has a look of

complete shock on her face, though she knew what was coming. Filomena imagines this from Gretel's point of view: her twenty-five-year-old best friend, and their twelve-year-old other best friend, and their other best friend, thirteen years old, who's passed out on a couch in the background.

"So it's true, what they say," she says, her grin as wide as the ocean she just crossed. "Guys really do take longer to mature!"

She folds Alistair in a long hug, then goes for Filomena. Shaking her head, Gretel walks into Filomena's bungalow and sits down at the kitchen table.

"Cute house, Mena—I mean Fil," she says, taking a bite of a croissant. "Mmm! Alistair, come on now. These are better than any I've had in Paris, and I'm not joking."

"Wow," Alistair says, also sitting at the kitchen table. "You guys actually got old."

"Hey now," Gretel says, wiping a crumb from her lip. "We're under thirty. That's way young."

"You know what I mean," he says. "This is so weird."

Filomena laughs. "You're telling us!" She pours three cups from the French press for them. "You just reminded us that an entirely different world exists! Wait, do you drink coffee, Alistair? Or will that stunt your growth?" She smiles a teasing smile, and Alistair rolls his eyes, taking a cup. The three sip and eat for a moment, looking at one another.

"So did you guys really forget us?" Alistair breaks the silence. "You forgot Never After?"

They both nod sadly.

"I never thought I would," Filomena says, touching her necklace's pendant again. "I swore I wouldn't! But somehow I did. I don't know when it happened. It just slipped away. I thought it was all a dream."

A sadness falls over them as they think of their years apart.

"How long has it been in Never After?" Gretel says. "Doesn't time move much quicker there than it does here?"

"It's hard to calculate," Alistair says. "You know, since no one gets older, things just change, move, but also remain eternal. It has felt like a long time, though."

"And you guys always remembered us?" Gretel asks.

"Always." Alistair smiles.

"Even Jack?" Filomena says softly.

"Especially Jack. That's, uh, part of why he's like this."

Gretel frowns. "What do you mean?"

"Well, things have been pretty good in Never After in general. You know, the occasional quest here and there, but it seems that when you called the dragons to Avalon to run Queen Olga and the ogres off the island—you remember that, don't you?"

Filomena nods. "I do now, since last night."

"Well, when you did that," Alistair continues, "it turns out the dragons didn't just run Olga off the island. They actually captured her. They thought that if they killed her, she might return somehow, or reincarnate—I'm not really sure. Marlon and Rosie can explain the whole thing better. So instead of killing her, the dragons captured her, and she's been locked in the Deep ever since."

"Wow," Gretel says. "That's amazing! That must be such a relief for Never After."

"Definitely. But anyway, back to Jack." He sighs deeply. "Before I tell you, Filomena, I don't want you to feel like this is your fault."

A shock runs through her body. "My fault?"

"I said it's *not* your fault!"

"But that sort of makes it seem like you think it's her fault," Gretel says, taking another bite of pastry.

"No! No. Just hear me out. The way this happened is, well, Jack tried to go through the portal."

"Oh wow."

"So it is true, what Marlon said way back when," Filomena says. "It really is dangerous to try to go through the portal now."

Alistair just nods.

"Why did he go through?" Gretel asks.

Alistair pauses. "He was trying to find Filomena."

A long silence falls over the table. Filomena pushes away her croissant. "So it *is* my fault," she says quietly.

"That's what I'm trying to say: It's not your fault!"

"But wait," Gretel says, "if the portal almost killed Jack, then how did *you* get here?"

"I was with Jack before he tried to go through. I was

waiting for him on the Never After side of the portal in case he needed help or something happened. Basically the portal spit him back out, and he was barely breathing. Right away, I hopped on Toto and took Jack to Marlon and Rosie, of course. Oh, they work together now, by the way. And they told me that the portals are what people in the mortal world refer to as black holes."

Filomena remembers thinking as much, back when she was using swoop holes and the portal.

"But since we moved Avalon to the mortal side and the portal was broken, it's much, much more dangerous to use it. They did tell me, though, that it is *possible* to go through and survive. Not likely, but statistically possible. It's kind of a random chaos thing. You don't know which way it's going to go."

"But why even try to come through the portal?" Gretel asks.

"Because Marlon and Rosie told me that the only cure for this kind of ailment, the kind Jack has, is in the waters of Avalon . . ."

"And the waters of Avalon are still on this side of the portal," Filomena finishes.

"Alistair, you risked your life going through the portal!" Gretel screeches.

He just shrugs.

"You really are brave, aren't you?" Gretel says, touching his arm.

"I would do anything for Jack. You know that."

Sitting around the kitchen table, the familiar feeling of familial love swells in Filomena. She knows that what Alistair did is what any of the four of them would do for each other. It goes without saying. Even if she and Gretel forgot it for all these years.

"So," Alistair says, "we need to take Jack to the waters of Avalon."

A slight panic seizes Filomena's chest.

"There's only one problem, Alistair," she says. "I have no idea how to get to Avalon."

CHAPTER THIRTY-NINE

ALISTAIR DISCOVERS TELEVISION

She remembers everything else, or most other things, about Never After and their adventures, so why not this?

"Is Avalon, like, a part of Los Angeles now?" Gretel asks. "Like a new neighborhood?"

"If it is, I haven't heard of it." Filomena shrugs.

They're sitting on the couch now. Filomena and Gretel are on either side of an unconscious Jack, and Alistair is in the armchair.

"I sort of remember this from when we were here before. Calvin was trying to explain this thing to me," Alistair says, pointing to the TV. "What is it again?"

"You are so clueless about the mortal world. It's so cute!" Gretel laughs. "Is this how we seemed when we were stumbling through Never After?"

"It's for watching shows," Filomena explains. "Imagine if tiny people performed little plays in a box. It's kind of like that, but you can watch it at any time. And that's the remote. You click it to turn it on."

Alistair picks up the remote and clicks the red button. The TV comes to life, and he jumps at the sounds and the visuals.

"This thing's magic! I'll have to tell Rosie about this. She'll freak out."

"Where . . . where am I? Am I dead?"

The voice comes from the unconscious boy, who is now apparently conscious. Filomena's eyes widen in anticipation and horror, excitement, thrill, fear, all of it. Jack's awake.

He pushes himself to a sitting position and rubs his eyes. The sunlight pouring through the windows disorients him. When his eyes finally open, he does a double take at Filomena, who's sitting next to him. Then his eyes go from open to saucer wide.

"Am I dead?" he says with a look of horror on his face.

"Hi, Jack," Filomena says shyly.

What a strange feeling. To see someone she was so in

love with when she was twelve and he was thirteen. *What would Jack at twenty-five look like?* she wonders.

"Alistair?!" Jack yells, not responding to Filomena.

Alistair waves from the armchair. "I'm here, Jack."

"What's going on? Am I hallucinating? Are we dead?"

"We're in the mortal world."

Jack frowns. "But . . . you didn't come through the portal with me. Ow." He touches his stomach, his shoulders, his head. "Everything feels horrible," he says, wincing.

"Yeah . . . ," Alistair starts. "The portal spit you back out, and you're . . . well, you're dying."

Jack doesn't seem to hear this, the fact that he's dying. He just stares at Filomena with a look of fear and confusion.

"Is this . . . ?" he says, not taking his eyes off her. He reaches out and touches her shoulder, then recoils quickly when it appears she's solid and not a hallucination.

Alistair explains what happened, but Jack's skeptical eye contact with Filomena remains.

"Wait, so this is real?" he says.

"It's real," Alistair responds.

"Filomena" is all Jack can muster.

"Hi," she says.

They look at each other for a long time.

Gretel laughs. "Well, this is awkward!"

"Gretel!" Jack says, turning to face the other direction, as if he just noticed her sitting there.

Gretel waves and smiles.

"I've missed you, Gretel," he says. "You both look . . . different."

"We went through this with Alistair already," Gretel says. "We're older, you're the same, yada yada."

Filomena has so many mixed feelings right now, she doesn't know whether to laugh or to cry. She and Jack finally found their way back to each other, and yet there's a gulf between them. Of age, of time, of experience, and also of health.

Jack tries to stand, but he gets too dizzy and has to lie back down. He sighs deeply, clearly frustrated with his condition. "I'm so glad to see you both," he says, wincing and looking at Filomena. "How are you? Are you happy?"

Is she happy? It's a good question. She's accomplished a lot in these past thirteen years. She has a college degree, she has a boyfriend, she has a home, and she has a potential career in political science. But is she happy?

"I . . . think so?" she says.

"Your hair is still short," Jack says.

She touches her chin-length hair. She never grew it out after Marlon cut it. She smiles, remembering how that happened. How Marlon cut off all her hair in a smooth sweep of a knife to use in a spell. How funny, that she forgot.

"Filomena has a very tall boyfriend," Alistair says, arms crossed. "Not sure how I feel about him, to be quite honest, but she says he's a good guy."

A look of resignation, a fear of an expectation that's come

to pass, falls on Jack's face. He nods, taking in this information. But then his eyes land on the emerald pendant, and his face regains a spark of light.

"You're still wearing the necklace," he says softly. A smile creeps onto his face.

Filomena touches it, an instinctual move, one she does a dozen times a day. How could she have been touching this emerald heart all this time and not remember where it came from?

As the four try to orient themselves in this new and strange dynamic, a TV commercial blares on the screen.

"*Come on down to Waters of Avalon Spa,*" the voiceover says. Images of waterfalls and pink sands fill the TV screen. "*Meet Hollywood's favorite health guru, the Lady of the Lake.*" A familiar face appears: a woman in a turquoise dress with intricate, delicate tattoos. Filomena's momentarily distracted from Jack, pulling her eyes away from him long enough to watch the commercial. "*Only those who believe are healed,*" the woman says with a smile, twirling a strand of long hair between her fingers. "*¡Vamos a Ávalon!*"

CHAPTER FORTY

BACK TO THE WATERS OF AVALON

They pile into Filomena's silver Honda, which is parked in her driveway. Gretel and Alistair both carry Jack, who's incredibly annoyed to need help. But every time he tries to walk, he collapses to the ground.

"Wait, so why do you think this spa is going to help Jack?" Gretel says, taking the passenger seat after calling shotgun.

Filomena pulls out of the driveway and starts driving.

"Gretel, don't you remember when we got Excalibur? When we went to the waters of Avalon and met the Lady of the Lake?"

Gretel squints, trying to activate her memory. "Oh, whoa. I forgot about Arturo! He was so cute."

Filomena laughs and rolls her eyes. That's *so* not the point. "I think, judging by that commercial, that the Lady of the Lake stayed in the mortal world after we moved Avalon here. And get this: I guess she started a spa!"

"So we're going to a spa to save Jack's life." Gretel nods, piecing it together. "Makes sense. Self-care is *so* important!"

"What's a spa?" Alistair says.

"Oh, Alistair, we have so much to teach you," Gretel says, turning around in her seat and smiling at him.

"Hold on, Fil," Jack says, "do you know how to get to the healing waters from here?"

A familiar feeling of thrill rises in her chest, hearing him call her Fil.

"No," Filomena responds, "but we have a stop to make first. I just realized I never returned Excalibur."

When they pull up to her parent's house, Alistair asks if he can come inside and say hi.

"I don't think we have time," Filomena says. "I don't know if they remember anything about Never After, either, and if they start to remember, it will just take way too much time. They'll have a million questions, and we'll be here for hours."

"Yeah, they'd probably order us takeout and want to hang out," Alistair says, "and that would be such a shame . . ."

"Uh, hey, best friend sort of dying over here," Jack says, raising his eyebrows at Alistair.

"Right, right, sorry. You go. We'll wait in this weird metallic carriage."

Filomena laughs and runs from the car to the front door of her parent's house, opening it with her spare key. She suspects that, since it's midday, they'll be deep into the day's chapters, writing in their offices, so she can sneak in and out unnoticed. Knowing how time works in Never After, she hopes she gets back in time for her mom's book launch party. She leaves a note explaining that she might be absent, just in case.

She goes to her old room. It's been a while since she's visited. Her parents have become less like homebodies in recent years; they'd often meet her at restaurants or bookstores or movie theaters to hang out. When she does come over, she doesn't often root through her old bedroom.

When she walks into her old room, she's transported back to the girl she was when she knew Alistair and Jack. All her copies of the Never After books line the bookshelf, along with her stuffed animals, her posters, her flashlight. She opens the closet, where she remembers she put Excalibur.

As she aged, she eventually misremembered this sword as a novelty toy from the Never After universe, assuming she'd got it at a book launch. She shakes her head, wanting to laugh and cry at how bizarre memory is, how she could ever have thought that the sword that saved her mother's life was just a toy. She picks it up, the opal blade and silver hilt, and the weight of it sends a shiver down her spine. She remembers the feeling of holding a sword, a Dragon's Tooth sword, slashing through ogres and defending her friends. Tears start to well in her eyes, but then she hears a car horn blaring.

Outside, Gretel is scolding Alistair. "Sorry, Fil, I told him not to!" she says.

"I was just curious what it did!" Alistair shrugs, playing innocent.

Then they see the sword.

"Whoa," Gretel says. "Now I really remember."

Filomena prays the sword will do something to Jack, and she opens the back door of the car, where he's sitting, and places it over him. She remembers how vividly and quickly it transformed her mother, bringing life back into her. But Jack just shakes his head weakly.

"It's been away from the waters of Avalon for too long," he says. "It's lost its healing power."

"Well, then we'll just have to use it as a bartering tool with Vilma," Filomena says, her heart sinking slightly. She puts the sword in the trunk and climbs into the driver's seat. "Gretel, can you look up 'Waters of Avalon Spa' on your maps app?" she asks.

Gretel does just that, and Alistair looks over her shoulder from the back seat, amazed.

"You can just look that up?" he says, eyes wide. "Wow, that would've saved us a lot of time on quests."

"The mortal world has its perks!" Gretel says, as she presses START on the app's navigation, and they take off driving.

"You learned how to drive," Jack says from the back seat when they're on the highway.

"Yeah! Almost ten years ago now." Filomena laughs. "Kind of crazy, right?"

"Now you can drive wherever you want, with whoever you want," he says.

At first, she thinks it's sort of a strange comment. It's accurate, but strange. But then she remembers all at once, like an impact of a car crash, their conversation under the jacaranda tree on that fateful night. She's pushed that memory so far, so deep, that even when she remembered all the wild things about Never After, she didn't remember that evening. It's too intense, too painful. The last conversation with Jack before they parted ways forever. Well, turns out it wasn't forever . . . They'd fantasized about all the dates they could go on if he stayed in the mortal world. She'd said that when they turned sixteen, they could drive anywhere.

She sighs. This is getting confusing.

"How did Calvin take all this, by the way?" Gretel asks, oblivious to the subtext happening between Jack and Fil.

"Not horrible . . . not great," Filomena says. "Mostly he just didn't understand, didn't see how I could be telling the truth. Honestly, he might just think I've lost my mind."

"Mortals," Jack mumbles from the back seat, seething slightly. "So closed-minded."

CHAPTER FORTY-ONE

THE DECISION, REPRISED

They can spot the signage from a mile away. Waters of Avalon Spa has an enormous entrance and seems to be set up like a luxurious hotel. From a distance, it doesn't look too unlike the Wicked Witch of the West's hotel, Exit West, back in Camelot. Filomena just hopes this trip will be less life endangering.

She pulls into the parking lot, and as she steps out of the car, a valet comes over to park it.

"Uh, just a second," Filomena says, popping the trunk to get Excalibur.

She's worried for a moment that carrying a large opal-bladed sword might draw attention to her, but she remembers that, luckily, they're in Hollywood, where eccentricity abounds. If anyone asks, she'll just tell them it's a prop for a movie she's working on.

"Shall we?" Gretel says, pointing to the large glass doors that form the spa's entrance.

Filomena and Alistair carry Jack, whose arms are slung around their shoulders. His energy levels seem to rise and dip at random, but right now, they're very low. Gretel carries the sword as they enter the spa.

Going beyond the glass doors, however, is like walking into a dream. It's Avalon! Just as Filomena remembers it.

When they're inside, she turns around to see the spa's storefront is just a film set's building: It's flat, two-dimensional, made of plywood for show, like buildings in an old Western.

"What's going on here?" she asks, puzzled.

"I think maybe Vilma's using a spa as a cover, but this really seems like Avalon, doesn't it?" Gretel replies.

They follow a shimmering pathway through a forest. That path definitely wasn't here the last time they visited. They walk along the pathway for a few minutes, and it leads them to the mermaids' lagoon.

"It's just like last time!" Filomena says. "Hardly anything has changed."

Just then, a mermaid with a light pink tail and long orange hair pops out of the water and takes a seat on a rock.

"Hello! Welcome to Waters of Avalon Spa. What services do you have booked for today?" She smiles serenely at them.

"Oh, we're actually here to see the Lady of the Lake," Gretel says.

The mermaid frowns cutely. "I'm sorry, we don't book appointments with the Lady of the Lake directly," she says.

Gretel sighs, then lifts up Excalibur. "You're sure she won't want to see this?" Gretel says.

The mermaid's eyes widen. "Oh my," she says. "Yes, let me get her." The mermaid dives off her rock and into the lagoon.

The four of them wait for a few minutes. Jack's weight is becoming more and more uncomfortable on Filomena's shoulders. She hasn't really taken in, until now, the fact that Jack could die. It just never seemed possible. He's immortal, first of all, and he's blessed by the fairies, second of all. He's the least likely to die of anyone she knows! And yet he risked death. Why? To come see her. What for? She wishes she could ask him, but he appears to be slipping in and out of consciousness now. He's having to exert a significant amount of energy to keep himself at least somewhat propped up.

The mermaid's head reappears, her orange hair spreading all around her shoulders in the water. "The Lady of the Lake would like to see you," she says. "Just follow the path around the bend, please."

They follow the path the mermaid points to.

"Do mortals see all this?" Gretel whispers to Fil. She just shrugs.

Finally they come to the lake with the pink sandy bottom and the crystal-clear water. The Lady of the Lake is waiting for them, sitting on the shore.

"Hey there. I wondered if it would be you," she says, standing up. Her long blond hair tumbles down her back.

How strange that, when Filomena first saw Vilma, she'd seemed so much older. Filomena remembers thinking Vilma was a true adult in her twenties. And now here's Filomena in her twenties. They're probably about the same age. Give or take a few millennia.

"Hi, Vilma," Filomena says shyly. It's been so long since she's interacted with anyone magical. It feels dizzying.

"*Mi hada*, what's going on here?" the Lady of the Lake says as Alistair and Filomena lay Jack down on the sandy pink shore.

"This is what we're here to see you about, actually. But first, I want to apologize," Filomena says. "Many years ago, I came to get Excalibur from you to heal my mother. And it worked! Thank fairies. But so much happened immediately afterward, with the portal closing and having moved Avalon to Hollywood . . . and eventually I forgot Never After ever existed."

Vilma nods. "It has been a long time, hasn't it?"

"Please accept my apology as we return Excalibur to its

rightful place," Filomena says. Gretel hands her the sword, and she holds it in both hands horizontally toward Vilma.

"Gracias, Filomena," Vilma says. "I accept your apology. Since we've been out of the fairy world, no heroes have come by on quests to get the sword, anyway, so it hasn't been missed." Vilma looks sad for a moment. Then her bright disposition recomposes. "But I've made it work! I started a spa here in Hollywood. It's hilarious; people love this place. They think the mermaids are a sort of gimmick, that I have girls dressed up in tails! And that I made all this for the spa experience." She motions to the lavender rocks, the waterfalls. "Mortals really will believe anything, huh?"

Vilma laughs a tinkling laugh, but Filomena can't muster even a giggle, seeing Jack lying unconscious on the shore.

"Vilma, we really need your help. Again," Filomena says. "Jack's dying. He tried to go through the portal."

Alistair finally chimes in: "Marlon the wizard told me that the waters of Avalon are the only way he can heal."

Vilma walks over to Jack and puts her hands on him. A few minutes go by as she touches various parts of his body, assessing the situation.

Filomena is filled with nerves. What if Jack dies? How will she live with herself? How will she go on, remembering that Never After exists but that Jack doesn't? She feels a pang of longing for Never After. For the adventures, for the magic it brought to her. The other life she might have had, the life she did have there.

Vilma stands.

"This is a very intense situation," she says. Her hands, with their hot-pink fingernails, are waving for emphasis. "Like, really intense."

"Can you help?" Alistair says desperately.

"I'm so sorry, but from what I can tell, there's only one way that Jack's life will be saved. The waters of Avalon can't heal him. He's too far gone for that. The only way Jack Stalker will survive is if Filomena goes back to the time of the Decision and chooses differently."

CHAPTER FORTY-TWO
Filomena's Choice

In some ways, it feels like a time warp is already occurring. Thirteen years later, Filomena stands on the shores of Avalon, desperate to heal someone she loves. But this time, the solution is far more complicated.

Vilma explained that the only way for Jack to be saved is to choose a different timeline. The timeline in which, after she saves her mother, Filomena decides to stay in Never After and Jack never goes through the portal to find her in the mortal world. But if she does that, if she goes back to when she was thirteen and chooses to stay in Never After, then everything that's happened in the last decade of her life will vanish, and she won't be able to go to the mortal world again.

"Whoa," Gretel says. "That's heavy."

Filomena feels dizzy. Jack is still unconscious. She can't talk to him about this decision, and she's not sure she wants to, anyway. He would probably just tell her to sacrifice him, that it was his choice to go through the portal, that she shouldn't have to give up her life for his.

"Gretel, what do you think I should do?" she asks.

Gretel just shakes her head. "I have no idea, Fil. I can't tell you what to do, especially when Jack's life is on the line. Will I lose you if you go back? Will it change my life? I don't know. But it's Jack, and it's you. I just don't know."

"Alistair?"

Alistair shrugs. "I know what I'd do, but it's not up to me. No one can answer this but you, Fil."

He's right. She's the only one who can make this decision. It's her life; it's her choice. She was forced to choose between worlds once, and now she's being forced to choose again.

This time, she knows what she has to do.

She has to go back.

Back, to thirteen years ago.

Back when she was twelve years old again.

ℰPILOGUE

With the portal sealed between two worlds
A decision had to be made.
Two realities existing
On the thin edge of a blade.
Would Filomena remain amid
Her family and the mortals
Or would she join friends in Never After
On the other end of the portal?
She made the Decision once,

Now she must make it twice,

But if she chooses differently,

The last thirteen years are her sacrifice.

She loved Jack Stalker before,

But does she still love him now?

And is that love the ultimate factor

In her choosing, anyhow?

The story is not over yet;

Do not laugh, do not weep.

For Filomena is not yet aware

that Queen Olga stirs in the Deep!

ACKNOWLEDGMENTS

Thank you to my forever Never After family—Kate Meltzer, Emilia Sowersby, and Jen Besser! Thank you to everyone at Macmillan! Thank you to my family and friends. Thank you to all my cute readers.

KEEP YOUR EYES PEELED
FOR THE EPIC FINALE TO
THE CHRONICLES OF
NEVER AFTER

Coming Soon!